GLORY BOX

ROAD TO BABYLON

SAM SISAVATH

Published by Road to Babylon Media LLC
www.roadtobabylon.com

Edited by Jennifer Jensen & Wendy Chan
Cover Art by Deranged Doctor Design

ISBN-10: 0-9978946-1-X
ISBN-13: 978-0-9978946-1-5

BOOKS IN THE ROAD TO BABYLON SERIES

Glory Box

Bombtrack

Rooster

Devil's Haircut

Black

The Distance

ALSO BY SAM SISAVATH

ABOUT GLORY BOX

FROM THE PURGE, A NEW BEGINNING.

It's been six years since a terrifying breed of seemingly unkillable creatures emerged from the darkness to topple the unprepared governments of the world, in the process knocking mankind down the food chain.

Survivors called it The Purge.

A few brave souls rose from the ashes of the old world to fight back, often against overwhelming odds. Led by indomitable heroes, they risked everything to achieve a final, stunning victory over the supernatural "ghouls" in The Battle of Houston.

Five years later, what remains of the ghouls have fled back into the shadows, and humanity now resides in isolated communities in relative peace. But human ambition and greed have also survived, and with no laws to stop those willing to pursue them, it's every man for himself.

Keo, one of the unknown heroes of The Battle of Houston, has found serenity in a small town in Texas. But he will discover that a violent past is not so easily cast aside when a madman rises to dominate those around him, and in the process shatters Keo's new life.

It's a brave new world, but monsters still exist—and thrive. And where there are evil deeds, good people must rise to stem the tide...on the Road to Babylon.

Author's Note About Potential SPOILERS

The Road to Babylon series is a follow-up to The Purge of Babylon, a 9-part storyline that introduced readers to the post-apocalyptic world that is further explored in GLORY BOX. Although it's not necessary to have read PoB in order to under-stand this book and future installments, it is nonetheless **highly recommended**. GLORY BOX goes to great lengths to avoid spoilers as it relates to PoB, but some things are simply unavoidable. So if you do decide to later visit the early series after reading this book, you may already have some very impor-tant plot points, like the fates of certain characters or the outcomes of pivotal battles, spoiled for you.

SIX YEARS AFTER THE PURGE

FIVE YEARS AFTER THE BATTLE OF
HOUSTON

RADIO BROADCAST FROM 5 YEARS AGO

"This is Lara, and if you're listening to this, then you've survived the unimaginable. It doesn't matter how you did it, just that you did when so many didn't. By now you've seen the endless piles of bones outside and you've heard the rumors. They're true. All of them. We've struck a crippling blow against the ghouls, but it's not over. It's far from over. They're still out there, along with the blue-eyed ones. But they don't control us anymore, and we know how to defeat them. It's their turn to be afraid. We're going to organize and we're going to hunt them down and destroy every single one of them, and they're going to find out that the night is no longer theirs. Make no mistake, this is the chance we've been waiting for—this is the start of a new beginning. For all of us. Because we're in this together, whether we called ourselves collaborators or rebels, or didn't call ourselves anything at all in the last year. None of it matters. Not anymore. A lot of very good and brave people paid the ultimate sacrifice to give us this second chance. Don't waste it like we *did before with endless bickering and petty grievances. Let the past die with the past. This is our chance to make the world ours again. Help me—join me—and we'll take it back. I'm Lara, and I'm a survivor. If you're listening to this, then so are you..."*

PROLOGUE

"Go to bed. Get some sleep. Wake up and do it all over again."

It was a simple enough plan, and for almost a year Keo had been able to make it work. Not tonight, though.

He was on the verge of REM sleep when the ghoul broke through the cabin window. Keo opened his eyes and slowed down his breathing, then listened to it crawling through the shattered glass pane. He imagined the sight of it—thin, frail, little more than a skeletal revenant of its former self. He could almost hear it breathing, smell the growing stench of rotting garbage starting to slowly, slowly fill up the air inside the living room.

Or maybe it was all in his mind. With the bedroom door closed, he couldn't really smell much of anything. And he didn't want to get up, not while snuggled comfortably underneath the thick blanket against the chilly night air. It was Texas, so even winter wasn't really winter, and nights where he got the chance to bundle up were a rarity. So he really, really didn't want to get up.

Keo sighed and pushed the blanket aside, then sat up when he heard the *thump* as the thing finally pushed its way through the row of iron rebar he had fastened over the windows. Just one of many improvements he'd made to the place after moving in. Not that the original owners minded; they were either dead or had found greener pastures. That was the best-case scenario, anyway. The worst case had them crawling around somebody else's house right now looking for a little blood to keep them going.

He had to think about the last time he had seen a ghoul. Almost eight months ago now, back in a town just outside of Oklahoma City. He still didn't know how the hell he had ended up in Sooner country, but there hadn't been very much to see, so Keo had retreated back south. Besides, winter was coming, and there was an old saying about the weather in Texas. Don't like the weather? Just wait a few minutes.

Or something like that.

Keo didn't wait a few minutes now. Maybe half of one before he got up from the full-size bed and reached under the pillow for the P220. He opened the nightstand drawer nearby and took out the suppressor and rolled it into place. There was no point in waking the rest of the world up. Unlike him, they were probably having a very nice sleep right now. And sound tended to travel far these days, especially unsuppressed gunshots.

He stood up and padded in his bare feet over to the door. He wasn't in any hurry. If the creature had the ability, it would have found its way to the bedroom by now. It could probably smell him already, maybe even hear the blood pumping through his veins, because that was what it had come here for. His blood. A single drop of it could sustain the thing for days.

His heartbeat accelerated slightly for the first time in a long time. But it wasn't out of fear. Keo wasn't afraid of them. He had stopped being afraid a long time ago. Once you've been stuck in an underground sewer with a few thousand of the things, one lone ghoul invader didn't even come close to igniting his fear-o-meter.

So why was he so excited?

It had been a while, that's all.

Yeah. Let's go with that.

There was enough moonlight in the great room that Keo saw it almost as soon as he stepped out of the back hallway. It was on the floor, pulling itself in his direction, and had been, from the looks of it, for some time now.

Keo glanced over at the window it had broken into in order to get inside. The two lower glass panes were shattered. The ghoul had squeezed through the broken portions but hadn't done a good enough job of creating an opening. There was thick black sludge along the edges of the hole where the creature had sliced itself as it entered. Coagulated blood covered portions of the windowsill and dripped onto the floor, leaving a trail behind as the thing pulled itself, one inch at a time, toward him. The rebars were equally oiled in black liquid.

It was a miserable-looking thing, malnourished and as pathetic as any he'd seen in recent years. One of its arms hung limply at its side while its right leg dragged behind it, just barely hanging onto the rest of its delicate frame. He imagined the ghoul getting snagged on a nail jutting out from the floor and not being able to pull itself free. Or maybe its useless leg would get caught and the creature would spend so much effort to escape it would simply pull the appendage loose.

There were a million possibilities, and Keo had seen most

of them with his own eyes. The ghouls were capable of doing just about anything, as long as there was a goal. Right now, that was him.

He lowered the SIG Sauer to his side and relaxed his grip on the gun before cocking the hammer. If the creature was afraid of the weapon, it didn't stop crawling—inch by inch by inch—across the floor toward him. There were silver bullets in the .45 semiautomatic. There was more silver around the house—in the kitchen, in the room he was standing in now, even in the bathroom—but if their presence meant anything, the creature was oblivious. Maybe it was too hungry to care, or maybe its senses were dulled by its weakened state. And yet, it had known he was inside the house.

It was weak, and though he'd seen weaker, this one was near the very bottom. He couldn't begin to identify the ghoul's sex even if he wanted to. It was beyond gender, beyond anything that once made it human. Pruned black flesh hung off a bony frame like a film of liquid instead of actual skin, torn and dirty. It was impossible to ignore the stench that radiated from its skin—like month-long garbage left to rot in the sun. He would have gagged if he wasn't so used to it, even if he hadn't been in the company of one in nearly eight months. It was one of those things you couldn't forget once you were exposed to it.

Keo winced a bit when the ghoul slipped into a bright shaft of moonlight, its badly-damaged head revealed for the first time in all its unholy glory. The thing had been forced to not only traverse the small hole it'd created in the window but also squeeze through the rebars. Even though its head was already small—it could have passed for a child's—it hadn't been small enough to get through undamaged. Blood dripped from its deformed skull, the sides forcefully flattened almost comically. Its eyes—black irises, like tar pits—bulged against its sockets, and it was missing most of its nose.

It had the appearance of a sickly child, but sizes could be deceiving. It could have been a fully-grown man or woman once upon a time or a giant whale of a couch potato in its former life. None of that mattered now, because at this second it was nothing but bones as it pulled itself toward him. It opened its mouth and stuck out its tongue, and saliva dripped freely. Caverns of jagged brown and yellow teeth showed themselves ("Meth teeth," someone once described them to Keo), as if it could taste him standing there watching it with morbid fascination.

It kept coming, an inch at a time.

An inch at a time...

He wondered how long it had been out there searching for someone—anyone—with blood pumping through their veins before it finally found him. If it had kept going, it would have stumbled across a town full of people. Instead, it'd found the cabin. Alone out here, close enough to what passed for civilization these days, and yet purposefully distanced.

"You've seen better days, huh?" Keo said out loud. "How long has it been since you had a little taste?"

It didn't answer him. Not that it could, even if it wanted to. Ghouls didn't speak. They could growl, and sometimes he swore he heard them screaming, but they didn't speak, though Keo knew of other variations of the creature that could, and did.

He thought of blue eyes and hissing sounds...

He shivered unwittingly. It wasn't from the cold or the fact he was standing in the draftiest part of the cabin in nothing but pajamas and a T-shirt.

The creature had made it halfway across the great room when Keo started thinking about the mess that awaited him tomorrow. There was just enough silver in the bullet to put the miserable thing out of its misery, and the sun would do most of the cleaning up in the morning, but there would still be the bones to take care of.

Now where did I put the shovel? he thought as he lifted the SIG Sauer and shot the ghoul in the forehead.

The *pfft!* of the suppressed gunshot wasn't nearly as loud as the empty cartridge that flicked into the air, arced for a bit, before falling back down to earth and *clinking* against the wooden floorboards. It rolled for a bit before finally coming to rest against the leg of an old stool.

The creature's upturned head *plopped* to the floor and it stopped moving completely, as if someone had hit a light switch and it simply...stopped.

Keo was used to the sight. Ghouls were practically unkill-able unless you shot or stabbed or cut them with silver. He'd seen headless ghouls, even ones missing half of their bodies, still attacking. It was the blood that coursed through their veins. The same disease that had infected them, turned them into monsters, made them vulnerable to silver. As long as the metallic element came into contact with their bloodstream, it was game over.

"Like magic," someone once said to him.

Keo didn't think it was magic. More like science. Not that he knew the answer, or cared to think about it too much. It wasn't exactly his field of expertise. Not even close. Besides, there were scientists and historians (the ones still alive, anyway) out there trying to figure it out right now, he was sure of it: Where the ghouls came from, how the infection worked, or why silver was so poisonous to them that even a tiny drop caused instantaneous death. The only thing more fatal to the ghouls was sunlight, but it was hard to wield the sun or wear it in a holster at your hip.

But those were questions for someone else to think about. He was tired and it was chilly, and he was going to have to dig a hole in the yard tomorrow. He wasn't looking forward to that at all.

Keo turned around and went back into the bedroom. He checked the wall clock before he slipped into bed.

3:14 a.m.

The hour of the wolf.

He smirked and went back to sleep, but the P220 remained on the blanket over his chest, clutched in his right hand. As someone else once said, *"Just in case."*

ONE

"How many were there?"

"Just one."

"What did you do with it?"

"You mean after I killed it?"

"Well, yes."

"I buried it in the yard."

"Was it hard?"

"Which part?"

"Killing it."

"Not with silver."

"I meant... How long has it been since you killed one of them?"

"It hasn't been that long."

"Right," Emma said. "I keep forgetting you've been here for less than a year. Before that, you were out there."

"What's it like?" Megan asked.

Keo looked over at her. Ten years old going on thirty, with her mother's green eyes and light brown hair. The girl picked at her plate of corn and meat loaf (her least favorite of Emma's cooking) and waited for an answer.

"What's what like?" Keo said, even though he knew perfectly well what she was referring to. He always wondered how long it would take her to finally ask, and apparently conversation between him and her mother about "out there" was the opening she'd been waiting for.

Smart girl.

"You know," Megan said. "Out there."

"There's nothing out there," Emma said.

"Are there a lot of them out there? Jim says there's a lot of them out there."

"Are," Emma said. "Jim says there *are* a lot of them."

"So there are?"

Emma sighed.

Keo smiled. "She's correcting your grammar."

"Oh," Megan said. Then, still to Keo, "How many have you killed? In total? Grace says you were in Houston when they killed the big one."

"Who's Grace?"

"Adam's sister."

"I don't know who Adam is."

She squinted her eyes at him, unsure if he was playing with her or not.

Keo shrugged. "Scout's honor."

"What's that?"

"What's what?"

"What's Scout's honor?"

Right. She may be ten going on thirty, but she spent the last five years living in Winding Creek and the five years before that being a kid.

"Just something people used to say," Keo said before looking across the table at Emma for help.

She gave him an amused smile. "You're the one who kept it going."

Keo turned back to Megan. She hadn't taken her eyes off him. "What did you learn about Houston, *wonsungi?*"

"The Battle of Houston. It's the reason we're not ghoul food right now," Megan said. "It's why The Walk Out happened, when all the ghouls—or most of them, anyway—came out of hiding and walked into the light during the daytime and got fried. You should know, since you were there."

"According to Grace."

"Who got it from her dad."

"Brian, Grace's father, is the school's history teacher," Emma said. "And English teacher. And, occasionally, math teacher when Christine's out sick."

"That's an awful lot of classes to teach," Keo said. "Makes sense he would get a lot of things wrong," he added, looking at Megan when he said it.

The girl didn't look convinced. "People who were there says a Chinese guy with a weird name was also there."

"Keo's not Chinese, Megan," Emma said.

"You know that, I know that, but most folks don't know that."

Keo grinned to himself. He liked her. He really did. She reminded him of someone else, who was always a little smarter than everyone around her.

"So, what's it like out there?" Megan asked.

"It's hot in the summer and cold in the winter, just like in Winding Creek," Keo said.

"That's all?"

"And dogs."

"Dogs?"

"They're making a comeback. All the animals are. Squirrels, raccoons, land animals that were almost extinct five years ago. If you can shoot, you can pretty much live off the land."

"Or you could just grow something," Emma said.

Keo looked over and smiled. "Or you could do that, sure."

Emma reached over and poked Megan in the arm with her fork. "Finish your plate."

"But it sucks," Megan said.

"It's Thursday. That means corn and meat loaf."

"Thursdays suck."

Emma sighed and glanced across the table at Keo for help.

He shrugged back at her.

She mouthed, *"Please?"*

He sighed and turned to Megan. "Finish your plate, and I'll give you one chance to ask me anything."

Megan's face brightened up. "About out there?"

"If that's what you want, sure."

"Deal," the girl said.

———

"Thanks," Emma said later.

"Happy to help," Keo said.

"Were you actually in the scouts?"

"I doubt they'd have me."

"What's so bad about you?"

"You wouldn't ask that if you really knew me."

"Does it have anything to do with that scar?"

"It doesn't *not* have something to do with this scar."

She rolled her eyes. "Sometimes I think having a grown-up conversation with Megan is easier."

Keo tightened his arms around her and inhaled her scent. She smelled of soap and water, but the fact it was coming from a beautiful and naked woman lying in bed with him made all the difference.

He blew at strands of her dark hair. "She's just going to keep asking about what's out there, you know."

"I know," Emma said quietly. "And she can keep asking as long as she doesn't act on it."

"You think there's a chance she would?"

"I don't know. She's a curious child. Brian says when he needs someone to ask a question, he doesn't have to look farther than her desk."

"She doesn't strike me as much of a teacher's pet."

"More like a teacher's pest."

Keo chuckled. "Now that I can believe."

"You can help me with that, too."

"How's that?"

"Convince her what's out there isn't worth seeing for herself." She rested her chin on his chest to fix him with a pair of serious jade eyes. "You've been out there longer than anyone in town. You know how dangerous it is."

"It's not for everyone, but it has its charms."

"Like what?"

"Freedom, for one."

"There's freedom here."

"Not like out there."

"And yet here you are, in Winding Creek."

"Yeah, well, there's a lot of things out there, but it doesn't have a gorgeous brunette who cooks for me and lets me sleep at her place whenever I want. Not to mention lie around in her bed while she's naked as a jaybird."

"Oh, is that all I am to you? A cook and a sex partner?"

"You're more than that."

"How much more?"

"You also do my laundry."

She sat up and glared down at him. "Get the fuck out of my bed, Keo."

He laughed. "You don't mean that."

"The hell I don't."

He pulled her down and kissed her. She resisted, pushing against his chest, but after a while she gave up and started kissing him back.

"Asshole," she said when he finally released her, and she lay back down on his chest.

"I've been called worse," Keo said.

"Like what?"

"You don't wanna know. You might start blushing and never stop."

"Is that before or after The Purge?"

"Before, during, and after."

"After?"

"And after, after."

"I don't know what that means." She paused, then, "You were really there, weren't you? In Houston."

"Yes."

"What was it like?"

"Can we not talk about it?"

"You don't want to?"

"No."

"Okay."

She didn't say anything else for a while, and Keo alternated between listening to her soft breathing, Megan's loud snoring in the bedroom next door, and what sounded like a wolf howling somewhere in the woods outside. He'd heard it last night, too, before the ghoul broke its way into his cabin. He had wondered if the creature had been alone. It used to be that where you found one ghoul, you usually found more.

"You never told me what you were doing out there for five years," Emma finally said.

"Looking," Keo said.

"For what?"

"I don't know. Just looking."

"If you don't know what you were looking for, how would you know if you ever found it?"

He chuckled. "I didn't say it was a very fruitful five years."

She sighed. "It's always a pleasure talking with you, Keo."

She went quiet again. He spent the next few quiet minutes enjoying the feel of her body, of her long legs sliding back and forth against his. He was almost 90% sure she wasn't doing it on purpose, but then women always were his weakness, and he hadn't found a total package that was more appealing than Emma these last few years.

"Stop it," Keo said.

"Stop what?" she said, but he could hear the slight amusement in her voice. So she did know what she was doing, after all.

"You're the one who said you had to get up early tomorrow."

"I don't know what you're talking about."

He sat up on the small bed and picked her up, then lay her under him. She smiled just before he tasted her lips, then

kissed her neck and kept going south. She let out a deep, satisfied moan, then bunched her fingers in his hair.

"Keo," she whispered.

"Yeah?" he said, moving lower.

"I've always wanted to ask…"

"What?"

"What kind of name is Keo, anyway?"

"Kevin was taken."

"Oh," she gasped. Then, her voice slightly pained, "Don't
leave tonight. Stay with me."

He didn't answer her.

"Keo," she whispered. "Stay with me tonight."

He still didn't answer her.

He'd almost said yes. Almost promised to stay the night
because her plea had caught him by surprise. In the months
since she welcomed him into her and her daughter's life, then
later into her bed, Keo had never stayed over. It didn't matter
how late he stayed at their house; he always left before
morning.

He did that again tonight, pulling on his clothes in the
dark as she slept. He picked up the holster with the SIG
Sauer inside from the dresser and clipped it onto the belt
behind his back. Then he grabbed his boots from the floor
and walked barefoot across the pitch-black room. He
didn't really need his night eyes because he'd been in the
room so many times and knew every nook and cranny by
heart.

He thought he might have heard her stirring behind him as

he opened the door, but he (quickly) slipped out before he could be sure.

It was cold outside, and he flipped up his jacket's collar before making sure the front door and the security gate over it were both locked behind him.

Winding Creek was deathly still an hour before midnight, but there was plenty of moonlight to show him the sidewalk and streets beyond Emma's front yard. It never ceased to amaze him how well-kept the town was, like an old 1950s painting of what suburban America used to look like. The only things missing were white picket fences and milkmen delivering door-to-door. That is, if you could ignore the security gates fastened over every door, and windows that were reinforced with rebar to keep out (*night-dwelling*) intruders.

He walked down the driveway and turned up the sidewalk, using the large white cross sticking up from the church in the main square as a beacon. Not that he needed the help since he'd made this walk so many times before.

Houses lined the streets to both sides of him, solar-powered LED lights at strategic intervals keeping the night at bay. The majority of the houses were dark, the people inside sleeping the way normal people should be. (*So what does that make you, pal?*) There was the occasional light from a den or second-floor bedroom, but no movements on the other side.

The world around him was so quiet Keo didn't have any problems hearing the soft *clop-clop* coming up the street behind him from almost a block away. He knew who it was and kept walking, hoping that maybe he could avoid a conversation if he reached the edge of town fast enough.

No such luck, as the horse picked up speed and the *clop-clop* grew louder.

He thought about making a run for it but decided the explanation he'd have to give in the morning wasn't worth the trouble.

Eventually, the horse and its rider caught up to him.

"Hey, Keo," a voice said just before a black mare pulled up next to him.

Keo nodded at Jim. The Winding Creek sheriff had a last name, but Keo didn't remember it. People were using last names again these days, unlike five years ago when just a first name was enough.

"What's the point of being sheriff if you can't give the midnight shift to the deputies?" Keo asked.

"Deputies?" Jim chuckled. "Deputy. I wish I had deputies. You wanna volunteer to help me and Duncan out?"

"Do you need help, Jim?"

"Well, no..."

"There's your answer."

Jim smiled. He was an easygoing man in his fifties, who had been, according to Emma, a cop before The Purge. He had kept that occupation, to an extent, when the town became a ghoul haven like hundreds (*thousands*) of places just like it six years ago. A year after that, with the ghouls' reign over, Jim was still wearing the uniform. Unlike a lot of self-appointed collaborator "authority," Jim was well-liked by the people he oversaw and had kept his position by unanimous vote.

"I've been meaning to look for you anyway," Jim was saying.

"Yeah?"

"Heard you ran into a ghoul last night."

"More like it ran into me. Or my cabin's window, to be exact."

"Just one?"

"Yeah, just one window."

"No, I mean, just one creature?"

"Just the one."

Jim didn't say anything right away. In the temporary silence, the only sounds were Keo's footsteps and the *clop-clop* of the horse's hooves. The animal's breath formed mists in front of it with every snort, and Keo thought it was giving him the side eye every few steps like it didn't trust him.

"There have been reports," Jim began.

"About?"

"Possible evidence of ghouls in the area. Duncan and I have been looking into them, but they were all dead ends."

"How long ago?"

"The first one was about a week ago. Just footprints in the ground that looked human but weren't."

"The ghouls used to be humans, Jim."

"I know. That's why we took it seriously enough to track it into the woods before we lost it." He paused again. "But with you actually having seen one, I think it might be wise to take another look at the reports."

"Have you told the others?"

"We thought it was prudent not to just yet. It might create unnecessary panic."

"How long has it been since a ghoul showed up in town?"

"Not counting your encounter? The last time was two years ago. There were five of them, and they made a nest in one of the homes."

"How did you kill them?"

"We burned down the house. Fried the whole lot."

"You can always do that again."

Keo glanced at the gun belt around Jim's waist and the six-shot revolver in the holster. *Cowboy cop,* Keo had thought when he had first met the man. You didn't see a lot of revolvers anymore, not when an automatic handgun could hold twice—most times much more than that—the rounds. When you were dealing with ghouls, numbers mattered—theirs, and the bullets you brought to the party.

Because where there's one, there's usually more around...

They continued in silence for a few more seconds before Keo finally said, "What's on your mind, Sheriff?"

"We could use your help," Jim said.

"Doing what?"

"Tracking them, looking out for everyone. That sort of thing."

"I'm not a tracker, Jim."

"But you're pretty good with that gun."

"A lot of people are pretty good with guns."

"Look, Keo—"

"You don't need me," Keo said, cutting him off. "There are thirty-seven able-bodied men in town for you to choose from. If you need more guns, just ask for volunteers. I'm sure you'll get plenty."

"I am. I'm asking you."

"That isn't me, I mean. Besides, it looks like you and Duncan got it all handled."

"Because it's been easy up till now."

"So what's changed?"

Jim didn't answer right away.

"Sheriff," Keo started, but this time Jim cut him off.

"I'm hearing about things going on out there that's making me a little nervous."

"Ghouls?"

"No. Other things."

"Can you be a little more specific?"

"I wish I could, but I don't have all the information. Something to do with Dresden and some other towns in our area. People are reporting gunshots. A lot of gunshots."

"Where?"

"From up north. You know how gunfire travels these days." He paused again. Then, "Dresden was also supposed to send some people over to trade last week, but they never showed up. I'm thinking about sending Duncan or someone up there to gather some intel. We could use an extra hand or two in the meantime."

Right. "Intel." Which always turns into a gunfight.

Keo shook his head. "That's not me anymore, Jim. Sorry."

"Does this have anything to do with what you did during the occupation? Because you're not alone, you know. We've all done things we regret, but we moved on. And, if possible, when the situation offers itself, we make amends."

Keo ignored him and kept walking, even picking up his pace.

"Keo—"

"No," Keo said. "And trust me when I say this, Jim: You don't *want* me."

Jim stopped his horse in the street and looked after him. "Emma and Megan live in this town too, Keo."

I was wondering when you'd bring them into this. Took you long enough, Jim.

Keo kept walking, turning at the intersection and continuing down the street that would, like every other time he took it, take him straight into the woods surrounding Winding Creek.

"Goddammit, Keo," Jim said from behind him, but Keo had already tuned him out.

Sorry, Jim. That's not me anymore.

He slipped into the woods and breathed a sigh of relief when there was nothing but shadows around him. Once upon a time the prospect of voluntarily walking into a forest of dark trees, with only the occasional shafts of moonlight to guide him, would have been unthinkable, but those days were long gone.

It was a brave new world, and a lot of things were possible again. Like, maybe, staying the night at a beautiful woman's place when she asked, without worrying about the repercussions.

Maybe I should have stayed, Keo thought, just before he broke off into a run in case he did something stupid...like turn around and go back to Emma's house to do just that.

TWO

She was at his cabin at noon after school let out, climbing the biggest tree in his yard and walking along the largest branch as if it were a tightrope. His first time seeing her up there had nearly given him a heart attack, mostly thinking about what to tell Emma, but it didn't take long before he recognized the natural climber that she was—just like he had been and still was when necessary.

"Get down here before you fall and break your neck," he shouted.

"Never gonna happen!" she called back.

"That's what they all say before they go *splat.*"

"Never, ever gonna happen!"

She tiptoed back to the tree, then slid down it, before walking over and plopping her backpack on the porch next to him. "What are you doing?"

"What does it look like?"

"It looks like you're trying to teach a stray dog to sit."

"Bingo."

She spent the next ten minutes or so watching him doing just that—trying to teach a ragged-looking mutt that had shown up this morning looking for food to sit. Keo had made the mistake of tossing the animal a biscuit, and the thing hadn't left since. There were plenty of wild dogs in the woods, much more now that there weren't hordes of ghouls waiting to feast on them.

Eleven minutes later, Megan groaned and said, "Give it up. He's never going to learn."

"I don't give up. You can ask anyone, and they'll tell you, 'That guy doesn't know how to give up.'"

"I think there's a word for that."

"Resilience."

"Nah, I think it's something else. Starts with an S."

"Stupendous?"

"Definitely not that, either."

"What do you know, you're only ten."

"My birthday's in two weeks. What're you gonna get me?"

He smiled. Leave it to Megan to shift topics without batting an eye. "Why should I get you anything?"

"It's tradition."

"People make new traditions these days. Ever heard of the phrase 'Out with the old, in with the new?'"

"No. Sounds stupid. Besides, I like the old ones better. So what're you gonna get me?"

"You'll see."

"You got me something already?" she asked, not quite able to hide the sudden rise in excitement in her voice.

"You'll see," he said again.

Keo held up a piece of bread to let the dog see. It was a scruffy-looking thing—mostly brown fur with patches of white

—and its nose was already wet before it wandered out of the woods and into his yard. Someone once told him that a dog with a wet nose meant it was a happy one.

"Sit," Keo said.

The dog cocked its head to one side and gave him a long, curious look.

"Sit," Keo said again.

"It's never going to sit," Megan said. "You should give up."

"I never give up."

"So you keep saying. But it's less about you and more about the dog, isn't it?"

He smirked. "Fancy English, for a kid."

"My English teacher is pretty good."

"Brian, Grace's dad?"

"Uh huh. You remembered."

"It happens." Keo held up the piece of bread in front of the dog again. "Sit."

The dog licked its lips, then lay down on its chin and began licking other parts of itself.

"Yuck," Megan said.

Keo tossed the bread next to the dog. The animal gobbled it up, then went back to enjoying itself.

"Gross," the girl said.

"It's only doing what feels good. It's natural."

"Doesn't make it any less gross."

"So, eleven in two weeks, huh?"

"Uh huh. What're you gonna get me?"

"I don't know. I'll see what I can find in the woods."

She frowned. "So you didn't actually get me anything yet?"

"Not yet."

"I was hoping for something less dirty."

"Oh, were you now?"

"Maybe something you might have gotten from the big cities while you were out there."

There it is again. I told you the girl wasn't going to give up, Emma.

"What do you know about the big cities?" he asked.

"I know they're still out there. That there are people in them."

"Who told you that?"

"Lots of people. Some who've even been there. Like you."

"The cities are better left forgotten, *wonsungi*."

"What's that mean anyway?"

"What?"

"What you always call me. *Wha-what?*"

He smiled. "*Wonsungi*."

"Yeah, that."

"It means monkey."

"Monkey?"

"My mom used to call me that."

"Why?"

"I was like you. I liked climbing trees when I was younger. I was pretty good at it, too."

"As good as me?"

"Better."

"I dunno. I'm pretty good."

He chuckled. "Maybe you're right. You might just be a better monkey than me. Happy?"

"I'm not sure," she said, and seemed to think about it for a moment. Then, "Why are the cities better left forgotten?"

"They're dangerous, that's why."

"Even to you?" she asked, looking over at him.

He nodded. "Even to me."

"Why?"

"Because besides assholes with guns and too much time on their hands, there are giant buildings filled with chemicals and other volatile goop with names as long as your arm and mine, just sitting around waiting to spring a leak. When that happens, everything goes *boom* and people die."

"You've seen it?"

"I've seen the aftermath. Trust me when I say you don't want to go anywhere near the big cities. There's nothing in them for you but trouble."

She seemed to think about it for a moment. Then, finally, "What else about the big cities scare you?"

"Did I mention the crazies with guns?"

"Not ghouls?"

"There aren't a lot of them around anymore, but there are still plenty of people. Trust me when I say this, kid; these days, the most dangerous thing you have to look out for are the creatures on two feet."

"Grace's father says sometimes the ghouls walk on two feet. He said they have blue eyes. Glowing blue eyes."

Keo didn't say anything.

"Have you seen them?" Megan asked.

Yes, I have, Keo thought, but he said, "Just make sure you don't trust people you don't know. It's dangerous out there. More than you know."

She nodded before tracing a dirty finger along the side of her face. "Is that where you got that? In the cities?"

Keo grunted. There were a lot of things in this life he couldn't outrun, and one of them was the big scar that ran down almost the entire left side of his face. It was a gift from a man named Pollard. That man, like so many others who had crossed Keo's path, was no longer among the living, but he had certainly left his mark while he was around, that was for damn sure.

Enjoying hell, Pollard? You and your kid? Good.

"You were really there, weren't you?" Megan asked after he didn't say anything for a while. "Houston? You were in Houston before The Walk Out."

"Yeah," Keo nodded.

"What was it like?"

He thought about it. Finally, he said, "It smelled."

She waited for him to continue, and when he didn't, "That's it?"

"Pretty much."

She frowned. Apparently, she had expected more of a story.

She was right—there was more to the story—but Keo didn't feel like telling it. Houston was the past, and just like most of his past, he preferred not to relive it because they inevitably brought back memories he'd rather push into the background.

He stood up to stretch instead and stared past the tall tree crowns at the sun in the distance. Afternoons—the brighter and warmer the better—were always his favorite time of the day, though they didn't always use to be.

"She does that, too," Megan was saying.

"What's that?" Keo asked.

"She stares at the sun. Sometimes her face would get really dark in the evenings and she reminds me that the night is still dangerous, that there are still things hiding in the woods waiting for some stupid kid to wander inside so they can gobble them up. That's why we always lock all our doors and make sure the windows are closed tight, every single night."

"You should listen to her."

"I do." Then, without a single hint, she shifted topics on him again. "How come you don't live with us?"

Ah, there it is.

"Your mom never asked me to," he said.

"That's because she doesn't want you to say no."

"What makes her think I'll say no?"

She shrugged. "She's just careful."

So am I, Keo thought, and said, "We never talked about it."

"You should move in," the girl said, looking at the dog as it went to work on a dirty patch of fur along its hind legs.

Keo smiled. The way she had said that, *"You should move in,"* like it was a statement of fact and not a question.

But it wasn't that simple for him. Out here, by himself, with only the cabin behind him to worry about, things were simpler. It didn't pay to become too attached to things, places, and most of all, people. It hadn't paid before The Purge, and it really hadn't paid during it, and it still didn't now.

He sat back down next to her. "We'll see."

"You should move in before my birthday," Megan said. "You already spend most of your time at our place anyway. Also, Mom smiles more when you're around. She doesn't think I notice, but I do."

Going in for the kill, huh, kid?

He admired her persistence, but he said, "We'll see what happens."

"My birthday's in two weeks."

"You've mentioned that."

"Just in case you forgot."

"I haven't."

"I know. Just in case. Get me something good, okay?"

"I'll see what I can do," Keo said, when two figures stepped out of the surrounding woods and into his front yard.

Ah, dammit, Keo thought as Jim and his deputy, Duncan, led their horses over by the reins.

Like his boss, Duncan wore a simple khaki uniform with his name stenciled on his chest and sported a gun belt. But instead of a six-shooter like Jim, the rangy twenty-something wore a 1911 pistol.

"Keo," Jim said.

"Jim," Keo said. He exchanged a courtesy nod with Duncan. "What brings you guys out here?"

"Just out for a stroll," Jim said.

Yeah, right. Out for a stroll, my ass.

Megan hopped off the slightly raised porch, brown leaves crunching loudly under her Nike sneakers as she landed. "I gotta be getting home anyway, before Mom puts together a search party. See ya."

"See ya, *wonsungi,*" Keo said.

She said to the dog, "Come on, boy!"

"I don't think he's going—" Keo said when the dog snapped up to its feet and jogged after her. "Or maybe he will."

"Tell your mom I said hi," Duncan said as Megan passed him.

"Sure, whatever," the girl said, before jogging into the woods.

"I don't think she likes me," Duncan said to Keo.

"Nah, that's just how she treats everyone she likes," Keo said.

"Yeah?"

"Absolutely."

"I don't think that's true."

Keo shrugged. "Probably not."

"Still haven't fixed that yet?" Jim asked, nodding at the cabin's broken window.

"I got an extra hammer, if you're interested in helping out."

"Maybe after we're done."

As smooth as molasses on silk, Jim, Keo thought, and said, "After we're done with what, Sheriff?"

Jim glanced back as if to make sure Megan was really gone. Then, turning back to Keo, "We found them."

"Them who?" Keo asked, even though he already knew the answer.

"Ghouls," Duncan said. "A whole nest of 'em."

Keo sighed. He had a feeling Jim wasn't going to give up after their chat last night.

"What exactly do you guys want from me?" Keo asked.

THREE

Keo didn't want to go with them, but he did anyway. Besides, they had a point when they said ghouls in the area were a danger to everyone in town, including Emma and Megan. But especially the girl, who regularly walked across the woods alone to see him at his cabin after school. Not that ghouls were any kind of a threat in the daytime, but Keo had seen how something small, like a single nest, could balloon into something bigger.

At least, that's why he told himself he was doing it.

"You sure you don't want a horse?" Jim asked.

Keo nodded. "I'm good."

"What do you have against horses?" Duncan asked.

"Nothing," Keo said. "I just don't like riding anything bigger than me."

"We can get you a pony."

"Funny. You're a regular comedian, Duncan. Duncan Comedian. That should be your stage name."

The deputy chuckled. "I'm just messing with you, Keo. Don't take it too personally."

"The last person who told me not to take something too personally hasn't said a word since."

"Oooh, tough guy." Duncan snorted, but Keo noticed that he snuck a wary glance in his direction.

Keo smiled and kept walking.

They had been moving through the woods around Winding Creek for the last hour or so, and by Keo's guess they were almost on the other side, with the farms and the stream that provided the town with all of its water nearby. It made sense that the ghouls would target the areas around the farms—that was where the livestock, the easier of the two types of prey (humans being the other), were.

It was around two in the afternoon when they finally reached their destination: a rundown shack smaller than the one Keo was currently living in. He knew of its existence because he had scouted this part of the woods long before he decided Winding Creek was worth taking a look at. There were three other habitable buildings in the area that had long been abandoned, and any one of them would have made just as good a nesting place.

They approached the house from the front, the two lawmen on horseback and Keo on foot. Keo was mindful of the tall grass around him, signs that no one had bothered to maintain the property for a few years now. The dead giveaway that someone (some*thing*) occupied the building were the filthy white blankets over the two windows flanking the door, blocking out the only thing the ghouls feared more than silver weapons—sunlight.

Jim climbed off his horse and tied the reins to a low-hanging branch. "Phil found one of his goats about half a mile from his property. It was all chewed up; looked like they'd been sucking on it for days. He didn't notice it was missing until this morning and went looking for it."

Keo didn't have to look far to see evidence that someone—more than someone, actually, but some*ones*—had been going back and forth from the cabin and the surrounding woods. Grass had been trampled, stepped over, and footprints led to the front door where clumps of dirt, some still damp, remained. The prints hadn't been made by a human being—or, at least, nothing that was still one. They might have been mistaken for bare feet if he didn't look closely enough or recognize their deformed nature. There were old specks of blood, dark black under the sunlight, but not enough to really notice if he wasn't already looking for them. That would be animal blood, or whatever it was the creatures had been dining on. Ghoul blood, like the undead things themselves, evaporated in sunlight.

He reached behind him and pulled out his SIG Sauer. He'd grabbed his knife before leaving his place, and it sat snugly on his left hip. Keo assumed both lawmen checking their own weapons next to him were also carrying the right weapons, not that he'd taken the time to make sure. They might have been insulted if he had; he knew *he* would if someone had asked him. Everyone was armed with silver weapons these days. Even Emma carried a knife with a silver-edged blade on her at all times.

"Ever thought about carrying something with more rounds?" Keo asked, nodding at Jim's six-shooter.

"That's why I brought this along," Jim said, pulling a sawed-off shotgun from a scabbard hanging off his horse's saddle. He grabbed a handful of shells and stuffed them into his pants pockets.

"Silver buckshot?"

"Of course," the sheriff said. "You?"

Keo nodded. "Of course."

The older man turned to face the cabin. "So, how are we going to do this?"

"You're asking me?"

Jim shrugged. "This is the first ghoul nest we've had in five years. We figured you'd have more experience taking them on."

"Well, it's not rocket science. We could just burn the place down like you did last time, but that might start a fire, and no one wants that."

"Nope. Too close to the farms."

"Uh huh. So let's just knock on the door and see what happens."

Duncan grunted. "Oh, I got a pretty good idea what's going to happen."

"Got a better idea, Deputy?"

"Didn't say that."

"Then less talking, more knocking," Keo said, and began walking toward the cabin.

The lawmen hurried to catch up, Jim walking to his left, while Duncan took his right.

You're doing this for Emma and Megan. Remember that.

It's a one and doner.

There was a metal security gate over the door, but it was hanging off two of its top hinges. Keo grabbed one of the rusted-over bars and pulled it back. The gate made a loud creaking sound, like something out of a bad horror movie.

Jim reached over and took the gate from Keo, allowing him to square up in front of the door. The slab of wood was dark brown, with a latch for a handle, and nothing resembling a doorknob. It looked thick enough that Keo was pretty sure he wasn't going to be able to kick it open, so he didn't even try. Instead, he pushed down on the latch and the door swung open with—unlike the gate over it—almost no sound at all.

He heard movement just before he saw them scurrying in the darkness inside. It was pitch-black, thanks to the blankets over the windows, and Keo gave himself a few seconds to let his eyes adjust.

He was still working on that when Duncan slipped past him and into the building and began shooting.

"Duncan!" Jim shouted, but he was about a second too late.

Keo sighed and pushed the door all the way in and followed Duncan inside. The deputy was still firing his 1911 Colt at a creature as it attempted to flee into a back hallway. It took three bullets, but one finally found its target and the ghoul —it was small, just barely bigger than Megan—seemed to slide before dropping, and lay still on the filthy floor.

Everything about the cabin's great room was dirty, with sheets of dust swarming them as soon as Keo took the first step inside, the rustic wood creaking loudly under his boots. The thunderous *bang! bang!* of Duncan's shots shook loose even more layers of dirt from the ceiling, and those landed on top of them.

Keo fought back a cough as something moved in the corner of his left eye. He turned, saw it bounding out of the dark corner. Its mouth was opening wide, showing jagged yellow teeth smeared with dark, old blood.

He shot it in the chest, and the creature flopped to the floor with a loud *thump.*

Then Jim was there, squeezing in between Keo and Duncan, and the massive *boom!* as he unloaded both shotgun barrels that left Keo's ears ringing. The walls and floor might have also trembled in the aftermath, but Keo couldn't be completely sure because he was trying desperately to fight through the shock of being so close to the blast.

Dammit, Jim! Not so close, you idiot!

The rest of the ghouls had fled into the bedrooms in the back. Keo couldn't quite hear them with his ears still buzzing, but he could *smell* them everywhere in the closed cabin.

"I guess we should finish it," Jim said as he reloaded his shotgun. Or Keo thought that was what he had said. The sheriff could have been reciting his grocery list for all Keo knew.

Jim took point, stepping over three twisted bodies lying on the floor toward the bedroom. Duncan followed, nervously changing up his grip on his pistol.

Keo gave the ghoul he'd killed a quick look before turning and following the two men into the back of the dark cabin, thinking to himself, *And you thought the days of going into dark rooms were over. Optimistic much?*

As it turned out, it wasn't much of a fight, and Keo didn't have to do very much. Jim did most of the work—or his shotgun did, as its double barrels full of silver buckshot tore into their victims inside the bedroom even before Keo or Duncan could enter after him.

In the end, Keo left the house feeling almost sorry for the creatures.

Almost.

Killing them proved easier than disposing of the bodies, which included dragging the bony carcasses outside. Keo managed two figures at a time while doing his very best not to imagine them as children, given how little they weighed and how small they both were. The sun was already eating away at their flesh even before he could get them off the porch and into the yard. He wished he could have said the stinging scent of evaporating ghoul skin, muscle, and everything else that covered their bleach-white bones was something new, but he was too used to it to lie to himself with any conviction.

Duncan and Jim grabbed rags from their saddlebags to wipe at the dust that covered them, while Keo ran his fingers through his hair and shook off the remains of vaporized ghoul —specks of gray cremated ash—that had been lifted into the air by the wind. He grabbed a bottle of water from Jim and poured the contents over his face and hair, then drank whatever was left.

"That was easier than I thought," Jim said as he wiped at his face and forehead with another bottle.

"I told you you didn't need me," Keo said.

"Maybe not this time..."

"This is the first and only time, Jim."

"What if more show up?"

"Then it's time to recruit more deputies. But this is it for me. One and done."

Jim nodded, though Keo didn't fail to notice the lack of verbal confirmation.

He glanced down at the pile of bones instead. It never

ceased to amaze him how white they looked once the sun got ahold of them, almost as if they were bleached by chemicals.

"Brings back memories," Duncan said, his hands on his hips. "How many bones did we bury after The Walk Out, Jim? A few thousand?"

"Maybe that," Jim nodded. "Maybe more."

"You weren't here, Keo, but they were everywhere. It was like someone had taken a digger and unearthed every cemetery in the world and dumped them around Winding Creek." The deputy shook his head. "I don't think I ever had to work so hard in my life. Not that I minded, mind you. No one did, because it meant these buggers were gone." He glanced around at the unmowed yard. "Hell, there're probably a few hundred of them under our feet as we speak. God knows we buried enough of them everywhere."

The Walk Out, Keo thought with a smile. He still remembered the shock of watching ghouls coming out of the buildings around the city as the helicopter he was sitting in hovered in the air. There was a seemingly endless wave of them—tens of thousands—obeying a command that only they could hear. *You did it, Will. You did it*, he remembered thinking.

Keo looked over at Jim and Duncan now as the two lawmen grabbed the multipurpose folding shovels they'd brought with them and walked back over. He doubted if either men knew who Will was or the things he'd done in the name of humanity. In the five years since, in all the towns he'd gone through and the people he'd met, not a single person had mentioned Will's name.

You died a hero, and no one even knows it except for those of us who were there.

It would have been a tragedy if the man himself cared. Keo

didn't know him—at least, not the man that he was before his transformation—but from everyone who did, he didn't think Will would have been the least bit bothered that no one even knew the sacrifices he had made that day under the HC Dome.

But Keo knew who Will was, and so did everyone who was there. And, more importantly, *she* knew, and he thought that was probably the only thing that mattered to Will at the very end.

Wish I could have known you better, pal. Maybe in another life...

"We only brought two," Jim was saying, holding up his shovel. "Didn't think you would actually agree to come along."

Neither did I, Keo thought, but said, "Two's all you need."

Duncan glanced down at the dozen or so remains. "You can always spell me. I'll dig and you shovel, how about that?"

"Nah. Besides, I got a long walk ahead of me."

"You're going already?" Jim asked.

"I gotta go take a shower or at least change clothes." He sniffed himself and shook his head. "I forgot how much they smell."

"You killed one of them two nights ago."

"One's different than a whole nest. The smell's more noticeable." Keo gave them a mock salute. "Have fun, boys," he said, and started off.

"Hey, Keo," Jim called after him when he was almost out of the clearing. Then, when Keo stopped and glanced back, "Thanks."

"Like I said, don't get used to it, Sheriff."

Jim smiled. "I'll tell Emma how helpful you were."

"Don't give her any ideas."

"What does she see in you, anyway?" Duncan asked as he shoved the spade into the ground and pushed it in with one boot.

"Must be my winning personality," Keo said.

"What personality?"

"You'll have to take your clothes off to find out, Duncan."

"Yeah, no thanks," the deputy said. "But I'll be sure to ask her when I get back from Dresden tomorrow." He winked. "I'll even bring back flowers. I bet she'll love that."

"Dresden?"

"Up north, to find out why they didn't show up as planned last week," Jim said. "He could use some com—"

"He doesn't need company," Keo said, cutting the sheriff off.

"Actually, I wouldn't mind, now that I think about it," Duncan said. "Maybe I'll ask Emma if she wants to come along..."

Keo turned and started off. "Good luck with the digging, boys," he said, and slipped back into the woods, glad to be moving as far away from the stench of dead ghouls as possible.

FOUR

He had gone nearly a year without shooting, stabbing, or maiming another human being, but Keo always knew that streak was going to end sooner or later. He was surprised it had lasted this long, and he credited most of that to his current situation—Megan, Emma, and a relatively quiet life he had stumbled across being the main reason.

Winding Creek was a hole in the wall, hidden from the world except for those who were brought here almost six years ago, and it had remained that way since. Life after The Purge was essentially the same for the townspeople—at least for those who had stayed behind when they no longer had to. Sometimes he wondered what life would have been like if he had found the place earlier in his travels.

Look at you, thinking about white picket fences. Disgusting.

His cabin was bigger and (definitely) cleaner than the one the ghouls had occupied, but it wasn't exactly luxurious. There was a single bedroom in the back with a great room taking up most of the space up front. It measured less than six hundred square feet in total (not that Keo ever broke out the measuring tape, but he eyeballed it at about that size) and would be smaller than most one-bedroom apartments in the city. But it was plenty big for just him, and besides, how much room did one man need, anyway?

He ran more water over his hair and face, then changed clothes after returning home, before heading back into the kitchen. From one of its windows and through the repurposed rebars, he could just make out the sun reflecting off the steeple of Winding Creek's church. It was the one constant sign that there was someone else out there beyond the ring of woods, that he wasn't alone.

You wouldn't need constant reminders if you'd moved in with Emma like Megan wanted you to, a voice said in the back of his head. *Rejoin civilization again, like a civilized human being.*

Oh, shut up, he thought, and pulled the curtains closed.

This was good enough. It had to be good enough. Committing now would only make things more complicated. There was a reason he still had a bug-out bag in his bedroom closet, because you never knew. You just never knew.

He stopped in front of the window that the ghoul had broken two nights ago and stared at it. There wasn't any blood left on the jagged shards of glass or on the windowsill. The sun had taken care of that. Too bad the sun couldn't fix the window for him, too.

He thought about Emma, about what she was doing now, and how she would react when he reappeared after sneaking out on her last night. It was the first time she'd asked, and he knew it took a lot of courage on her part. Emma, like him, was wary of getting involved, and yet she had taken the risk...only to have him skip out on her like a thief in the night.

What a manly thing to do.

God, you suck.

To keep himself busy and from thinking about all his faults, Keo spent a few minutes digging out the .45 bullet from the floorboards. It was mostly lead, with just enough silver stirred into the final product to kill ghouls. You really didn't need much—certainly nothing like the silver-coated buckshot Jim had used back at the ghouls' nest. Just a little silver would do it. How the hell did it work, anyway? Maybe one of those scientists Keo was sure were still out there would figure it out and tell him one of these days.

He tossed the salvaged material into a bowl already filled with other metals, things that could be turned into bullets later. There were still plenty of weapons and ammo just lying around even six years after The Purge, but they weren't going to last forever. Keo had learned to be prepared.

Just in case...

There was one advantage to being so close to civilization again—coffee. Winding Creek was the first town he'd come across that knew how to grow the stuff, and getting a whiff of freshly-brewed coffee in the air one morning while scouting the area had made him temporarily question his sanity. That was also how he'd met Emma.

Stop thinking about her. Jesus.

Keo was grinding the beans with the water heating up on the kettle behind him when he heard it: a very faint *popping* sound.

His head snapped up.

It took him a second—maybe a second and a half, or

possibly even two—to fully process what he had just heard. By the time he knew what the noise was with absolute certainty, two more identical sounds had echoed.

Pop-pop!

Then, quickly after that:

Pop-pop-pop!

Keo abandoned the beans and rushed to the nearest window and looked south toward the skinny white steeple in the distance, poking out from the tree crowns like an unwanted appendage.

Pop-pop!

They seemed to be getting louder with each one, maybe even getting closer. Or maybe now that his brain had fully recognized the noises for what they were, they just appeared louder, more urgent. Maybe—

Brap-brap-brap! Brap-brap-brap!

Keo went deathly still, and this time he didn't have to waste a second trying to decipher the new noise. He knew exactly what it was.

The water had begun to boil when Keo ran into the bedroom and grabbed the P220 from under the pillow. He shoved it into his front waistband, then grabbed one side of the bed and tossed the mattress and box springs over. The dusty rug that he hadn't touched in over five months came next; Keo jerked open the trap door, reached in, got a good grip on the side handles, and lifted the box up and deposited it next to him.

It wasn't much to look at: a three-quarters thick pine rectangle, twenty-three inches long, nine inches wide, and nine inches deep. There was no lock, since Keo assumed if someone knew where it was, they wouldn't have any trouble cracking the lid anyway. He pulled it open and stared at its contents.

Almost a year. He'd almost gone a full year...

"*Daebak*," he said out loud to the empty room.

Pop-pop-pop!

The gunfire got louder as he closed in on the town limits. From the many times he'd gone back and forth, Keo knew he had another hundred or so paces ahead of him. Of course, since he was running at almost full-speed (*Faster than a donkey but slower than a cheetah, pal!*) and was extending his normal stride, it was more like fifty (give or take) steps left.

The steeple was growing in size to his left, and he steered clear of the spur road that connected Winding Creek to a two-lane country blacktop. His mind swirled with possibilities (Who was attacking? Who was doing the shooting? And *why?*) as he dodged branches and went around gnarled tree trunks and hopped over shrubs.

He gripped the MP5SD in front of him, sweat from his palms glistening off the black matted exterior of the Heckler & Koch submachine gun. It felt a lot heavier than he remembered, but then he hadn't held it in over five months. But he didn't worry about its ability to function again when he needed it. After all, no one made guns like the Germans, and this particular model had served him well before, during, and after the world went to shit.

Pop-pop-pop!

He was getting closer.

Thirty steps...

He flicked off the safety on the weapon.

Twenty...

Beads of sweat stung his eyes, but he blinked through it.

Fifteen...

Thirty rounds in the magazine. Two more spares in his back pocket.

Ten...

The SIG Sauer P220 pressed snugly against his front waist had seven rounds, which wasn't good, but he did have two spares in his front pockets—

Shit!

Keo was lifting the submachine gun when the first figure burst through the thick foliage in front of him, the sound of heavy footsteps registering just a second too late. (*You're getting slow, old timer!*) The man was breathing hard—gasping, really—and Keo really should have heard it well before he spotted the man himself, but Keo's own breath was pounding in his ears from the running and had camouflaged it.

Excuses, excuses!

The man was dragging a little girl behind him. She was the same age and height as Megan, but she was wearing a dress, something Megan wouldn't be caught dead in. Tears flooded down the girl's cheeks, her entire body seeming to convulse as she was pulled out of the thick brush and onto the other side—

"Oh, Jesus!" the man said when he saw Keo in front of him a split second later. "Keo? Thank God it's you."

That's a first, Keo thought, lowering the weapon and stepping closer.

He focused on Mark. Blood poured down one side of his face from a wound along his temple that Keo couldn't quite make out with the shadows around them. Mark was wearing his apron, still stained with fresh flour, which meant he had been at work in his bakery when the chaos began.

"What's happening in town, Mark?" Keo asked.

Mark stared blankly at him, as if he couldn't quite figure out the question. His daughter, Angie (or was it Angela? Abbie? Something with an *A*, Keo was (mostly) sure of it) stood silently at his side gripping his hand as her own chest heaved with every breath. The girl looked ready to scream but was somehow keeping it in. Keo couldn't imagine how, but maybe, like most kids her age who were still around, Angie/Angela/A-something had practice being quiet in stressful situations. She was around ten and would have lived through The Purge.

"People with guns," Mark said. He bent over at the waist to catch his breath. "They just started shooting. Jim, Duncan... They're dead. They're both dead."

Well, shit, that's not good.

The last Keo saw of the lawmen was the two of them getting ready to dig graves for the piles of ghoul bones outside the cabin on the opposite side of town. While Keo had to circle around Winding Creek to get back to his cabin without going through the town itself, the sheriff and his deputy would have only had to walk the short distance back and would have arrived in town long before he made it back to his place.

Just in time to get killed.

Keo crouched in front of Mark and snapped his fingers in front of the other man's face to get his attention. Mark glanced up, his chest still heaving, seemingly in sync with his daughter next to him. The baker hadn't, Keo saw, let go of his daughter's hand, and Keo didn't think anyone could pry the two apart.

"Who were they?" Keo asked.

Mark shook his head. "I don't know. I don't know..."

"Strangers?"

"Yes..."

"How many?"

"I don't know. I don't know..."

"How many did you *see?*"

"Five..."

"But there's more?"

"Yes..."

"How many machine guns did you see?"

"What?"

"Machine guns. How many did you see?"

"I don't know. I don't know..."

"Vehicles?"

"Horses. They were riding horses."

"All of them?"

"Some were on foot..."

"No vehicle?"

"I didn't see any. I didn't see any..."

Keo nodded. The lack of vehicles would explain why he hadn't heard them while he was still back at the cabin. Vehicles meant engines and engines made noise. A lot of very loud noises, especially out here where the preferable mode of transportation was horses or on foot. Horses were easy to feed—there was green everywhere you looked—whereas cars needed fuel, which was as rare as a decent porterhouse steak these days.

Then Keo asked the question he'd been dreading. "Emma and Megan. Did you see them?"

Mark shook his head. "No..."

"Are you sure?"

"Yes..."

"Are you *sure,* Mark?"

The baker seemed to think about it before answering. Then, "I ran. God help me, I ran out the back with Angel. I didn't see anyone. I'm sorry, Keo, I'm sorry. I just ran."

Angel. Close enough.

"Okay," Keo said, when the *pop-pop-pop* of automatic weapons fire made Mark spin around so fast that he almost pulled his daughter off her feet.

"Oh, God," Mark said breathlessly. "Oh, God..."

"Go," Keo said.

Mark turned back around to look at him. "Go where?"

"My cabin. Go."

"What if they find us there?"

"Then I guess you keep running."

Mark stared at him like he was having difficulty processing Keo's last statement.

"*Go,*" Keo said, harder this time so it would get through to the terrified man. Then, in a calmer voice and with just a ghost of a grin that was directed at Mark's daughter, "And try not to make too much of a mess, okay? I just cleaned the place this morning."

Mark nodded, might have been on the verge of saying something—maybe even to thank him?—but stumbled forward past Keo instead.

The girl followed her father but looked back at Keo, tears streaming down her face. She really did look a lot like Megan in every way but the eyes. Megan was, Keo thought, an old soul like her mother.

Keo smiled back at the girl. It was probably a terrible attempt at being comforting, but the girl returned it anyway, just before she and her father vanished around a large tree, with only the very loud (*Too loud*) *crunch-crunch* of their foot-steps left in their wake.

He turned back around.

The shooting had slowed, with only the occasional *pop!* followed by long beats of silence before another gunshot could be heard. Keo wasn't entirely sure if that was good or bad. But he was sure of one thing: He wasn't going to find out standing here underneath the very comforting shade of a large tree.

He unslung the MP5SD and took the first step toward the tree line.

———

Winding Creek wasn't the biggest place Keo had been in before, during, or after The Purge. In fact, it wasn't very big at all. Like most locations in the state of Texas that had been repurposed in the weeks and months after the ghouls took over, it was a small community most people had never heard of, but one with all the right ingredients to make it stand out—surrounded by thriving farmland, and close enough to a water source that allowed it to thrive. Of the six hundred or so people who had been settled here, most of them either went home or went in search of greener pastures.

The place wasn't anywhere close to "home" for Keo, but then most places weren't. There were really only two reasons he stayed, and their names were Emma and Megan. He was thinking of them now as he reached the edge of the tree line and went into a crouch, his breath hammering against his chest.

You're out of shape. Time to get back on the treadmill!

Keo leaned slightly forward and looked through two

towering oak trees with trunks bigger than five of him combined. That was plenty of cover as he peered out toward the north end of Winding Creek. A paved road led into Main Street through a series of buildings, their backs facing him at the moment. All the action was taking place on the other side, as far as he could tell. The houses would be farther back, but to get to them he would either have to cross Main Street or spend another thirty minutes going around it.

The church tower was fifty meters or so directly ahead—a brick-and-mortar rectangle that ended in a sharp point topped by a white cross. The middle of the structure was hollowed and held a large bronze and copper bell at the center. Keo was used to that thing banging away an hour before every sundown and even more often on Sundays. Apparently people still went to church in Winding Creek, which made the place a novelty in a post-Purge world.

Pop-pop!

Automatic rifle fire coming from his right, somewhere near the town square.

Bang!

A single shot, likely from a handgun.

Bang! Bang!

Two more shots, also from handguns, but these came from a separate pistol than the first.

Two shooters. Exchanging gunfire? Maybe. To find out for sure, he'd have to leave the safety of the woods and venture out. Either that, or go around and pray that Emma and Megan were home when the attack began. What were the chances of that—

A flash of movement in the corner of his left eye, and Keo slid back to put a thick bush between him and two men on horseback as they tore across the open flat field. He glimpsed civilian clothes, fingerless gloves clutching reins, thick boots in stirrups, and black urban assault vests. Gun belts and holsters, pouches, and AR rifles thumping against their backs. If Keo had to guess, both men were strapped with enough spare magazines to weigh two full human beings each.

Can't say they didn't come prepared.

Both horsemen flew across Keo's line of vision before disappearing through two buildings—a bakery (*Mark's*) and an apartment where he knew a few people that called the place home. The men on horseback were clearly reacting—and now heading—toward the new reports of gunfire.

Who are these guys?

He remained very still, the MP5SD clutched in front of him, and listened for more hints about what was happening in the part of the town that he couldn't see from his position. The air had gone eerily quiet since the sudden bursts of shooting two minutes ago. Even after moving closer toward the brush, Keo still couldn't pick up any new sounds.

No shooting, no voices. A big, fat nothing.

That can't be good.

What were the chances the good folks of Winding Creek had managed to fight back against their attackers and won, and were now taking stock of their losses?

Yeah right.

Keo sighed, and thought, *Like you had anything better to do today anyway,* and pushed back up onto his feet before taking the first steps into the open fields.

FIVE

Mark's bakery was the most obvious point of entry via the back door, and though Keo found evidence of a struggle inside the place, there was surprisingly very little blood. A few drops here and there, including a broken glass countertop and a couple of overturned chairs. Given Mark's state, Keo had expected much worse and had envisioned him fighting for his life before tearing out of the back.

He eased through the small building, using the counter and then the chairs for cover. The bakery had a glass door and two curtainless windows that looked out into the streets. He kept low and made it all the way to the front without being detected. Keo pushed against the wall, then slid up to his full six-one height before peeking outside.

He searched for that machine gun he'd heard earlier, the *brap-brap-brap* that had gotten his attention more than anything. Keo had gone up against a lot—guys with guns, a lot of guys with a lot of guns—but he despised having to face an MG. It was unfair, really, like bringing a knife to a gunfight when the other guy told you only knives were allowed.

Or something like that.

He couldn't locate the machine gun (something like that would be welded onto the back of a technical or being lugged around by a beefy guy with arms the size of his thighs, most likely), but he did locate where the two horsemen he'd seen earlier had gone. They had stopped in the street and were standing over a body.

The motionless figure had on dark pants and a white shirt and was definitely male. (*Not Emma or Megan. Thank God.*) Two more figures stood on the street, one crouched over the body. Jeans and khaki cargos, and similar black assault vests like the two horsemen. Except now that Keo could get a better look at the men without them moving in a blur, he was able to spot the rough white circle emblems with what looked like the capital letter *M* in the middle. The images looked as if they were made with white markers and drawn in by hand, and appeared at random locations on the front and back of the vests. One of them had his *M* higher up and over one of his pouches, while another had his closer to the center.

Now where have I seen that before?

One of the men was prodding at the dead figure's temple with the muzzle of his rifle while the others looked on. They might have also been exchanging quips, but Keo couldn't make out words from inside the bakery, but their reactions—one might have laughed—seemed to lend credence to that. He eyeballed the distance at about seventy meters, give or take.

The dead man could have been anyone. There were exactly one hundred and twenty-seven people in Winding Creek. Of those, thirty-nine were adult males and the rest were women and kids. Keo hadn't gotten to know all of the men—not that he would have been able to tell who was lying on the street at the moment from where he was hiding anyway, with the man's face turned in the wrong direction.

The fact that the town had more women than men wasn't strange at all. Most towns these days had the same slanted numbers in favor of the fairer XX sex. The majority of those females also had children, with most of them under the age of five. It was a young population boom designed purely to serve masters that were now gone.

Well, mostly all gone, anyway.

Keo was still thinking about numbers, trying to decide how much of this mess he was willing to get himself into in order to save a woman and a ten-year-old girl who hadn't known he existed (and vice versa) until less than a year ago, when he heard the screaming.

He wasn't surprised to hear it. It was inevitable. He'd seen it in other places, sometimes while it was happening, but most of the times just the bloody and filthy aftermaths. There was no reason Winding Creek would be spared once someone stronger and with more guns discovered its existence.

The screaming came from the apartment complex next door, and the fact that it was a woman made damn sure Keo couldn't ignore it. Not that he would have anyway (*Yeah, keep telling yourself that, pal*), but thoughts of Emma—or worse, Megan—flashed across his mind's eye even as he darted back across the bakery to the same door he'd entered only a few minutes earlier.

He sneaked a look out first before exposing himself, then crossed the short distance to the apartment. There was an alleyway between the two structures, and Keo made sure the four heavily-armed men down the street weren't looking in his direction before he jogged across the empty space. They weren't, he saw, either because they couldn't hear the screaming or they didn't care because it wasn't anything they hadn't been expecting.

The apartment had a back door and it was already slightly ajar when Keo reached it. He pushed it open with the suppressor attached to the end of his submachine gun, ensuring that the weapon took the lead and saw whatever—if anything—was waiting for him before he did so he wouldn't need to lift it first to fire.

His forefinger tested the trigger of the H&K. He'd found it three years ago in a dump just outside of the Dallas-Fort Worth area, next to a dead man who was wearing cowboy boots for some reason. The gun hadn't been very well maintained, but that was easily remedied. Keo had used a lot of weapons in his time, but he had a real love for the German-made MP5SD. If he were a more superstitious man, he might even consider it his good luck charm.

The back door opened up into a hallway, with a view of the front lobby about thirty meters ahead. The super's office, long ago converted into a storage room, was to his right. There were a few empty boxes on the floor leading to the front doors that Keo stepped over so he could sneak a quick peek into the office. Looters had taken everything they could (food and weapons) and left the rest (clothes and farming supplies).

Keo faced forward, then continued on.

He didn't have to see it to know it was coming, because he could *smell* it long before he made it to the other side of the corridor. The air was thick with it, and though it had been a while, it hadn't been that long ago.

He stepped over a pair of empty bullet casings scattered among the tossed boxes, then had to go around a thick pool of blood near the mouth of the hallway. Trails of blood led him to five figures stacked on top of one another like hastily assembled campfire logs near the center of the room. The man on top was lying on his back, and there was a very neat bullet hole in his forehead. The three rounds in his chest, that were still dripping blood onto the men underneath him, weren't nearly as orderly. Thick lines of blood, fresh enough that they tickled at his nostrils, connected the pile to the stairs five meters to his left.

Five bodies. All adult males.

More screaming, coming from above him. It was loud enough that Keo instinctively went into a slight crouch and pushed against the hallway wall as he looked out the open lobby door and into the street. Of the four heavily-armed bodies he'd seen out there earlier, the two on horseback had vanished, leaving just the two on foot to go through the dead man's pockets. The screaming, again, hadn't been worth their attention.

Keo stood up and slid out of the back hallway and around the random pools of blood blocking his path to the stairs. He avoided the heavy trails of red as well as the bloody boot prints that traveled randomly in and out of the thick liquid by sticking to the side and taking the steps one at a time, the submachine gun leading the way the entire time.

There was no way to tell from just the screaming who the woman was. It could have been Emma for all he knew, though it didn't make sense for her to be here, unless she had fled here from her home during the attack. But more likely it was one of the many women in Winding Creek that he'd never gotten around to meeting. There were certainly plenty of them.

But the fact that it *could* have been Emma—regardless of how remote—was enough to keep him moving instead of responding to the very real instinct to bug out. Go back to the cabin, grab his bag, and *get the hell outta here.* Because this wasn't his fight, and it wasn't like he'd never seen a town being taken over by force before. It was always bloody, always violent, and the men always ended up dead and the women in...worse shape.

So why didn't he stop and turn around and obey his instincts to get the hell out now while he still could? Now, while no one had any idea he was even around? Because this was stupid. This was so, so goddamn stupid.

It might be Emma. It probably isn't, but it might be her.

Then he was at the second floor without realizing it, and instead of turning around, Keo stopped and listened to the woman. She had stopped screaming and was sobbing now. He couldn't tell if she was in pain, but it was clearly distress. It didn't take a genius to figure that one out, which was good because no one had ever accused him of being smarter than the average bear.

He heard male voices, too—more than one—occasionally drowning out the woman. They were talking amongst themselves, and there was an edge to them. *And excitement.*

Keo took the last step and went into another crouch before leaning around the corner.

There were three of them, lining up along the wall outside an open door almost exactly halfway up the hallway from the staircase. Their backs were to him, and like the ones he'd seen in the streets, they wore civilian clothes and black assault vests, the sloppily (*Hand-drawn? Looks like it.*) circled white *M* emblem on different parts of what was clearly some shabby attempt at a uniform...ish. They had their rifles slung, and the bloody boot prints he'd been painfully avoiding on his way up led to the figures in front of him now.

Keo gripped the submachine gun tighter, when one of the men (in the middle) said, "Fuck, how long's he going to take?"

"Shut up," the one at the front said. He was leaning casually against the wall, patiently biding his time by tossing a bloody knife from hand to hand.

"I'm just saying," the first guy said.

"You say too much."

"You don't think he's taking too long?"

"No."

"He's ruining her."

"You'll get your shot."

"I just don't want him to ruin her before I do, that's all."

"Finders keepers," a third one said.

The first speaker glanced over his shoulder. He was young —early twenties, with shaggy hair and light blue eyes. "Finders? He didn't find shit."

"How do you know?" the third one said. Keo couldn't see his face, but he had a mullet that went down past his collar.

"Because I was outside clearing the fucking church with him when they found her."

"Well, why didn't you say so?"

"I just did."

Mullet *harumped* but let it go.

"He's taking way too long," Shaggy said as he turned back around.

"Shut up," the one up front said again.

"I'm just sayin'..."

A fucking Three Stooges routine, these assholes, Keo thought as he climbed the last step.

He might have made just a little bit more noise than he had intended to. He blamed it on the sudden rush of adrenaline pouring through him because his body knew exactly what he was about to do even before his mind accepted it.

A year. Almost went a whole year...

The woman screamed again, louder this time (though maybe that was just because Keo was now on the same floor and she just sounded louder), and drowned out any noise he might have made as he straightened up and the magazines in his front pockets *clacked* softly against one another.

He took one step, then two—and when the Three Stooges still hadn't turned around to acknowledge his presence—Keo went faster, and faster, and *faster* up the hallway.

There were ten doors to his left and ten more to his right. He passed the first closed apartment door without trouble and was almost at the second one—three doors down from his target—when Mullet, at the very back, began to turn around.

The man's eyes widened at the sight of Keo sneaking up behind him, and he opened his mouth to say something. Keo shot him in the forehead, the gunshot bouncing off the narrow passageway as a barely audible *pfft!*

Keo heard it just fine, but the other two never turned around.

It was an easy shot from less than nine meters away, and even as Mullet was slumping to the floor, Keo fired again, his second round slamming into the back of Shaggy's head before the submachine gun's first bullet casing had the chance to *clink* against the wooden floorboards underneath him.

The first man, at the front of the line, reacted faster than Keo had anticipated. He put his knife away and was spinning around, his right hand stabbing down to his hip for his holstered sidearm at the same time. It was a slick move, and clearly he had practiced it before. But it wasn't fast enough, and the man was wrapping his fingers around the gun when Keo shot him, striking him in the throat.

Blood gushed out in an arc, spraying the wall as the man stumbled but didn't go down. Keo tracked him and nailed him in the face with a second bullet. Keo was already running forward, stepping over Mullet, then Shaggy, before the third body crumpled completely to the hallway floor.

The open door allowed Keo to quickly turn and slip into the apartment—

And almost stumbled over a body lying on the carpet.

Rick, Keo thought at the sight of the upturned face.

There were thirty-nine men in Winding Creek, and Keo only knew a handful of them. Rick was a familiar face because Emma knew his wife, and they'd had something approaching a double date once.

Keo stepped over Rick, sweeping the room before picking up speed toward the open bedroom door on the other side. He had a feeling he already knew who he had been listening to screaming as he got closer.

The woman was sobbing when Keo stepped through the doorframe. The sobs were mixed in with someone else's pained grunting. The latter was coming from a man, his pants huddled around his knees as he thrashed on top of the pale figure underneath him. An assault vest, along with a gun holster, lay in a pile on the floor next to the bed. An AR, elaborately painted with camo, leaned against an armoire nearby.

The woman saw Keo over the man's right shoulder as he entered the room, and recognition flickered across her eyes.

Wendy. Rick's wife.

Keo thought about putting the man out of his misery, but there was a chance his bullet could go right through his target and hit Wendy. So instead of squeezing the trigger, he slung the MP5SD and pulled out his knife and stepped toward the bed.

Either the man heard Keo or he realized something was wrong—or it could have just been the fact that Wendy had stopped making any sounds at all, or even fighting him— because he ceased both grunting and thrusting and raised himself off his victim. He hadn't gotten very far when Keo grabbed him by his oily wet hair and jerked his head back, lifting his sweat-slicked body further off Wendy, before he shoved the extremely sharp point of the Ka-Bar into the nape of the man's neck.

He pushed it deep, deep, and *deeper*.

Wendy might have grabbed at her mouth in horror if her hands weren't bound with duct tape and tied to the bed post behind her. She was stretched out on the bed like some kind of sacrifice, and maybe she was, Keo thought, remembering the three men lining up outside the apartment for their turn.

The man's body spasmed as Keo pushed the knife downward with one hand. When the guy stopped moving completely, Keo rolled him off Wendy and over the side of the bed. He landed with a loud, sickening *thump* on the floor even as blood poured out of him.

Keo glanced back at the bedroom door—then past it and into the living room beyond—to make sure no one had sneaked in while he was busy. After all, if there were three waiting outside there could easily be four or more, with the lollygaggers just now showing up.

But there was no one but Rick out there.

He turned back to Wendy, who attempted to cover herself with her legs. Her eyes were bruised and there were red marks around her neck. Keo took pity on the both of them and grabbed a blanket and put it over her. There was blood on the cotton fabric, but he didn't think Wendy cared. Keo hurried over to the headboard and cut her hands free, and she quickly scrambled away from him, clutching the sheets to her breasts.

He wiped the blood from the Ka-Bar on a white shirt hanging off the bedpost and put it away before unslinging the MP5SD again. "Wendy, right?"

She nodded, her eyes going from him to the door. No, not the door, but the body outside. "He's dead," she whispered.

Keo nodded. "I'm sorry."

"He's dead," she whispered again.

She was in shock. It didn't come through in her voice—barely below a whisper—but he recognized it on her face, in the way she sat clutching the blanket and stared at Rick's unmoving form.

Keo gave the open doors another quick check before moving across the room to the window. He peeked out from behind the curtain and searched for—then found—the same body in the street. The two guys were still there, still rummaging through the man's pockets. What the hell were they looking for that it was taking so much time?

From a higher position he could see more of the town—and the bodies. There was a dozen or so more of them farther up the street and along the sidewalks. Mostly men from their shapes, but he saw a few women sprinkled among them.

Thankfully, no kids—or, at least, nothing small enough to be a kid. It almost looked like the victims were fleeing *to* the town square when the invasion happened. Why?

He glimpsed more men in black urban assault vests moving around. (*Christ, where'd they all come from?*) There were four on horseback and seven (maybe eight) on foot. They were patrolling, while a dozen or so were going in and out of a large warehouse on the other side of the square, a constantly moving line of people carrying boxes and bags to a pair of waiting U-Haul trailers hitched to horses. Keo recognized the building where Winding Creek stored its goods—everything they had harvested from the land, including those coffee beans that Emma had offered him the first day they met.

He glanced back at Wendy. She hadn't gotten off the bed. He couldn't even be sure if she had moved at all since scrambling away from him.

"Wendy..." When it didn't look as if she had heard him, Keo said louder, "Wendy."

She finally turned to face him. Her hair was in her face, and she looked on the verge of crying hysterically but somehow, somehow didn't.

"Emma," he said. "Do you know what happened to Emma and Megan?"

"Emma?" Wendy said, still whispering. He wondered if she was even aware of that.

"Did you see what happened to them?"

Wendy shook her head before her eyes wandered back to Rick in the living room.

"What about the others?" Keo asked.

"Others?" she said, and this time didn't look over at him.

"I see bodies outside, but that's not everyone. It's not even close. What happened to the rest?"

"They took them."

"They took them?" he repeated.

"The babies," Wendy said. "They took all the babies."

"*All* the babies?"

"All the babies," Wendy said again. "They took all the babies."

The children. She means the children. I think.

He glanced out the window again, at the men in assault vests raiding the storage warehouse on the other side of town, at the ones roaming the streets and sidewalks. More heavily armed figures were going in and out of buildings. The houses were on the other side. What were the chances Emma and Megan were still there? What were the chances they had managed to survive the assault at all?

Keo turned back to Wendy. "What about the women? Did they take them, too?"

"Yes," Wendy nodded. "They took the women. And the babies. God, they took all the babies."

"Where?"

"Where?" Wendy said.

"Where did they take all the babies?"

Wendy shook her head. "I don't know..."

"But you saw them. Take the babies. The children."

She nodded.

"What about—" Keo started to ask when Wendy finally climbed off the bed and stood over the dead man on the floor. "Wendy?" When he didn't get a response: "Wendy, are you okay?"

She was still clutching the blanket to her nude body, but

her bare back was to him, so Keo couldn't see her face. Not that he needed to in order to know what was going through her head at the moment.

"Wendy," he said. Then, when she didn't answer, he said again but louder, "Wendy. Over here. *Wendy.*"

She crouched down until he could only see the top of her head on the other side of the bed.

"Wendy," Keo said. "It's okay. We'll get out of here. I promise—"

He hadn't gotten *promise* completely out when the sound of a gunshot interrupted him and the top of Wendy's head that he could see disappeared out of view.

Keo ran back to the bed, but even as he rounded the floorboards he already knew what he was going to find on the other side.

There was blood, along with clumps of other things dripping from the bedsheets, and Wendy's body was curled up on the floor almost in a fetal position next to her assaulter. The blanket was somehow still clutched to her body, keeping her clothed as she fell. A handgun lay nearby, as did the pile of clothes and weapons the dead man had taken off.

Well, shit.

SIX

Depending on how far the closest bad guys were, Keo figured he had anywhere from thirty seconds to a full minute before he was overwhelmed. Maybe even more time if he was really, really lucky.

Yeah, right.

Winding Creek had settled into an eerie calmness after the initial bloodbath, and the gunshot was loud enough it wasn't going to take a lot to figure out where it had come from. His only real chance was that the men racing toward him now would do it cautiously and take their time entering the building. Of course, he could be dealing with a bunch of assholes with more balls than brain cells, which meant they would throw caution to the wind and storm the place at full speed.

Keo snatched up the dead guy's fancy AR and slung it—you never knew when an extra weapon would come in handy—and shoved a pair of spare magazines for it into some empty pockets on his cargo pants. He picked up the equally fancy Colt .45 1911 model semiautomatic Wendy had used to end

her life from the floor and grabbed two spares for that. By the
time he had zipped up another pants pocket, he could already
hear them coming up the stairs, the *bam-bam-bam* of their
heavy boots like hammers against the floorboards.

More balls than brain cells it is!

He rushed out of the bedroom, moving slower than before
thanks to the added weight. Not by much, but enough that he
noticed. He had thought about grabbing Rapist Number One's
assault vest so he didn't have to cram everything into his avail-
able pockets, but that would have cost him an extra ten seconds
or more, and right now that was ten seconds more than he had
to waste.

Keo reached the open living room door and stepped over
Rick's lifeless body. He pushed against the doorframe and
leaned out, then looked left toward the top of the stairs at the
end of the hallway.

The men he'd killed lay where he last saw them—three
inconsequential lumps of human waste that he wasn't going to
lose any sleep over. He heard them coming well before he
actually saw them, their boots sledgehammering against the
wooden staircase steps. He might have also heard voices but
couldn't be sure over the pounding footsteps.

Definitely more balls than brains.

The first one had taken two steps onto the second floor,
sunlight from the window down the hallway to Keo's right
glinting off his smooth, bald forehead, when Keo shot him in
the chest with the MP5SD. The man looked surprised, but
Keo had seen that expression before: they didn't know where
the sudden pain was coming from because they hadn't heard
the gunshot. That usually lasted for half a second (sometimes it
was just a barely noticeable flicker) before their legs turned to

jelly and they collapsed, like this one did. The man was holding a submachine gun of his own, and he pulled the trigger unwittingly as he fell, spraying 9mm rounds into the nearby wall.

The second man was on the stair landing when he reflexively started ducking at the sound of gunfire. He was bigger than the first, wearing a Houston Texans jersey underneath his assault vest, and he was turning to flee back down the stairs when Keo shot him twice, the second bullet hitting his target just under the base of the skull.

He dropped.

Someone shouted, "Fuck!" from the steps below, followed by new rounds of pounding footsteps—except these were heading back down.

Maybe some brains after all.

Keo took advantage of the moment to glance to his right. There was a wall with a window back there but no curtains, so he could see a wall of green trees on the other side. He gauged the distance at twenty or so meters of open space, which wasn't nearly as intimidating as the God-knew-how-many number of men waiting for him on the other side of the corridor.

He turned back left, toward the staircase.

Hushed voices, signs of someone trying to take control, but there were no further movements up or down the stairs. They had probably stagnated somewhere in the middle of the steps—

A head leaned around the corner, and Keo instinctively snapped off a shot at it.

Keo managed to glimpse a thick patch of white hair pulling back just as his 9mm round slammed into the corner about a foot above the man's head.

"Next one goes into your right eye!" Keo shouted.

Silence.

Five seconds, then ten.

Then, finally, "Who the fuck are you?" a voice asked. Male, guttural.

"I'm the Easter Bunny," Keo said. "Can't you tell?"

"You're pretty damn well armed for a kid's mascot."

"I'm the Easter Bunny who can't find his eggs. I'm really mad right now."

The man chuckled. Keo thought it sounded reasonably genuine. *Mostly.*

"Got a name?" the man asked.

"EB."

"EB?"

"Something wrong with your hearing?"

Five more seconds of silence. Then, "I get it. EB. Easter Bunny."

Keo smirked. *Took you long enough.*

"Buck," the voice said.

"Buck you, too," Keo shouted back.

Another chuckle. "No. Buck. That's my name."

"You don't say."

"Seems only fair you'd tell me yours."

"I already did."

"I don't believe you."

"Yeah, well, believe what you want. It's a free country."

"Have you been out there? It hasn't been a free country in a long time."

Jackass has a point.

The same head of white hair was leaning out into the open again—or, at least, enough to get one eye up the hallway and in his direction. Keo fought against the urge to take another shot.

The chances of hitting his target was minimal, and he had so, so many questions.

"The babies," Wendy had said. *"They took all the babies."*

Why the hell did they take "the babies?"

"You're all alone up here," the man named Buck said. He looked to be in his fifties, with something that might have been a scar across his forehead. If the five dead men between him and Keo meant anything to him, Buck didn't seem all that bothered by it. At least, not enough to stop shouting back and forth with him.

"Not true," Keo said. "I have friends."

"Oh yeah? And where might they be?"

"Right here with me. Their names are Heckler, Koch, Colt, and my bestie, Ka-Bar."

Buck snorted. "You a vet?"

"Almost, but I got kicked out of school for dissecting a live turtle."

"What?"

"Vet school. Wasn't that what you were talking about?"

"No."

"Ah. The other vet."

"So you are one."

"Nah."

"No?" the man said doubtfully.

"I'm more of the lone wolf type. Like Chuck Norris. Minus the facial hair."

"They got memes about you, too?"

"I don't know what that is."

"What's that?"

"Memes."

"Viral shit."

"Now that's something I'm glad I don't have. Sounds painful."

Buck snorted. "You Chinese or something, EB?"

"Or something."

"You look Chinese."

"Then I guess I must be Chinese. Wouldn't wanna make you feel bad."

The man with white hair leaned back behind the wall, and Keo heard whispers.

That's my cue!

He quickly pulled back from the door, turned, and jogged across the living room and into the bedroom. He grabbed one of the blankets crumpled on the bed and one of the pillows, then unhooked the assault vest. This one had the circled *M* almost near the top and in the middle of two pouches.

A perfect bull's-eye to aim for. Swell.

He hugged the bundle to his chest and hurried, moving as silently as he could—which took some doing while wearing boots—back to the front door. When he stuck his head quickly out into the hallway, it was as empty as last time except for the five bodies between him and the stairs on the other end.

"You plotting against me, Buck?" Keo shouted down the narrow corridor.

Buck poked his head around the corner, just one eyeball visible like last time. If nothing else, the man knew how to stay hidden. "What makes you say that, EB?"

"I dunno. You've been awfully quiet. Plus, I'm naturally the suspicious type."

"Hey, whatever helps you stay alive."

"Why Winding Creek?" Keo asked as he piled the blanket, pillow, and assault vest on the floor and unslung the AR, before relieving himself of its spare magazines, then did the same to the Colt. He definitely wasn't going to need all that extra weight for what he had planned.

"Why Winding Creek what?" Buck said from down the hallway.

Keo removed all the bulky gear from the vest, then slipped it on and pushed the clasps into place, careful to do it slowly to minimize the *clicking* sound of the pieces locking.

"Why did you attack Winding Creek?" he called out.

"Because it's here," Buck said.

"Come again?"

"Because it's here. Because they had what we wanted. Because it was easy. *Because.*"

Keo didn't know why he was even the slightest bit surprised. He'd seen what happened to Winding Creek repeated in a dozen places ever since he went off on his own. Towns like this had something someone else wanted, and they were willing to do whatever it took to take it. He remembered telling Emma that they couldn't hide from the world forever, that sooner or later someone who wasn't interested in trading would stumble across them. He had even told Jim once or twice. They hadn't listened. And he didn't really blame them, either. Besides the fact that he was no one—a stranger, even now—they had been isolated for so long—years—that there was no reason to believe they couldn't keep doing it.

But nothing lasts forever, Emma. I told you that.

"Hey, EB," Buck shouted from down the hallway.

Keo picked up the pillow. It was big and fluffy and actually felt pretty good despite the heavy sweat stains. "Yeah?"

"You still with me?"

"What are we, friends now? Fuck off."

Buck chuckled. "Don't be that way. Look, I got a proposition for you. And no, I'm not going to ask you to be my Demi Moore."

"Your what?"

"Demi Moore."

"I don't know who that is."

"From that movie with Robert Redford?"

"I don't watch a lot of movies."

"You knew who Chuck Norris was."

"Everyone knows Chuck Norris. I was in Kathmandu doing this thing a few years back, and *they* knew who Chuck Norris was. Kathmandu, Buckaroo. Kath, you dig it?"

"My point is, I have a deal for you."

"So, let's hear it."

"Give up your weapons and surrender."

Not bloody likely, Keo thought, but said anyway because he needed the extra time, "And then what?"

"I promise you'll get a fair hearing."

Keo wanted to laugh but didn't. "A fair hearing, huh? For what?"

"Oh, I don't know. How about killing five of my men?"

Six, actually, Keo thought, but said, "Your men? You in charge of these scumbags, Buck?"

"I guess I am."

"You don't sound so sure. Are you or aren't you?"

"I am."

"King Alpha, huh?"

"Of these boys? You bet."

Keo pushed the pillow against his chest, then picked up the blanket and slipped it around him. He slung the MP5SD, using the strap to further fasten the fabric against the pillow and his body. It felt good, but he wouldn't know if it was enough until he walked away from this. *If* he walked away from it.

"How about a counter proposal?" he shouted into the hallway.

"I'm listening," Buck said.

"You and your men surrender your weapons to *me*, and I promise to only shoot ten of you in the balls."

Buck laughed, and he was still laughing when Keo burst out of the open doorway and turned right and ran.

He ran as fast as he could and kept running even when he heard Buck shouting, clearly startled, *"Fuck!"*

Haha, sucker!

He made the first five meters before Buck noticed and got another five in before the first bullet *zipped!* past his head.

Keo added another five meters, his breath hammering away in his throat, then managed two more when the walls to the left and right of him began exploding, chunks of it flying all around his head. He couldn't tell how many were shooting—it could have been one or two or all of them, including his new best friend Buck—because at that very second all he could hear was his heartbeat crashing against his ears, pushing just about everything into the background as a slight buzzing noise.

Lights splashed in from the window (*Don't run into the light!* Keo thought, and might have even laughed out loud), like a beacon calling to him.

I'm coming, window, I'm coming!

He was almost there, almost home free, when there was a stab of pain from his right thigh and he thought, *So close. So close!*

He would have screamed if he wasn't too busy grunting

and gasping for breath as he continued to pour on the speed, knowing that the split second after he stopped moving he was a dead man and one (or two or a dozen) bullets slamming into the walls and floor and ceiling around him at the moment would finally locate their real target.

So he kept running.

Faster, faster, FASTER!

And hit the window with everything he had, and it disintegrated like cardboard.

Suddenly there was nothing but open, chilly air, and then he was in free fall.

SEVEN

This is such a bad idea. Such a bad, bad idea.

Of course, it was too late to do anything about it because he was currently plummeting out of the air like a bird with its wings clipped, and there was just one second before—

He slammed chest first into the ground below.

He was wondering if that had been a six meter (*give or take*) drop or more like fifty as he rolled onto his back and let the blanket unwind. Every part of his body was screaming, but at least he was in one piece. Or mostly in one piece. But the alternative was worse—broken and dead. He wasn't sure how much the blanket and pillow had spared him by absorbing some of the fall and if the padding in the assault vest had even done anything.

But he was *alive!*

The only part of him that wasn't aching was his right thigh, and that was only because it was too busy bleeding. He would have spent twenty or so seconds making sure he didn't bleed to death if he'd had them to spare. The truth was he probably had

less time than that before Buck and his boys made it across the
hallway and—

A head, sticking out of the window directly above him.

Keo drew the P220 from his waistband and squeezed off
two rounds, but the head—with a nice thick bush of brown hair
—jerked back into the building as soon as its owner saw Keo
taking aim. But the shots did what he needed them to—
momentarily keeping the people up there from raining gunfire
down on his helpless form.

He rectified his vulnerable position by scrambling up, did
everything he could to ignore the stabbing pain from his leg,
and took off running toward the woods. Thank God there was
nothing between him and the trees except the same open field
he'd crossed a few hundred times before.

Not that Keo thought he was going to make it to cover
without having to dodge gunfire, and he was right. (*Dammit,
couldn't you be wrong for once in your life?*) He was only
halfway across when they started shooting, bullets punching
into the ground around him and *zip-zip-zipping!* over his head.
Even though he knew it wasn't going to do a lick of good, Keo
still instinctively raised both hands over his head like a shield.

His other instinct—to run in a series of random zigzag
patterns—was probably what saved his life, but even then one
round came dangerously close to detaching his left ear from
the rest of his head. The round had gotten so close he swore he
felt the *heat* of the bullet's trajectory as it went past his earlobe.

Christ!

The tree line in front of him was disintegrating branch by
branch, leaf by leaf, chunks of the gnarled trunks flickering
into the air like mini missiles. Keo wasn't sure if there was
going to be anything left by the time he reached it—

Yes!

He didn't so much as jump into the woods as he lunged violently inside, crashing into a tree and bouncing off it like a ping-pong ball. He didn't care about the immensely inelegant entry and righted himself (or as much as he could, anyway) and kept going, because the only direction left was farther into the thick shadows underneath the sea of heavy oak tree crowns.

He could already hear them coming behind him—the shouts and screaming of very, very angry men. A few of them were still shooting, but Keo was so deep into the woods now that he didn't even care branches were snapping in half around him.

Save your ammo, boys! he wanted to shout back but didn't, just in case he was overestimating just how safe he was. All it would take was one stray bullet and he was done. He could see himself going a good distance with one leg wound—

Shit. The leg wound.

He shifted down into a brisk walk so he could glance back.

Yup, he was leaving behind small drops of blood. Not a lot, but enough to track him if all the trampled grass and broken branches he'd left haphazardly in his wake weren't enough. Keo put one hand over the small wound—it wasn't much, just a bullet graze (*Thank God for small wounds*)—to stop the bleeding.

He upshifted until he was once again running. He was picking his way through the woods at a fairly decent speed until he realized he was going in the wrong direction and righted himself. He'd made the trek back and forth between the cabin and Winding Creek so many times that he knew the area circling the town like the back of his hand.

He couldn't hear them behind him, but he knew they were coming. Sooner or later—

The *thump-thump-thump* of rhythmic movement on the dirt ground broke through his thoughts, confirming what he had been dreading—the ones on horseback had taken up the pursuit.

Keo could see himself outrunning his pursuers on foot even with one slightly gimpy leg (hell, he'd done it before, and in far worse conditions), but men on horses were a different story. He could even imagine a few scenarios where he could outmaneuver vehicles, but horses could go under, around, and through things that cars or ATVs couldn't.

So Keo slowed down and used the opportunity to catch his breath. He wiped his bloody palm on his pants. The area around the small crease in his right thigh was still soaked with blood, but it wasn't dripping anymore. Still, he was going to have to tend to it. From experience, he knew that the only thing more dangerous than bullets to a man's health was unchecked infection.

He'd been running at full speed for a good two to three (*five?*) minutes, and every breath he continued to take echoed slightly in his ears. The fact that he could still detect the *thump-thump-thump* of horseshoes pounding the dirt ground at all was a good clue the adrenaline wasn't completely over-powering his senses, but it also meant his pursuers were close. *Too* close.

Keo didn't stop completely until he had reached a big tree that stood out from the rest. The trunk was a good five feet across and plenty big enough to hide his entire body as he leaned against it, pushing his back up against the ancient bark.

He continued to slow down his breathing as he waited.

The upside to running for his life was that he didn't have time to stop and acknowledge the aches. Even the slight throbbing pain from his right thigh had started to ebb into the background.

Keo closed his eyes and listened, the MP5SD gripped loosely in front of him. The trigger felt heavier than usual when he tested the pull with his forefinger, but maybe that was probably because he was a little weaker.

You're bleeding, remember? Not to mention that second-story fall. You're lucky you didn't break your neck. What the hell were you thinking?

He wasn't thinking was the answer.

Well, that wasn't entirely true. He was thinking—he just didn't have any choice, just like *now*.

He pushed off the tree and spun to his right, into the bigger space between oaks because it made sense that was the direction the closest horseman would also take—the wider and easier route.

It was the correct choice, because as soon as Keo showed himself, the horseman jerked on his reins and the horse pulled up, the reins digging so tightly into its skin that Keo thought the animal was on the verge of rearing up on its hind legs. But it didn't, and instead turned around sixty degrees to present its rider to Keo.

Just like Christmas! Keo thought, when the man shouted, "Wait!"

Keo almost laughed. *"Wait?"* Why the hell would he *"wait?"*

He squeezed the trigger—and missed from five meters away!

Impossible. How the hell...?

The round sailed high and snapped off a branch behind its intended target. The rider actually ducked even as he groped for his sidearm, but his mount was moving so erratically he was struggling to maintain his balance in the saddle at the same time.

I missed! I actually missed! How did I miss?

He was still thinking about that (he blamed it on the adrenaline, on firing too fast, on everything including the pain) when he shot the man again, and this time hit his target in the throat even though he was going for the face. (*Beggars can't be choosers!*) The man made a gagging sound, immediately forgot his gun, and seemed to slide off his saddle and fell, landing with a loud *thwump!* on the slightly damp ground. Blood sprayed from his neck even as he rolled around, splashing autumn leaves.

But Keo didn't have any chance to wallow in his success before the second horseman appeared in the background. The man already had a pistol in his hand, and he pulled his ride to a stop twenty meters away and fired. Like the first horseman, this one had his rifle slung over his back, but unslinging it would have taken more time than just drawing the sidearm at his hip.

The first round from Buck's man hit the trunk of the tree Keo had been hiding behind. Bark flicked at Keo's face, and he swore a few shards had pierced one of his eyeballs, but that was impossible because something like that would have definitely killed him. Or, at least, blinded him.

Except he could still see just fine out of both eyes as he took a quick step to his left even as the man got off a second shot. Unlike Keo's own gunshot, both of the man's exploded like thunder in the crisp air.

The second round came closer, but it still missed Keo by a good foot or two.

Keo didn't give the man a third chance. He spent a second aiming (*Don't miss again! You might only get one shot!*), lining his target in his red dot sight before squeezing the trigger. The man jerked back in his saddle but didn't fall. Instead, he somehow still remained upright when Keo put another round into him, and this time knocked the man off the horse—but not entirely. One of his boots got caught in the stirrups, prompting the animal to turn and flee, dragging its dead rider on the ground with him.

The first horseman was still on the ground, but he had stopped moving and now lay crumpled against a tree trunk. Keo was looking at the man, trying to decide whether to waste a bullet to make sure he was really dead or not, when he heard shouting coming from the direction where the horse and its rider had disappeared. Either someone was trying to stop the runaway horse or giving orders.

Oh, who the hell cares!

Keo turned to go—and almost walked right into the horse that had lost its rider.

The animal stood in front of Keo, staring at him with large brown eyes that matched its skin. Its legs were big enough that if it wanted to, Keo had no doubt it could crush his head under its hooves. The fact that it hadn't bolted like the other one either meant the horse was used to gunfire or it was too stubborn to be scared by it.

More shouting from behind him, and the voices were definitely getting closer.

Keo turned back around.

The horse was still there and didn't look as if it had even moved an inch.

"You got a problem?" Keo asked.

The horse stared back at him. Keo couldn't decide if that was annoyance or boredom in its eyes. Did horses get annoyed or bored?

"Scram."

It didn't.

"Whatever," Keo said, and slid past the horse.

He waited for it to spook and run off—or worse, attack him —but it remained calm and let him pass.

He had gotten in a dozen steps before Keo glanced back.

The horse was still looking, large brown eyes trained on him as if *it* didn't completely trust him to keep walking.

Weird horse, Keo thought, before turning around and picking up his pace until he was jogging through the woods again. He would have launched into a full sprint if the slightly buzzing pain from his right thigh didn't remind him that it wasn't a good idea. Keo reached down and put his bloodied palm over the wound to stanch further bleeding.

Even as he ducked under a branch, Keo wondered if the riderless brown horse was thinking the same thing as it watched him run off.

"Now what, genius? You should have stayed away from town, but you didn't. So now what?"

Good question, horse. Really good question...

EIGHT

Mark and his daughter Angel weren't at the cabin, though there was plenty of evidence they had found it just fine if the half-empty pantries were any indication. Ol' Mark had run off with as many goods and nonperishables as father and daughter could carry, but he had either generously left the bug-out bag or he never bothered to check the bedroom.

Keo didn't blame the guy, not after what he'd seen at Winding Creek. The baker was looking out for his daughter, and Keo was still just a guy who lived outside of town who Mark traded bread with once a week.

After taking quick stock of what was left in his kitchen, Keo's first priority was taking care of the bullet graze on his right thigh. Mark also hadn't taken the first aid kit in the drawer under the sink counter, and Keo went to work cleaning then dressing the wound, with his pants huddled around his ankles. Not the prettiest sight if someone were to walk in on him, but it was better than lying dead on the floor from an infection.

Keo didn't bother cleaning up after he was done, but he did wipe his bloody hands and grab the kit before leaving. He kept his ears open the entire time, knowing that sooner or later the bad guys (*Heh heh, "bad guys"*) would either track him to the cabin or accidentally stumble across it. If they launched a manhunt, it wouldn't be hard because there was only so much space around town.

Either way, the results were the same. He guessed he had a few minutes' head start on them, maybe more if Buck's boys took the death of the two horsemen as a sign to slow down. But that wasn't something he could rely on.

Keo grabbed the bug-out bag and added extra jerky and bottled water to what was already inside. It was a good forty-something pounds by the time he was done, but an extra forty-something pounds to haul around was better than starving or dying of thirst a few days from now. Mark had also bypassed the water purification tablets in the kitchen, either because he didn't know what they were—they were bundled up in unre-markable-looking brown packaging—or he was being nice.

Either/or works for me.

Even better, Mark had also missed the stash of painkillers on the top shelf of the closet (*Just in case*). Keo shoved them into the pack after snapping one open and downing two of the white pills to help with the lingering aches and pains. It was good stuff that he had stumbled across and hoarded away for just such a rainy day about two years ago.

"*What about Emma and Megan?*" a voice asked in the back of his head.

That stopped him in his tracks, and Keo stood still in the middle of the cabin.

What about them? He couldn't do anything for them, not

against that army in Winding Creek. How many men did Buck actually have that Keo never got to see? How many shooters did you need to take a town? Even one as domesticated and easy pickings like Winding Creek? Twenty well-armed soldiers? Fifty? It would take something close to those numbers to pacify a town of just over a hundred people in less than a few hours.

Few hours? Try one.

Barely an hour. Winding Creek never stood a chance.

"But what about Emma and Megan?" the voice asked again.

Going back into Winding Creek was suicide. He had no idea what had happened to Emma or Megan or anyone else for that matter. Whatever element of surprise he had was ruined when Wendy shot herself. After that, they would be expecting him; there would be guards around the town perimeter and more men on horseback. And if he was *really* unlucky, that machine gun he'd heard earlier but still hadn't caught sight of would be waiting to punch a few hundred holes into him.

No, there was nothing back for him in Winding Creek. No Emma or Megan, or even information about their whereabouts. He'd done his part; he'd gone back to find out only to end up being run out of town. What else could they possibly expect from him?

Nice one. You almost convinced yourself that time, pal.

Keo ignored the voice and forced himself to move again.

He didn't bother with extra clothes but did head back into the bedroom to grab two more magazines for the MP5SD. He checked the front windows just in case there were shooters outside, and when he didn't see one, he grabbed the door and threw it open—

It stared at him, brown eyes as big as his fists.

Or, at least, it seemed that large because the animal was standing so close to the front door that he wasn't quite sure how it had managed not to knock on the slab of wood with its forehead.

"The hell?" Keo said out loud.

It was the same horse from the woods. Had it followed him to the cabin and waited out here this entire time?

Its long black mane hung off its neck like a thick rug, and there was something majestic about the animal that made Keo think it would have gone for a pretty penny pre-Purge. But the most interesting part was that Keo hadn't heard it moving around out here. He hadn't even seen the damn thing until he opened the door. Were horses supposed to be able to move so stealthily? The thing was easily over a thousand pounds, and combined with its horseshoes, it should have made *some* noise while moving around out here.

"What do you want?" Keo asked.

The horse took a couple of steps back and lifted its head slightly up and down before resuming its staring at him.

"Man, you're weird."

Keo looked past the animal at the thick wall of woods beyond the clearing. The horse may have tracked him easily to the cabin, but apparently Buck's boys were having more trouble. Either that, or his instincts were right and they were being more cautious after he wasted the last two.

He turned back to the animal in front of him. "Can you hear them out there? Are they coming?"

The horse snorted and bent its head to graze the grass at Keo's feet.

"I don't know what that means."

Keo watched it eat for a moment, then took a chance and reached for the reins dangling off its shoulder. He expected the creature to resist, but it continued to feed.

"Easy, boy," Keo said. It seemed like the thing to say to a horse that could stomp him into the ground if it so chose.

Keo ran his hands along the animal's flanks. It was like running his fingers through a tangle of silk. He flicked playfully at the stirrups, and when the horse still didn't lift its head in protest, he wrapped one tentative hand around the saddle's horn.

"Okay?"

The horse ignored him.

"I'm going to climb up now..."

Silence.

"Don't do anything I wouldn't do, like throw me off, then try to kill me."

When the horse still didn't respond, Keo sighed and thought, *Beats walking on a bum leg,* and put one foot into the stirrup before starting to pull himself up—

The animal lifted its head and looked back at him. It was such a casual glance, like it was wondering what the hell he was doing, and Keo froze in mid-climb with one foot in the stirrup and the other leg halfway over the saddle.

He wasn't sure how long they stared at each other in that pose. Maybe it was just a few seconds, or an entire minute had passed. By the time Keo decided he was already committed, it felt like a lifetime, and he threw his leg over the saddle and settled down.

The horse went back to grazing.

"Okay," Keo said, with probably a bigger sigh of relief than he had intended. "Okay, this'll work, this'll work..."

He was pretty sure the horse was a thoroughbred, one of those animals born to be fast, though how old it was he had no clue. Could it have predated The Purge? That would mean it had somehow managed to survive against all odds. Most horses Keo had encountered in the years since were young, the vast majority of them having been born and raised post-Purge. It was a lot easier to survive now—for humans and animals alike —with the ghoul population reduced to a tiny fraction of its former self.

Not that the horse was going to give him any hints about its past. There was nothing on the saddle to indicate who its previous owner had been, and as far as Keo was concerned, it didn't matter. Its previous rider was dead, and the horse hadn't seemed all that concerned about it, given how easily he had allowed Keo to take over.

Adapt or perish, right? Even the horses know that.

They had been traveling through the woods for just a few minutes before the horse suddenly stopped in its tracks and lifted its head high. It let out a short snort and Keo glanced over his shoulder, back in the direction they'd come.

There was nothing back there. Nothing but oak trees.

He had purposefully steered them clear of the country road that he knew led to Winding Creek's front doors. Those same narrow lanes would have been the ones Buck and his men had used to launch their attack, but there was a back door in. More of a hiking trail, really, but it could host horses and men on foot, along with vehicles as long as they weren't too wide.

He wondered if Emma and her daughter had been taken

along one of those roads. *If* they had survived the initial onslaught on the town. What were the chances of that? Decent, because Emma would be smart enough to hide when the attack began. And Megan was well on her way home before the chaos ensued.

Keo hoped, anyway.

But in the absence of their bodies, the *possibility* existed that both women were still out there, alive. Or, at least, that's what he kept telling himself.

The horse let out another snort, and Keo leaned forward and patted its shoulder with his free left hand. "What is it? You hear something?"

He didn't know why he expected the thoroughbred to answer, because it didn't. Instead, it turned its head back around and faced forward again and resumed moving, this time at a slow walk.

Keo straightened up in the saddle. "Guess not."

They continued on for another ten minutes, the horse occasionally picking up speed only to slow down again. There wasn't any pattern that Keo could discern, because each time the animal changed gears, Keo went low and listened. Really, really listened. Except all he could hear were the birds chirping in the trees and the surprisingly loud scurrying of furry animals along the dangling branches.

Eventually, Keo started to notice the drop in temperature, which prompted him to check his watch. He hadn't been keeping track of time since the mess in town, but it had been two hours since he barely escaped the apartment building. His body wasn't aching nearly as much as it had before thanks to the pills he'd downed, but he still got reminders of what he had come to call his Plummet of Death every now and then. But aches were better than gaping wounds.

After about another thirty or so minutes of aimless jogging, then walking, then jogging again (*Make up your damn mind, horse.*), it occurred to Keo that by avoiding the roads but at the same time keeping parallel to it for the sake of familiarity, it meant he was getting closer to Princeville, the closest big city to Winding Creek by far.

Keo had never actually gone through Princeville, but he had skirted along its edges on his way south. Twenty thousand-plus people had called the place home before the Purge, and there was enough of a population that Texas A&M University had built a satellite campus there. He had also spotted an airport to the east, though the closest Keo ever came to spending time in the city was hunkering down for a few days in a farm along a state highway that ran right through town.

The horse had stopped moving again and gone back to grazing on the generous grass. Animals were getting fat on the land these days, with more than enough food to go around. The ones that could feast on nature, anyway. It was easy for horses, deer, and the other land-based population to rebuild now that there wasn't a constant horde of ghouls to feed on them. There was still the threat of humans, but those were far and few. Not everyone had learned the valuable skill of hunting. Most of the people at Winding Creek had belonged in that category.

Thoughts of the town's populace brought him back to Emma and Megan. Everything brought him back to Emma and Megan.

They were out there, somewhere. Maybe dead, maybe still alive but captured.

"They took the women. And the babies. God, they took all the babies..." Wendy had said.

By *babies* she had clearly meant the children. (*Probably.*)

Keo could understand taking the women, and even the teenagers. He had learned long ago that men were cruel and base creatures, and like the ghouls they'd fought to survive six years ago, men could do unspeakable things to one another as long as it satisfied their primal urges. Keo had seen plenty of it happening even before The Purge. The fall of civilization only gave them more opportunities and less consequences. Wendy, and those men who had lined up outside her apartment, were just reminders of that sad fact.

"They took the women. And the babies. God, they took all the babies..."

The women and the kids? But especially the kids. What were Buck and his people going to do with kids?

Then again, maybe he didn't want to find out. Maybe it was better for him if he let it all go. It hadn't gone very well when he ran off into Winding Creek without a plan. He'd almost died. *Should* have died except for his Plummet of Death. Talk about doing something stupid and getting away with it.

Barely.

Still, it gnawed at him.

"They took the women. And the babies. God, they took all the babies..."

Why the hell had they taken the kids? But maybe the better question was, did he really want to know?

"And it was such a nice morning, too," Keo said out loud.

The horse stopped grazing long enough to lift its head slightly and exhaled through its nose.

Keo smiled. "For you too, huh?"

He patted the thoroughbred on the neck, then smoothed down its mane with his free hand. It seemed to like it and let out a soft whinny in approval.

"Sorry about shooting your previous owner. I guess you weren't all that fond of him, huh?"

He looked back just to be sure there wasn't anyone sneaking up on him (or worse, who had been eavesdropping while he was talking to a horse, which would have been even more embarrassing).

Then he spent a few minutes thinking about what to do next.

Going forward would take him toward the southern tip of Princeville, but west would lead him away from it. The smart move would be to avoid the city altogether. There was nothing for him there except trouble. Potentially a lot of trouble, if it turned out Buck and company had set up camp there, which was a good bet. What were the chances he might be able to find the spoils of their attack—including the women and children—with them? He hadn't spotted the captives in town, which probably meant they had already been moved by the time he arrived.

What were the chances they were in Princeville *right now?*

At the moment, it was his best option, because going back to Winding Creek to look for traces of the women was suicide.

Keo sighed. He hated when he had choices, because he invariably chose the wrong one. It was a curse. Or maybe he just wasn't smart enough to always make the right choice. He knew a few people who would readily agree it was the latter.

I suck at this, he thought, before giving the horse a soft tap on both sides of its belly. The animal stopped eating and continued walking through the woods.

Even as they slipped out of dark patches of shadows and into bright sunlight and back again, Wendy's voice continued echoing inside Keo's head, and he couldn't shake it no matter how hard he tried.

"They took the women," she had said, in that flat, almost monotone whisper as if she were afraid of being overheard. *"And the babies. God, they took all the babies..."*

And each time, without fail, he would ask himself, *Why did they take the kids? What the hell is going on out there?*

Or maybe the question he should have been asking himself was, just how much was it going to cost him to find out?

NINE

Princeville, Texas, looked serene from a distance, especially through the clear lens of a five-hundred-dollar pair of binoculars. It was three in the afternoon, and sunlight flickered off its gravel-topped buildings and empty roads. A McDonald's arch was the most obvious thing at this end of the city, but farther in Keo could spot a bank and a strip mall. There were a couple of hotels in the distance, but he was too far away to make out details. Highway 77 popped out of the flat ground to his right and ran straight north, disappearing behind an apartment complex and what might have been a two-story (or possibly three) hospital.

The place looked deserted, but appearances could be deceiving, and Keo stayed far enough out of sight that he felt relatively safe he could disappear back into the trees at the first hint of trouble. He had settled on the west side, with a large, open field between him and the city limits. Tall, swaying grass brushed against his shoulders while he crouched and would have been tapping at his waist if he were standing.

Keo took a moment to look back at the horse. It was chewing grass a few meters behind him, still inside the woods. He'd tied the reins to a branch, but that wasn't really going to stop the thoroughbred if it decided to take off. The animal was big and strong enough to snap half a dozen branches if it wanted to say *adieu* to him, and the fact that it hadn't...

Weird horse, Keo thought, before looking back out at Princeville.

He'd always avoided cities like Princeville in the past, and instead opted to trade and at times linger around the smaller towns. There had been a lot of Winding Creeks, and each one had served their purpose. Food, supplies, and company.

So why had he settled at Winding Creek, of all places? The answer to that was an easy one: Emma. She was a beautiful woman, and Keo was a sucker for beautiful women. Maybe that was why he had run headfirst into town when he heard the shooting and why he was still here now, looking for signs of where Buck's people might have taken her and the girl. He owed mother and daughter that much: To *try* to locate, and if possible, help them. To do any less would be an asshole thing to do.

"Don't be an asshole, Keo," someone once said to him not all that long ago, and Keo had spent a lot of effort trying not to be one.

At least, not anymore.

A sudden snort from behind him, and Keo glanced back to find the horse with its head raised high and looking at him.

"What?" Keo said, about a second before he heard it.

He turned around and refocused on Highway 77 across the expansive field with the binoculars, locating the familiar source of the noise without any problems. It was, after all, the only thing moving around out there besides the grass.

There it is. I knew it had to be out there.

It was a technical—a civilian truck with a machine gun mounted in the back—heading toward Princeville. A man in dark clothing, a balaclava protecting his face against the cold winds, stood in the truck bed manning the MG. There were two other figures inside the vehicle—

Shit, he thought when a second, then a *third*, technical appeared behind the first. They had the same configuration—men in front and a gunner in the back behind a mounted weapon that could fire a few thousand rounds in his direction in the space of less than a minute if they had any inklings he was around.

A Toyota and two Fords, all beat up from heavy use. The four-lane road they were traveling on was smooth enough and completely abandoned so they could afford to drive at top speed into the city. The men in the back were wearing civilian clothes with the familiar black urban assault vest—the same kind he was currently wearing—though he couldn't make out their circled *M*'s from all the way out here.

Keo lowered the binoculars when the last of the vehicles disappeared one by one out of view. He remained crouched for a moment, listening to the fading car engines. Soon, it was just him and the horse again.

Three technicals. Three machine guns. Maybe more already in Princeville that he couldn't see. A place like that was big enough to hold—whether temporarily or permanently —a lot of people with a lot of guns.

A hell of a lot of guns.

Keo sat down and dug out a bag of deer jerky from his bag.

He was chewing on one of the sticks when he felt a nudge against his shoulder and looked over to find the horse's brown eyes staring back at him. To his unsurprise, it had snapped the branch he had tied its rein to without any effort.

"What? You tired of eating grass?"

The animal seemed to nod toward the jerky in Keo's hand.

"I guess you deserve it. You did let me ride you."

He held up the half-eaten meat, and the horse snatched it out of his hand. Keo smirked, then dug out another one, and the horse also gobbled that one up.

Keo fished out a third piece for himself. "Go easy there, pal. Jerky don't grow on trees, you know."

The horse turned and walked back to where it had been grazing.

"You're welcome, by the way," Keo said, before looking out at Princeville again.

Now where was he? Right...

Three technicals. Three machine guns. Probably more inside the city.

Those were some bad odds. What made it worse was that he didn't know for sure just *how bad* his odds really were. There could be a few hundred guys like Buck in the place right now. Or a thousand. Okay, maybe not a thousand. At most it was a few hundred. But at least more than twenty or so, if the leftovers he'd seen back at Winding Creek were any indication. That was still a heck of a lot of guys.

Keo sighed and wondered what *she* would say if she knew what he was about to do.

"*Don't be an asshole, Keo,*" she had once said to him. "*If you won't stay with us, if you won't come back to the Trident with me, at least promise me you're not going out there just to get yourself killed. Tell me you'll at least* try *to make it back, and mean it."*

This wasn't quite the same situation, but it was damn close. He was about to embark on something that could very well get him killed when the much better alternative was open to him and all he had to do was take it.

Except he couldn't. Emma had welcomed him into her life, into her home, and into her little girl's life. Her ten-year-old-going-on-thirty little girl, whose birthday was less than two weeks away.

"My birthday's in two weeks," she had said. *"What are you gonna get me?"*

"Why should I get you anything?" he had answered.

"It's tradition."

"People make new traditions these days. Ever heard of the phrase 'Out with the old, in with the new?'"

"No. Sounds stupid. Besides, I like the old ones better. So what're you gonna get me?"

"You'll see."

"You got me something already?" she had said, trying and failing to hide the excitement in her voice.

He was all set to go look for a birthday present, too, but that was going to have to go on the back burner.

Now where was he?

Ah.

Three technicals. Three machine guns. Probably more waiting for him inside Princeville.

Yeah, those were some really bad odds. Real shitty odds.

So what else was new?

He couldn't just walk away. He wished he could—and maybe, not all that long ago he could have pulled the trigger and even found ways to justify it in his mind—but those days were long gone. He couldn't decide, though, how much that should worry him.

Oh, who are you kidding. It should worry you lots, pal.

He was still chastising himself as he slid along the two buildings toward the voices up ahead. Two guys going back and forth. It wasn't the most stimulating conversation ever, but then it was hard to find good conversationalists these days. Most people would point to him as a prime example.

"How many?" one was asking.

"Five dozen, I think," the other one said.

"Shit, that's a lot."

"That's a hell of a lot, yeah."

He wasn't sure what they were talking about—what the "five dozen" was referring to—because he'd stumbled across them in mid conversation. A part of him wanted to keep going until he found just one guy, but he'd been moving steadily up the back streets of Princeville for the last thirty minutes before he located these two and didn't feel like trying his luck deeper in the city. Besides, he needed information, and sooner or later he'd have to talk to someone. These two bozos might as well be those someones.

He walked casually out from between the two buildings, the submachine gun slung over one shoulder and one hand playing with the cheap metal lighter he'd found half-buried in the ground while sneaking his way into town.

They were standing on the sidewalk with an empty strip mall across the street. As far as Keo could tell, there wasn't another living soul around for miles, but of course that wasn't true. Princeville was big enough that Buck's men had to spread out to cover every part of it. That was exactly what Keo was counting on. That, and the fact Buck had a lot of men, enough that maybe not all of them would recognize that Keo didn't belong. After all, who knew everyone in a hundred-or-more men army?

At least, that was the plan. If he was wrong about even just one of those assumptions, he was probably a dead man.

Keo sighed, thought, *This is such a bad idea*, and stepped out from between the buildings.

The first of the two chatterboxes to hear his approach spun around, hands tightening on the AK-47 clone in front of him. He was young, mid-twenties, and looked like he was losing the battle to grow a mustache. Like his buddy, he sported a rough circled *M* on the front and back of his assault vest.

"Hey," Keo said. "You guys got a cigarette?"

The second one was taller with a buzz cut, but about the same age. He, too, had startled at Keo's sudden arrival and lifted his rifle slightly. "The fuck you come from?"

"Got a cigarette?" Keo asked him.

"What?"

"Cigarette," Keo said, and held up the lighter for effect.

The two men stared at him, then exchanged a confused look. But neither one raised their weapons in alarm.

So far, so good...you big, dumb idiot.

The two were reacting exactly as Keo had hoped—confused. The fact that he wasn't in any hurry and was walking casually toward them as if he belonged, combined with the black assault vest he'd stolen from the man he'd knifed inside Winding Creek, added to the role he was playing: He was just one of them, looking for a cigarette. And a man who belonged didn't have to be afraid of two guys standing guard.

"Where'd you come from?" Failed Mustache said, but even as he asked the question, Keo noticed the man unclutching his fingers around his weapon.

Eureka.

"Buck told me to check the woods," Keo said.

"What for?"

"Fuck if I know. Just in case someone followed us from Winding Creek or something, I guess." He shrugged indifferently. Then, adding just the right amount of impatience, "You guys got cigarettes or not?"

The taller one with the buzz cut also relaxed his grip around his AR. Even better, he slung his rifle before answering. "Don't smoke. It's a filthy habit; bad for your health."

"Yeah, well, who wants to live forever?"

"Me," Failed Mustache said, and he and Buzz Cut chuckled.

Keo gave them a dramatic eye roll. "Whatever. I'm gonna go see if anyone has some I can bum." He started to walk off before stopping and glanced back. "Buck still at the same place? I gotta report in in person."

"At the mall, yeah," Buzz Cut said.

Keo nodded and turned to go.

"Hey," Failed Mustache said. Then, when Keo glanced over his shoulder, "You see anything in the woods?"

"Yeah. Plenty."

Failed Mustache waited for Keo to answer, and when Keo didn't, the man said, "So? What'd you see?"

"Trees. Tons of the stuff. Don't know where they came from."

Buzz Cut snorted. "Wise guy."

Keo gave them a half-assed salute and continued up the street.

He didn't breathe easier until he had put at least twenty paces between them, and even then he kept waiting for gunfire.

Twenty paces became forty, then fifty, then a hundred.

Christ, that worked. I can't believe that worked.

Keo put the lighter away and calmly moved the MP5SD until it was thumping in front of him instead of slung behind him. The submachine gun was now within easy reach if the other Buckies weren't quite as easily convinced as Failed Mustache and Buzz Cut. The prospect of having to shoot his way up Princeville just to get some information wasn't something he was looking forward to, but at least he'd gotten past the first hurdle.

Highway 77 ran somewhere to his right, on the other side of a series of empty buildings and apartments. Sunlight beat down on him, and he glanced at his watch just to make sure he still had time left before sunset. Buck's men hadn't looked all that concerned about the coming nightfall, which told him they had been out here long enough to know how to deal with any ghouls they ran across. Chances were good their bullets, like the knives in their sheaths, had silver in them. You didn't survive this long without knowing what the ghouls feared the most—sunlight and silver.

Keo took mental notes of everything he crossed, including the abandoned businesses to his left. There were more to his right across the two-lane road, but they were harder to make out with the sun in his eyes. He had to walk around the occasional bones on the sidewalk, remnants of The Walk Out that hadn't been brushed away by wind and elements or taken by animals.

Unlike smaller towns like Winding Creek, there hadn't been anyone in Princeville to clean up the mess after the ghouls exposed themselves to sunlight five years ago. It would take years, he guessed, before these left-behind remnants were either completely devoured by insects and animals or turned into dust in the wind. In the years since Houston, he had come across bones that had simply fallen apart, almost as if whatever had turned the ghouls had also weakened them to the very, well, bone. It was one of those things that Keo was more than happy to let the scientists sort out. Assuming there were even guys in lab coats still around.

Like most cities, Princeville had seen its share of looters over the years. It used to be that Keo could find nonperishables and water without having to try very hard. Most survivors had abandoned the towns where they had been held against their will, and that translated into more people claiming what used to be so abundant for roamers like himself. The dwindling resources was one reason Keo had stuck around Winding Creek. The town fed itself from the fields, and though it didn't completely ignore the leftovers of the world around it, its citizens didn't treat them as necessities. The people had more than they needed to survive; they had become comfortable as a result. *Too* comfortable, as it turned out, considering how easily the Buckies had pacified them this morning.

A growl, and Keo stopped and turned left.

A dog squatted in the alleyway between two buildings, a bleached white bone on the ground in front of it. The animal gave him a warning look before snatching the bone—it looked like a deformed hand, with long, delicate fingers just barely hanging on—with its long, sharp teeth and hopping onto its feet, then turning and jogging away.

Keo couldn't help but smile. Five years ago, the dog would have been running from ghouls, but now it was surviving on their bones.

What goes around, comes around.

He turned and continued up the sidewalk.

He hadn't gone more than a few feet when he tensed up slightly as a car flew down the street in front of him. It went from being a small dot in the distance to a black Toyota in the blink of an eye. He couldn't be sure if it was one of the three he'd seen earlier, not that it mattered, because one technical was the same as another—deadly if that MG was pointed at him.

Keo willed himself to walk normally, neither moving fast nor slow or making any overt attempts to hide from the oncoming vehicle. He glimpsed people through the front windshield—two in the front and three more squeezed into the back. But it was really the guy manning the machine gun, its tripod welded to the truck's cab, that got his attention because the barrel was pointed in his direction.

A thousand rounds a minute. A thousand rounds a minute...

He waited for the technical to get closer, fighting every instinct to dive into the same alleyway where he had spotted the dog, or lift the H&K into a shooting position.

The gunner. He would have to take out the gunner first—

No. Whatever you do, don't do that.

When the truck was within ten meters, Keo gave it an acknowledging wave with one hand. The guy in the front passenger seat returned it before looking away, as did the gunner in the back.

Crunch! as the front tires of the truck obliterated a stray femur on the road just before it blasted past him and vanished in the opposite direction.

Damn, I think I just pissed myself.

He fought the urge to look back to make sure the truck was really gone, and instead kept walking. At this rate, he wasn't sure how many more encounters he could get past before he let one slip and peed his pants.

He gave himself one hour to find out what he could before locating the first exit and getting the hell out of Dodge.

TEN

Buzz Cut had said Buck was at *the* mall, which meant there was only one mall in the entire place. That was surprising, given the twenty thousand-something people that once called Princeville home. In Keo's experience, even small towns usually somehow managed two malls. Americans loved their malls.

But one or two or a dozen malls didn't matter because Keo wasn't interested in actually finding Buck. He had managed to stay under the radar and fit in because no one knew who he was or recognized his face. Buck was the exception. Keo liked to think he had an Everyman face, but the truth was he probably stood out.

"You Chinese or something?" Buck had asked him back in Winding Creek as they stared at each other across a second-floor hallway.

Or something.

How many men did Buck have under him who were *"Chinese or something?"*

The question was moot if he could continue to avoid Buck, but he couldn't dodge every single Bucky that he came across, because that would defeat the purpose of coming here in the first place. That didn't exactly leave him with a lot of options, but he was at least comforted by the fact he had been right when he didn't think Buck's people knew everyone in their group. Which also confirmed Keo's theory there were a lot of them.

That was both good and bad.

Good in that he could probably interact with more Buckies without being recognized for the infiltrator he was; bad in that once he was exposed, he was going to have to deal with a lot of bad guys.

A shit burger however you look at it, pal.

But he was already inside the city, and there was no turning back, so Keo kept going, moving toward a group of vehicles parked outside a Walmart. Like most big box retail stores he'd crossed paths with in the past, there were plenty of old abandoned cars in the parking lot, but the ones he paid attention to were the two technicals parked near the front. There were more U-Haul trailers hooked up to horses, and people were going in and out of the large building carrying boxes and bulging bags.

Keo stayed on his side of the street, keeping the massive parking lot between him and all the activity. If anyone saw him walking by, no one cared enough to spend more than a second glancing in his direction before going back to work. He counted at least two dozen men, not including the ones hanging around the trucks. Around thirty or so, and this was just at one spot.

He left the Walmart behind and walked past an empty

Pizza Hut, then a bakery and a small strip mall with a Family Dollar and an AT&T retail store. Nothing he hadn't seen in a hundred cities as he crisscrossed Texas, never really sure what he was looking for but unable to scratch the idea that he didn't belong in one place.

The street continued on, and Keo passed more empty buildings and store fronts and cars that hadn't moved in years. He could see subdivisions in the background, homes surrounded by what looked like jungles for lawns. Pretty soon he wouldn't be able to see the houses unless he was standing right in front of them—

"Hey!"

Keo turned around and looked across the street at a guy standing in the parking lot of a budget hotel. The man had one hand raised to get Keo's attention. Despite the distance, Keo could make out red hair under the sunlight.

"Yeah?" Keo shouted back.

"Get over here!" the man said, before turning and walking off.

Keo stared after him. The way the man had told him to *Get over here*, like he was used to giving orders and having them followed, probably meant he was one of Buck's lieutenants. Or however the Buckies distinguished their leadership from their grunts. If true, that would mean the man might have information Keo needed.

On the other hand, he hadn't been able to see the guy's face clearly, so it was a good bet the guy hadn't been able to see his, either. Which meant Keo could take off right now while the Bucky's back was turned, and redhead wouldn't be able to identify him later.

So what was he waiting for?

Too late, he thought when the guy stopped a few seconds later and glanced back and shouted, "Hey! I said to get your ass over here!"

Keo sighed and jogged across the street toward the motel.

It was an ugly building, designed in an N-shape with an open parking lot in the middle. There were ten rooms on one side, five more in the back, and five more to his left, with the manager's office twice as big as the individual rooms. Unlike most of the businesses Keo had walked past, there were only a couple of cars inside the lot, all of them with dirt-caked windows and grimy bodies. The only vehicle that looked in any shape to still drive was the white Ford F-150 parked near the center, where the man who had called Keo over was walking toward now.

Keo casually reached down and flicked the fire selector on the submachine gun to semiautomatic just as he reached the parking lot. He kept his hand draped over the weapon in an almost lazy manner, nothing that would indicate dangerous intentions.

The redhead had walked over to the parked Ford and leaned into the open front passenger-side door. He was reaching for something inside, but Keo only had eyes for the M240 mounted in the back of the vehicle. The M240 was an older model machine gun, but it was still fully capable of slicing him in half in the blink of an eye. Fortunately, there was no one manning it at the moment, which was the only reason Keo didn't turn and run.

"What's going on?" Keo said as he got closer.

The Bucky came out of the open door with a bottle of water and took a sip. He had a receding hairline, which looked odd against his almost glowing red goatee. He sighed with relief when he was done. "What's your name?"

"Jay," Keo said.

"You're one of Fenton's guys?"

Keo nodded and thought, *I am now*, before saying, "Yeah. What's up?"

"I thought all of Fenton's guys were supposed to be gone by now?"

"Supposed to, but Buck's got me running around in the woods just in case there were some strays from Winding Creek."

"Whatever," the man said, and finished the last drop of water before tossing the bottle into the truck bed. "Give me a hand with this."

"With what?"

"Just follow me."

Keo fell in behind him. "I didn't catch your name."

"Wagner," the man said.

"Where is everyone, Wagner?"

"They went to grab a bite. Why did you think I called you over?"

So you're all alone, huh? Good to know, good to know.

Keo followed Wagner to the motel rooms on the right. All the doors looked identical, but Wagner led him to the one marked *15*. The curtains were drawn, and there were fresh drops of blood on the ground connecting Room 15 with the Ford behind them. Someone hadn't gone inside willingly.

"How many did you get back in Winding Creek?" Wagner was asking him.

"How many did I get what?" Keo said.

Wagner stopped and looked back at him. "How many did you kill?"

Keo recovered and answered as quickly and confidently as he could manage, "I wasn't really keeping score. Why?"

"I thought you Fenton boys were hardcore killers," Wagner said, grinning at him. That was either an inside joke at Keo's expense or...something else.

Keo shrugged indifferently. "Not all of us."

"That's not what I heard."

"You heard wrong."

"Maybe," Wagner said, and turned around and continued to Room 15. "Let's see how you would solve this problem of mine. Do a good job, and I'll put a word in for you with Buck. We're always looking for guys to be a permanent member of the team."

"I'd appreciate it," Keo said, even though he didn't have a clue what Wagner was talking about.

Wagner opened the door and stepped inside Room 15, and Keo followed.

It wasn't nearly as bad as he was anticipating, but it wasn't very good, either. It was far from anything even remotely approaching "good," in fact.

There were two of them, and one was either dead or on his way there. Keo had never seen either man before. Their wrists and ankles were bound with duct tape, but that had little to do with why one of the men was lying awkwardly on his side, blood dribbling from his mouth and broken nose, and down to the dust-laden carpet.

The other one looked to be in a better spot, though not by very much. His face was black and purple, his right eye so big Keo thought he was wearing sunglasses with only one lens when he first saw the man. His nose was broken, and blood trickled out of it and into his mouth, not that he seemed to notice. He had dark black hair, but the most curious thing about him—and his partner nearby—was that they were dressed almost identical to Keo and Wagner: cargo pants, civilian shirts, and black assault vests with the circled *M* emblems. They were also wearing gun belts, but the holsters were empty.

Wagner had walked over to the full-size bed where he picked up a white blanket to wipe his hands. Keo hadn't seen it before, but he had blood on his fingers and knuckles, though he was probably getting his hands dirtier considering the filthy state of the blanket he was using. Keo decided to keep that to himself.

"Who are they?" he asked instead.

"The half-dead one's Vince, the not-quite-dead one's Lewis," Wagner said. "You know about the missing people?"

What missing people? Keo thought, but shook his head and said, "I was kinda busy doing something else. What happened?"

"The numbers didn't add up. There's about twenty missing heads from Winding Creek." The redhead tossed the blanket on the floor and put his hands on his hips before staring at Vince and Lewis. "We think these two managed to sneak the ones in the subdivision out of the south end of town during the attack."

Keo looked back at the two men. If they could hear the conversation, neither showed any obvious signs. Especially

Vince, who looked practically dead—if he wasn't actually dead. Lewis looked in remarkably better shape by comparison.

"Why would they do that?" Keo asked.

"They're from Winding Creek," Wagner said. "Used to be, anyway. Of course, we didn't know that until this morning when someone spotted Vince there with a couple of women and kids that later went missing. Then, when asked about it, he denied it." Wagner walked over and crouched in front of Lewis. "This one put up quite a fight."

"You did all this?" Keo asked.

"Nah, just this one," Wagner said, nodding at Vince. "Some of it, anyway. The others took their shots before they went to get something to eat. I wasn't very hungry."

Not for food, from the looks of it.

Wagner stood back up and glanced over at Keo. "The other one kept his mouth shut through the whole thing. Brave motherfucker. I don't think he's going to say much even if we cut off his balls. This one," he added, pointing at Lewis, "I think is more willing. Just needs a little coaxing, is all."

"Coaxing, huh?" Keo said.

"Something like that." The redhead grinned before that quickly vanished, and he suddenly gave Keo a suspicious look. "You don't know them, do you? They're Fenton's boys, too."

"Nah, I don't know them."

Wagner nodded. "Good. So, you up to do a little tuning?"

"What exactly do you expect him to tell you?"

"Where the ones that escaped went. Buck thinks they must have some kind of a safe house somewhere out there. But even if they don't, Lewis here probably knows where they went. He had to send them somewhere."

"You said twenty people escaped the attack?"

Wagner shrugged. "Give or take."

"Women and kids?"

"Some women, some kids, some guys."

"You don't sound all that sure..."

"I'm sure."

"How?"

"'Cause we know how many were in that town, and the count doesn't add up," Wagner said.

They were spying on Winding Creek before the attack. Jesus Christ. I'm lucky they didn't know I was around the area, too, or they would have definitely hit the cabin at the same time, Keo thought, when he realized Wagner was staring at him.

"What?" Keo said.

"You're from Fenton," the redhead said. It wasn't a question.

"Yeah. We already went over that. What about it?"

"How many people from Fenton joined us for the raid?"

"What?"

"It's an easy question," Wagner said, and his hand moved not-so-casually to his holstered sidearm. "How many of Fenton's guys came with us to take Winding Creek...Jay?"

Keo feigned thinking about it. "Fuck if I know," he said, just before Wagner grabbed his gun.

The man had the disadvantage of having to grip, then pull the semiautomatic from its holster, while Keo only had to turn the submachine gun slightly with his right hand and pull the trigger.

Wagner glanced down at his chest, where the 9mm round had struck him. He looked confused more than anything, but that quickly gave way to pain about the same time his legs surrendered underneath him and he crumpled to the filthy floor.

Keo turned around and hurried to the windows and looked out.

The Ford F-150 was still parked outside where he last saw it, and it was still just as empty with no one in the back. He peered left toward the street, but there was nothing out there except an empty stretch of city and abandoned cars.

"Who are you?" a voice asked.

Keo looked over his shoulder and found Lewis, his left eye open and staring across the room at him.

"Who are you?" the man asked again.

Keo walked back, stepping over Wagner's body, and crouched in front of Lewis. The man's one good eye tracked his every movement, which was a good indicator ol' Lewis had been playing possum up until now.

"Nice one, convincing him you were half dead," Keo said.

Lewis blinked at him but didn't confirm or deny.

"The people you and your buddy helped escape from Winding Creek," Keo said. "Were two of them Emma and her daughter, Megan?"

Lewis didn't answer. His eye shifted from Keo to Wagner's body behind him, then back to Keo.

"What?" Keo said. "You think I'm trying to trick you?"

No answer.

Keo reached back with the submachine gun, pointed it at the back of Wagner's head, and pulled the trigger. Lewis flinched when the round punched through Wagner's skull and exited the front of his face, brain matter splashing the parts of the carpet lit up by the sunlight.

He looked back at Lewis. "See? Not a ruse. He's really

dead, and I really did kill him. Now, Emma and Megan. Did they get away?"

Lew looked conflicted. Unless, of course, Keo was reading him all wrong. There was a pretty good chance of that, given how badly bruised and bloodied Lewis's face was. The guy could have been thinking about yesterday's breakfast, for all Keo knew.

"Come on, man," Keo said. "They're my friends. Emma's... more than that. Did they get away this morning? Do you even know who—"

He must have been pretty convincing, because Lewis said, before he could finish:

"They got out. Both of them. They got out..."

ELEVEN

"Are you sure?" Keo asked. "Emma and Megan? Blondes?"

Lewis stared suspiciously back at him with his good eye. Or, at least, that's what Keo thought the man was doing. Lewis could have just been looking at him normally, or as "normally" as he could muster, given his current pulpy state.

"No," Lewis finally said.

"No?" Keo repeated.

"Brunettes. Both."

"Blue eyes?"

"Green. Both."

Keo smiled. "Just had to be sure."

"Sure now?"

"Maybe. You could still be lying. Blondes. Brunettes. Fifty-fifty, right?"

"What about redheads?"

"Thirty-seventy." Keo shrugged. "You'll forgive me if I don't believe you. People have a bad habit of lying these days. Blame it on the state of the world. Or reality TV. Same shit."

"You gotta trust somebody, sometime."

Not if you've seen the things I've seen, pal, Keo thought, but said, "Are you saying you trust me?"

"No. Not even close."

"Good answer."

Keo stood up and glanced back at the curtainless windows. He could see the F-150 in the parking lot, that very dangerous M240 still pointed harmlessly up at the sky, and no signs of any of Wagner's buddies having come back from their lunch.

"They'll be back," Lewis said.

"How many?" Keo asked, looking back at him.

"Three."

"They did this to you? And your buddy here?"

Lewis nodded (or was that a flinch?), before turning his one good eye over to Vince. "Is he dead?"

Keo crouched in front of Vince, but he hadn't even put a pair of fingers against the side of his neck before he knew the answer to Lewis's question. Vince wasn't moving at all, much less breathing, and his skin was clammy to the touch.

"He's gone," Keo said.

Lewis sighed and looked like he was about to go to sleep —or die.

Neither option was acceptable, so Keo put his hands on the man's shoulders to keep him upright against the wall. "Where did they go? Emma and Megan?"

"With the others," Lewis said.

"I got that part. But where, exactly?"

Lewis blinked at him.

"You know, right?" Keo asked. When Lewis nodded but didn't say anything, "But you're not going to tell me, is that it?"

"I'll show you where they went."

"You can barely walk."

"I'll manage."

"That's doubtful, my friend."

"I'm not telling you."

"Why not?"

"We're back to trust again."

"Didn't you just say that we all have to trust someone sometime?"

"I'm still not going to tell you."

"I just killed Wagner to save your life."

"Thanks, but I still don't trust you." He shook his head. "This could all be a trick. I know how Buck operates." Lewis shot a quick glance at Wagner's still body before refocusing on Keo. "Take me with you, or you'll never find Emma and Megan."

Keo stared at the man. What were the chances Lewis was trying to sandbag him? Just because he knew what Emma and her daughter looked like—or their hair color, anyway—didn't mean he wasn't above lying about them surviving. He was desperate, and Keo had met plenty of desperate people who did desperate things.

"They'll be back soon," Lewis said. "They'll kill you for what you did to Wagner. Or worse."

"Oh yeah? What's worse than dead?"

"You're looking at it," Lewis said.

Keo smirked before standing up. "You realize, of course, that if you're lying to me, I'll have to sew that good eye up. Mind you, not that I'd get any pleasure out of it, but it's the principle of the thing, you understand."

Lewis stared back at him but didn't say anything.

Must be my lucky day, Keo thought when he peered into the parked Ford and saw the key dangling from the ignition.

He pulled out of the truck and looked past the empty parking lot at the street beyond. There was no one in sight, though he could hear voices and activity in the area. Princeville was big enough that Buck's men had to spread out in order to loot the place, though Keo wondered how much was still left after nearly six years. Plenty, apparently, if those busy bees at the Walmart were any indication.

Keo left the F-150's driver-side door open and hurried back to Room 15.

Lewis was leaning against the open doorway with Wagner's pistol now stuffed in his formerly empty holster. Keo didn't think it was possible, but the man looked in even worse shape with the warm sunlight against his face highlighting that fist-size bump over his left eye.

The former Winding Creek resident peered back at him through the narrow slit that he called his right eye. "Keys?"

"Inside," Keo said. He slipped one arm around Lewis's waist, and the other man practically fell against him. "You gonna die on me, Lewis?"

"Not if I can help it," the man said with a grunt.

Fortunately, Lewis was a lean one hundred and fifty-something pounds, and Keo was able to shoulder him without either one of them collapsing from exertion. Lewis did the best he could to assist, but the beating had taken its toll not just on his face but the rest of him. Keo could hear him grunting and see the grimace on his face with every step. Wagner and his pals hadn't been gentle on the guy, that was for sure.

"Where did they go, anyway?" Keo asked, hoping to keep Lewis from focusing too much on the pain. "The other three?"

"The food truck," Lewis said.

"Food truck?"

"Yeah. Basically what it sounds like. All the food is kept there."

"Where is it now?"

"Wherever Buck is."

That'll be the mall.

"Who's this Fenton guy?" Keo asked.

"It's not a guy, it's a place," Lewis said. "Fenton, Texas."

"Never heard of it."

"Neither had I, until five years ago."

Keo reached over and opened the truck's passenger side door and helped Lewis inside. The man almost fell down on the seat before righting himself with some effort, then spent the next few seconds blinking his good eye against the sun pouring in through the cracked windshield. No, not cracks. There were a couple of bullet holes in it, where the driver sat. Which, Keo thought, probably explained the (very old, from the looks of it) dried blood on the upholstery behind the steering wheel.

Now that's a bad omen if I ever saw one.

"Maybe I should go into the back, man the machine gun," Lewis was saying.

Keo grinned. "Maybe you should focus on not dying first, pal."

"Yeah, that's probably a better idea."

"Strap in."

Lewis nodded and pulled at the seat belt while Keo hurried around the truck, giving the streets another look—

The roar of engines preceded a pair of vehicles by a good ten seconds, and Keo was opening the driver side when they slashed up the street—two trucks, both technicals, with men in the back. If they even knew Keo was in the motel parking lot, no one glanced over or slowed down, which prompted Keo to think, *What's their hurry?*

The answer came in the form of a series of *pop-pop-pop* sounds from farther up the road. Half a mile, at least, and the gunshots echoed in the crisp afternoon air for a long while, mingling in with the sounds of engines.

It went on for five, then ten, seconds before going silent.

Keo was sliding into the truck when the gunfire started up again, and this time someone opened up with a machine gun, the *brap-brap-brap* sending a slight shiver up and down his spine. He got (mostly) through it by slamming the door shut and turning the key in the ignition.

The Ford leapt to life without a problem. The gas gauge was half empty (*Let's go with half full this time, shall we?*), and the mileage was in the six digits.

"What's going on?" Lewis asked in the front passenger seat. He was turned slightly to the left in the direction of the gunfire that had just stopped again.

"I don't know," Keo said, "but I'd rather hear it from a distance than up close and personal."

"What the hell was that?" a voice asked.

Keo exchanged a look with Lewis before they both turned around and discovered the portable two-way radio jammed into the armrest on Lewis's side.

Lewis pulled it out, just as the familiar voice said, "What was all that shooting?"

The voice was slightly distorted coming through the tinny speakers, but it was the same guy from Winding Creek.

My old buddy Buckaroo.

"Found a ghouls' nest in one of the strip malls, sir," someone answered through the radio. "About a dozen black eyes in the back of one of the buildings. They didn't want to come out, so we had to do a little convincing."

"You done?" Buck asked, sounding slightly irritated.

"Just about, sir."

"Finish up. We're heading back to Fenton in an hour."

"Roger that."

"That's a hell of a lot of silver ammo just for a dozen black eyes," Keo said.

"Buck's not hurtin' for ammo," Lewis said. "Neither is Fenton."

"Silver?"

"They've been stocking up, raiding the surrounding towns for whatever they need. Fenton is a booming city, getting fat off everyone else." He had said that last part like a man who knew from first-hand experience.

Keo grabbed the truck's gear stick. "So, where we going, Lewis?"

"South, out of town," Lewis said.

"Then what?"

"I'll let you know when we're safely out of town."

Keo thought about Buzz Cut and Failed Mustache, waiting for him at the south end of Princeville. "Can you shoot?"

"Yeah..."

"You sure?"

"Point and pull the trigger, right? Not rocket science."

"Not what I was referring to."

"Oh." Then, after a moment, "I'll manage."

Keo put the truck in reverse. "Just make sure the gun is pointed out the window and not at me."

"Gee, is that how it works?"

Smartass, Keo thought, while Lewis drew Wagner's sidearm and put it in his lap, forefinger in the trigger guard.

Keo backed out of the parking lot. "How many men did Buck take Winding Creek with?"

"He brought forty or so of his own, and about twenty or so more from Fenton," Lewis said. "It was overkill. Winding Creek never stood a chance."

Tell me something I don't already know.

Keo stepped on the brake and lingered with the back bumper almost in the street, but not quite. He glanced left, then right—then stared up the road where the shooting had come from. There hadn't been any more communications through the radio, so he figured whatever ghouls had been unlucky enough to run across Buck's crew were long gone and things were back on track for the raiders.

"You were in Fenton," Keo said. "You and your buddy back there in the motel room."

Lewis nodded. "When we learned they were going to hit Winding Creek, we volunteered. Vince and me."

"To warn them."

"Yeah..."

"Why didn't you just send a message?"

"Like what, pick up the phone and call them? Send a homing pigeon?"

Keo chuckled. "Good point."

He reversed completely into the street, then turned right,

back in the direction he had come. Fading sunlight reflected off a technical parked along the curb in the rearview mirror, but the vehicle wasn't close enough for him to get a better look. Which meant they couldn't see him any clearer, either.

Keo stepped on the gas anyway, comforted in the knowledge that speeding wasn't going to get him noticed in Princeville, considering how every vehicle he'd seen so far was hauling ass for one reason or another.

"You left Winding Creek five years ago," Keo said. "After The Walk Out."

"Yeah," Lewis said.

"Why?"

"It wasn't our home."

"Where is home?"

"Dallas."

"So how'd you end up in Fenton?"

"It was on the way, but Vince and I decided to check it out. Then one week became a month, and before we knew it, it'd been a year. But that Fenton isn't the same as the Fenton that's out there right now."

"What was it like before?"

"Decent. In a lot of ways like Winding Creek, but bigger. Copenhagen changed everything."

"Copenhagen?"

"He's the one calling the shots. Has been for the last five years. He's the guy driving that place. What it is now is because of him. It mirrors his personality. His...ambitions."

"I thought Buck was the HMIC."

"Buck's like his general; he runs the paramilitary group. The ones with the circled *M*." He glanced over at that emblem now, on the front of Keo's assault vest.

"It's not mine," Keo said.

"Where'd you get it?"

"The owner didn't need it anymore."

Lewis nodded, understanding.

"Why did they take the kids?" Keo asked.

"Not just the kids. The women, too," Lewis said.

"But not the men?"

"No. Not the men."

"Why?"

"I don't know."

"You don't know?"

Lewis shook his head. "This is the first time we volunteered for a raiding party. We never knew they were taking women and children from the towns until we got to Winding Creek and we got our orders. We always thought it was just supplies and guns."

"I didn't see any of them in Princeville. The women and children they took from Winding Creek. Where were they keeping them?"

"They're not here. They took them on ahead of us almost as soon as the fighting ended," Lewis said. "Buck's men. They're the only ones he really trusts. Guys like Vince and me are just volunteers. They don't tell us much."

"How is it you didn't know they were bringing people back with them from the raids?"

"Fenton is separated into two areas—the one where Copenhagen and Buck live and operate, and the rest of town. We don't have a clue what goes on in the restricted area. Not a clue."

"And you never volunteered until you found out they were targeting Winding Creek?"

"Yeah."

"NIMBY, right?"

"What?" Lewis said.

"Not In My Back Yard. It's fine when it's the other guy's backyard, but when it's yours, fuck that shit, right?"

"I guess."

Keo didn't have to ask Lewis about this Copenhagen. He knew guys like him—men who stepped in to fill the vacuums of power. If it weren't Copenhagen, it would have been someone else. The names changed, but the men didn't.

Same shit, different day.

They drove past the Walmart where Keo had seen all the activity earlier, but it was now a barren wasteland of abandoned cars. There were no signs of the trucks or U-Hauls attached to horses or Buckies looting what was left of the superstore.

Something *crunched* under the truck's tires—probably more bones—but Keo didn't stop or slow down.

"Who is he? Buck?" Keo asked.

"I don't know," Lewis said. "He showed up one day about two years ago with that little army of his."

"When did the raids began?"

"Only a few months ago."

"You could have warned Winding Creek earlier."

"I know," Lewis said, and didn't say anything else.

And Keo guessed there was nothing else *to* say. He had a feeling Lewis had been thinking about that for some time now. Keo had seen the aftermath of the slaughter in Winding Creek —the bodies in the streets, the ones he could spot through windows inside buildings, people like Wendy—but Lewis and the now-dead Vince would have seen it up close.

Shoulda, woulda, coulda, pal, Keo thought as he slowed down when he saw a pair of familiar figures slowly growing in size in front of him.

Except they weren't alone this time: A technical sat on the curb nearby with a tall lanky man in black, like a specter of death against the setting sun, staring back at Keo from behind a mounted machine gun.

TWELVE

"Daebak," Keo said.

"What?" Lewis said.

"Nothing."

He had two options: Speed up and make a run for it and risk getting skewered by that MG, or slow down.

Keo slowed down.

"What are you doing?" Lewis asked, his voice rising with alarm. He fidgeted in his seat even as his one good eye peered out the windshield at the group of men.

"Relax," Keo said.

"Relax?" Lewis repeated, as if the word was completely alien to him.

"Yeah, relax."

"That's a machine gun."

"I noticed that, Lewis."

"So what are you *doing?*"

"Re*lax*," Keo said. "And let me do the talking."

"What are you going to say?"

"I don't know yet."

"You don't know yet?"

Keo sighed. "You need to calm down and don't do anything stupid."

"Like what?"

"Like start shooting."

"Okay," Lewis said.

"Okay?" Keo said, glancing over at him.

The other man nodded. "Yeah, okay."

Now why don't I believe you? Keo thought, watching how Lewis continued moving around in the front passenger seat.

Keo didn't really blame the guy. In his shoes, after what he had been through at the motel, he wouldn't have been all that ready to "relax," either.

Easy does it. Easy does it.

It wasn't much of a blockade, with just one truck and two guys on foot. There might have been two more inside the truck —a red Chevy that, as Keo neared, had bullet holes along the sides and Kansas license plates—but two or three (or even ten) didn't really factor into his thought process.

He focused almost entirely on the tall guy in the truck bed standing behind what looked like an older model belt-fed M240. The gunner wasn't actually pointing the weapon at Keo as he approached in the Ford, but it wouldn't have taken very much for him to swivel that thing over and pull the trigger. The prospect of a torrent of 7.62 rounds making even bigger holes in the windshield in front of him left Keo feeling a little...cold.

He might have shivered slightly and hoped Lewis didn't notice.

"We can outrun them," Lewis said suddenly.

"Them, but not that machine gun," Keo said.

"I can take him."

Keo glanced over at the Glock in Lewis's lap, at the way the man was nervously clutching and unclutching it.

Yeah, right, Keo thought, but said, "Just relax, Lewis. And remember to let me do the talking."

Lewis didn't answer, and he also didn't put the gun away.

"Lewis…" Keo said.

"Yeah, I know, let you do the talking," Lewis said.

"Exactly," Keo said as he continued slowing down, before stopping completely in front of Failed Mustache, who stood in the middle of the road with one hand raised and the other holding the AR slung in front of him.

Keo kept one foot on the brake but didn't put the gear into park. Instead, he leaned out the window as Failed Mustache walked over. Buzz Cut had remained near the Chevy, chatting with the driver. There wasn't a second man inside the other truck, Keo saw now, which meant four in all—Failed Mustache, Buzz Cut, the driver, and the machine gunner.

But that machine gunner, though…

That very dangerous man, visible just a few yards in front and to the right of Keo's line of vision, had glanced over momentarily to get a better look at the Ford from his high perch. The man either didn't find anything overly interesting or wasn't alarmed, because he glanced back up the road while leaning back against the Chevy's cab with his elbows draped lazily over the roof.

Keo turned his focus to Failed Mustache as the man approached his side of the truck. All the while, Keo had picked up the MP5SD and laid it across his lap, with the muzzle pointed toward the door. Not that he expected to shoot through the door, but with one hand on the weapon, it wouldn't take too much effort to lift the submachine gun and squeeze off a round or two out the already open window.

"You again," Failed Mustache said.

"Me again," Keo said.

"Where you going now?"

"Patrol."

"Looking for more trees?"

"You know how many trees there are out there? Buck wants me to check every single one of them."

Failed Mustache chuckled. "Hey, don't worry about it. It's all just hazing. You wanna join the main crew, you gotta do the grunt work first."

"I got no problems with that."

"Well, at least you're not walking this time."

"Got that right."

The man peered past Keo and at Lewis in the passenger seat. "What the hell happened to you?"

"Ran into a doorknob," Keo said.

"Must have been a big fucking doorknob," Failed Mustache said.

Keo grinned and was about to say, *"You bet your ass it was,"* but before he could open his mouth, there was a deafening *bang!* from his right and Keo thought, *Well dammit, Lewis, now you've done it!*

The sound of the gunshot was thunderous inside the close confines of the truck's front seats. Keo didn't even want to think about how loud it might have been if their windows weren't open, because even now he thought he might have gone slightly deaf.

Outside his door, Failed Mustache was collapsing out of view when Keo gunned the gas.

Buzz Cut, in front and to the right of the truck, was whirling around, reaching back for his slung rifle, when Keo hit him with the grill of the Ford. Keo wasn't entirely sure what had happened—had Buzz Cut been fast enough to turn and jump into the truck's path or had Keo swerved into the guy, knowing that two Buckies was better than three?

Either way, just as he glimpsed Failed Mustache going down with the corner of his left eye, this time he saw Buzz Cut going *up* and *back* with the corner of his right.

"Drive, drive, drive!" Lewis was shouting in the passenger seat.

What the hell do you think I'm doing, Lewis ol' pal? Keo thought as he bent forward and slightly over the steering wheel even as the accelerator slammed into the floor and stayed there.

The Ford lurched under him, the two front tires threatening to give way, but broadsiding Buzz Cut must have done something, because the truck quickly righted itself and they were blasting up the road—

Then Keo heard it, the noise he'd been dreading:

Brap-brap-brap! Brap-brap-brap!

"Shit!" Lewis shouted.

"I told you to fucking let me do the talking!" Keo shouted back.

"I did! I didn't say a word!"

Keo smirked (*Well, I guess technically he's not wrong.*) when the rear windshield behind them shattered and the *ping-ping-ping!* of rounds smashing into the back and right-hand side of the truck filled the air.

And technically I'm about to get my ass shot to ribbons!

Keo didn't take his foot off the gas and kept his body almost completely slumped over the steering wheel as he struggled to maintain control while the Ford picked up more and more speed, even as the machine gun continued, the *ping-ping-ping!* overwhelming Keo's eardrums. That last part was a hell of a feat, given that both his ears were still ringing from Lewis's very close-quarters gunshot.

"Drive faster!" Lewis shouted.

"What the hell do you think I'm doing?" Keo shouted back.

He had put thirty meters—*forty*—on the blockade and the still-firing M249 when Keo finally risked a quick glance at his side mirror. It was still intact, which made sense since the machine gunner was positioned on the other side of the vehicle when it opened up.

The driver of the Chevy was standing in the street looking after them while screaming into a radio. Or, at least, Keo assumed he had to be shouting into the two-way; how else was he going to be heard over the *brap-brap-brap* of the machine gun firing nearby?

And then, mercifully, the MG fell silent.

Hallelujah!

Keo glanced down at the speedometer. Seventy miles and climbing. He took his foot off the gas and the truck slowed down, the speed decreasing about the same rate as Keo's racing heartbeat.

Close one. Christ, that was a close one.

Let's never do that again!

"You could have at least given me some warning," Keo

said. Then, when Lewis didn't respond, "You hear what I said?"

He looked over at Lewis, only to see a lot of blood.

Aw, shit. And things were going so well, too.

Lewis was slumped over his seat, held in place only by his seat belt, or else he would have been crumpled on the floor right now. Blood pumped out of the side of his neck in thick clumps, spraying the upholstery and dashboard. Keo would have noticed the massive amount of blood loss earlier if he wasn't so concerned with trying not to get tagged himself.

He sneaked a look at the rearview mirror—except there was nothing up there but a piece of the black plastic that used to hold the mirror in place. That explained all the glass he heard *zinging* around his head. He twisted in his seat to peek out through the big rectangular hole behind him instead.

Princeville was getting smaller in the background, and Keo couldn't make out the Chevy or its occupants anymore. The lack of pursuit was definitely good, though it probably wouldn't be that way forever. Sooner or later, Buck was going to send people after him. And sooner or later, someone was going to stumble into the motel and find Wagner's body.

Keo reached over and put one hand on Lewis's neck, pressing his palm against the wound. Without the gunfire and the sounds of bullets punching into the Ford, Keo could now hear Lewis's labored breathing. He pushed hard, heard the man grunting—which was what he was hoping for, because grunting meant Lewis was still alive.

For now.

"Hey, hey," Keo said. "You still with me? Lewis ol' pal, you still with me?"

Lewis wheezed, even as more blood pumped against Keo's

palm. Wetness began oozing through his fingers and down the length of his arm underneath his long-sleeve thermal sweater, until he could feel them against his armpit.

"Lewis, Lewis," Keo said. "Where are the girls? Lewis, where did the girls go?"

Keo slowed down just enough to give Lewis a quick look—saw the other man staring back at him with his one good eye that he was barely able to keep open.

"Lewis," Keo said, "you're going to die. I'm sorry, man, but you're going to die. You know that, right?"

Lewis didn't say anything. Keo wasn't even sure if he could, even if he wanted to.

"You're bleeding way too much," Keo said. "And it's not going to stop. I can't make it stop. You know that, right? Lewis?"

He alternated between looking Lewis in the eye—to let the other man know he was dead serious—and keeping the road ahead of him. The last thing he needed right now was to rear-end an abandoned vehicle. There was little chance of that out here in the countryside, but all it would really take was one stray chunk of metal in the road to end their little escape attempt.

"You're gonna die, and I can't do anything about it," Keo said. "So you gotta tell me where the girls are. I can't help them if I can't find them. You understand? Lewis, you understand? *Where are the girls?*"

Lewis's eye was glassy, and he was clearly struggling to keep it open. Finally, he somehow managed a slow nod.

Keo breathed a sigh of relief. "Where are they? Where's Emma and Megan and the others?"

"Jonah," Lewis said. Or croaked.

"Jonah?" Keo said. "What's that? A guy? A city?"

"Jonah," Lewis repeated.

"I don't know what that is, Lewis. What's Jonah? A town? Is it a town? Did the girls escape to another town called Jonah?"

Lewis didn't answer. He had closed his eye, and his body had become heavier as it pushed against Keo's hand.

Keo shot his side mirror another quick look. There was nothing behind him but smooth, paved road. The taller buildings of Princeville were still visible in the distance, but there was still no sunlight reflecting off incoming vehicles.

He eased his foot off the gas and stopped the Ford in the middle of the road and put the gear in park. He twisted in his seat and concentrated on Lewis, on keeping his hand against the other man's neck so Lewis didn't bleed out on him faster than he already was.

Keo leaned across the seat, ignoring the damp upholstery under him, the wetness seeping through his clothes. If he wasn't already covered in blood, he might have grimaced at the warm contact.

He gave Lewis's cheeks a couple of taps to wake him up, and when the man opened his eye again—or halfway, anyway —Keo said, "Jonah, Lewis. What's Jonah? Who is Jonah?"

"South," Lewis whispered.

"South? Jonah is down south? So it's a town?"

"South...east."

"Southeast?" Then, when it looked like Lewis was going for a nod, "Along the coastline?"

There, an honest to goodness nod.

"It's a town?" Keo asked. "Jonah is a town along the coastline?"

But Lewis had closed his eye again, and his body slumped against Keo's hand. Even the blood seemed to stop gushing against Keo's palm, and when Keo took his sticky hand away, Lewis didn't notice—or move at all.

Keo sat back in the driver's seat. He was covered in blood, but none of it was his.

"Swell," he said when he saw the gas gauge on the truck's dashboard. It had been half-empty the last time he looked, but the needle was already scraping the red now. The M249 puncturing the gas tank had been a very real concern given the man's firing position, but Keo had been hoping...

He sighed and put the truck back into drive. He checked the side mirror before stepping on the gas. They were going to come after him, which meant he had to put as many miles between him and his pursuers as possible before the Ford gave out.

Another mile, if he was lucky. Two, if he was *really* lucky.

THIRTEEN

There were no Buckies on his tail, which was the good news; the bad news was the leaking gas tank that allowed him to drive for another five miles before he hit the *E* and the truck simply died on him. But five miles was more than he had been hoping for, so maybe it was *great* news instead of just *good*.

Maybe my luck's finally changing. Let's hope.

Keo grabbed his things and the extra Glock from Lewis and jogged off the road and humped it to the woods. It took him half a minute to cross the field of waist-high grass, and he kept expecting a technical or two (or a dozen) to bear down on him at any second. Except they didn't; there weren't even hints that Buck had sent anyone in pursuit, and Keo reached the tree line unmolested.

Losing Lewis was a blow; not the man himself—Keo didn't know him well enough to care one way or another—but the information in his head.

"Jonah," Lewis had said.

It could have been anything. A town, a store, or someone's

name. But at least Keo had a direction—southeast, which would take him to the coastline. It wasn't exactly a map he could hold in his hands, but it was more than he had before he stepped into Princeville.

Jonah. Somewhere along the coastline. Either a town or a place, or someone who lived down there.

A lot of maybes.

He was still covered in Lewis's blood when he stepped one foot, then another dozen into the woods and immediately noticed the major dip in temperature, the tall tree crowns around him keeping the sun from contact with his skin. He'd chosen a corner with too many shadows, and Keo's antenna went up even though it had been ages since he was afraid of the dark. Not since that time in Houston, anyway.

His instincts were to keep going, to put as much distance between him and the road as possible, but he didn't. Instead, Keo turned around to face the tree line and went into a slight crouch and waited.

He had a much longer wait than he expected—almost twelve minutes, to be exact—before the first vehicle showed up. It was, predictably, a technical, and the machine gunner in the back swiveled the MG around from left to right. A second vehicle came up quickly behind the first. One of the trucks turned slightly so it covered the woods where Keo was currently hidden inside while the second one faced the other direction, creating an almost V-shaped defensive posture in the middle of the four-lane road.

A man in a Houston Texans ball cap climbed out of the first truck while three other figures from the two vehicles swarmed the abandoned F-150. Fading sunlight reflected off the barrels of their rifles as they circled, then crowded around the Ford. Ball Cap peered inside, probably to check Lewis for vitals, before leaning back out. He said something—Keo was much too far to hear what, and the man hadn't bothered to shout for his benefit—and the others relaxed, though they didn't put their weapons away.

The machine gunners, Keo saw, had remained alert throughout.

Not bad for a bunch of amateurs.

But were they really amateurs? No, not really. Maybe Vince and Lewis had been, but not Buckaroo's men. These guys clearly had some military training.

Ball Cap walked a few yards down the road and, hands on his hips, glanced around. It wasn't Buck, even though Keo couldn't see his hair with the hat on. But the man was younger and longer in the face, and he unclipped a portable two-way and said something into it before waiting for a response.

Keo was secured enough inside the woods that he wasn't afraid of being spotted. Of course, if one of the machine gunners decided to spray and pray in his direction he was a dead man, but Keo doubted they would do that if he didn't give them any reasons to. After all, what idiot would stay behind to watch?

Just you, pal. Just you.

He waited for the men on the country road to spread out and continue their pursuit. He wanted one of those vehicles, even if it meant having to go head-to-head with an MG. After all, it couldn't shoot him if it couldn't see him.

But instead, his pursuers climbed back into their technicals and turned their trucks around. Keo watched them disappear back in the direction they'd come until he couldn't see or hear them anymore.

He had to admit, that was unexpected. Who was on the other end of that two-way, and what had they said? Buck, most likely. So why hadn't Buck ordered them to pursue him? He had just killed Wagner and likely Buzz Cut, too, while Lewis had taken out Failed Mustache. Of course, Buck didn't know Keo was responsible for those bodies unless someone at the roadblock had managed to get a good enough look to describe him to their leader.

What were the chances Buck could put two and two together? Maybe the better question was, would a guy like Buck care? He seemed to have plenty of men to spare. Or maybe, unlike Keo, Buck wasn't prone to giving in to petty revenge.

Don't look a gift horse in the mouth, Keo thought, and stood up and headed farther into the dark woods.

He glanced up, peeking through the thick crowns at the sky on the other side. It was hard to tell how much light was left from what little he could see, so he glanced down at his watch instead.

Two hours before sunset.

He picked up his pace, every inch of him warm and sticky with Lewis's blood.

———

Jonah.

Jonah-what? Jonah-who?

You couldn't have given me more than just a name, Lewis ol' pal? Or at least tell me what it's a name for?

Keo didn't know anyone named Jonah, or a place called Jonah, and he didn't have a map on him, either. There was one back in the cabin, and that was where he was headed now. According to Lewis, Emma and Megan (and however many had made it out of Winding Creek with them—twenty or so, if Wagner could be believed) had headed southeast away from town during the attack.

At least he had a direction, and soon he'd have a map to help out with a "what."

Jonah Town? Jonah City? Jonah's Fun-o-Rama?

It could have been anything. Or anyone. This was Texas, and Keo had met plenty of guys with strange names, and "Jonah" wouldn't even count as the strangest.

Two hours wasn't going to be nearly enough time for him to beat nightfall, though. (Was that why the Buckies hadn't pursued him? Were they counting the clock, too?) At least, not on foot. The stuffed backpack already weighed him down, slowing his progress, and without the thoroughbred to pick up the slack, he would be lucky to make half the distance to the cabin before darkness caught up to him.

Fortunately, Keo was familiar with the miles between Winding Creek and Princeville and knew of a few good candidates to bunk down for the night. But not yet. It took him half an hour to circle back to where he had stashed his bug-out pack before heading into town. He pulled it out of a large bush and took a quick peek at the trees above him. The dwindling light was all the incentive he needed to pick up his pace. He couldn't remember the last time the prospect of being caught outside after sundown left him this anxious.

The more things change—

Keo stopped and pivoted, the MP5SD swinging up to chest level, and he peered through the optic at his target.

He'd heard it a few minutes earlier—something occasionally moving behind him—but it had come and gone, and he wasn't sure if it was just his imagination. But then there it was again, except much closer this time, and Keo didn't understand why he was still alive unless whoever was back there didn't have a gun, because they were certainly close enough to put a round into the back of his head.

Except no one fired a shot—including Keo himself—because the only thing staring back at him was...the horse.

The same thoroughbred he'd acquired from one of Buck's people outside of Winding Creek, that Keo had let go before entering Princeville. He was pretty sure it was the same one, too, given its color and those curious brown eyes peering back at him from thirty paces. It had been quiet as a mouse except for the times when it accidentally stepped on a dry twig or bumped into a low-hanging branch.

A friggin' ninja horse, Keo thought as he lowered his weapon.

"I almost shot you. You know that?"

The animal seemed to relax in turn before starting to walk over.

"What are you doing?"

The horse, of course, didn't answer.

"I asked you a question. What do you think you're doing?"

It stopped momentarily to chew on some grass before continuing over to his position.

"Stupid animal. You're probably safer out there by yourself. Do you realize that?"

It peered at him with its big brown eyes.

"Okay, don't say I didn't warn you."

Keo turned and resumed his way southeast through the woods.

He walked for about a minute before sneaking a look back. The horse was still back there, but it didn't look like it had gotten any closer. When it saw Keo looking back, the animal stopped and stared.

"Well, come on then, if you're gonna come."

He resumed walking, and it took another five minutes before the horse appeared beside him. Keo looked over at it and got a sideways glance in return.

"You're an odd duck, aren't you? What's the matter, got so used to human company and now you don't know how to do without? Is that it?" Keo chuckled. "What am I saying? I'm the one talking to a horse."

He kept walking, and the horse kept pace beside him. For such a big animal, it was amazingly quiet and light on its feet.

"I'm gonna have to put a bell on you. That'll keep you from sneaking up on me again."

It snorted in reply.

"Or two bells. Don't think I won't."

Sunlight was fading faster than Keo had anticipated. Even the horse seemed to sense the coming darkness, if its constant sniffing was any indication. Then again, the animal could have just had something in its nose, for all Keo knew. It wasn't like he was a horse expert or anything.

Keo found what he was looking for with twenty or so minutes to spare: an old bungalow near the same stream that fed into Winding Creek's farms. They were still about five or so miles from town and Keo wasn't thrilled about being so near what had been, until very recently, a thriving place, but was now nothing more than a graveyard. But at least Emma and Megan weren't two of the casualties, and that eased his mind tremendously.

He did a quick circuit around the old building, looking for signs of occupancy. He paid attention to the smell, which was the first sign there were ghouls nearby. The creatures reeked of decay and dead things, and the longer they stayed in one place, the stronger the odor.

The air was relatively clean, and he found the front door intact. The windows were devoid of glass or any barriers, and just about anything could have climbed into the place at any time. But the smell wasn't there and, when Keo made his way inside he found the great room in shambles, the floor littered with dust and elements from the woods outside, but the house was otherwise uninhabited.

When Keo stepped back outside, the horse was waiting near the door. It gave him a look of anticipation, which Keo couldn't quite figure out.

"What?"

The animal seemed to look up at the darkening skies.

"You want to come in, is that it?"

It stared at him.

"You are housebroken, right?"

It sniffed the air between them.

"Fine. But wipe your hooves. Unless you were raised in a barn. You weren't raised in a barn, were you?"

Keo went back inside and the horse followed, its horse-shoes *clop-clopping* against the wooden floorboards. Keo closed the door, but instead of a lock, there was a two-by-four on the floor that could be slipped into a latch over the bigger slab of wood. He did that now, though he did have second thoughts since the windows were unprotected and anything that could climb three feet up the wall could break their way in through those entry points. Keo had seen ghouls climb a lot higher than that.

He headed straight into the back hallway, still mindful of the many shadowy corners. But again, the air smelled fine, and even the horse didn't seem spooked by anything in front of them as it followed behind him. He was pretty sure the animal's sense of smell was much better than his, and if it wasn't worried...

"We good?" he asked the horse.

It sniffed the air and remained calm.

"I'll take that as a yes."

There were two bedrooms, both the same size, and Keo chose the one farthest back. There was only one window, and it already had a dresser pushed up against it. The mostly cherry red furniture looked intact, and it was heavy enough that it took a lot of effort for Keo to even budge it. Whoever had placed it there had chosen wisely.

He closed the door, pushed the deadbolt into place, and settled into one of the corners. There was no bed or even a cot, so someone had "liberated" the place before he showed up. He didn't mind sitting on the floor, though, because Keo wasn't sure if he could get any sleep anyway.

Keo could feel the darkness creeping up on the bungalow even if he couldn't see the woods through the blocked window. It was in the way the room slowly darkened as natural sunlight faded and the air chilled.

The horse had laid down on its stomach in the very center of the room, and with its eyes on the door the entire time, rested its jaw on the floorboards.

It's definitely done this before, Keo thought, wondering how long the animal had been out here, surviving. Maybe that was why it preferred human company; an extra layer of protection against the things that still hid in the night.

Smart. Much smarter than most people I know.

"Keep an eye out. Make a sound if you hear anything."

The animal turned its head in response to his voice.

"I'm counting on you, horse. Horse. That's your name from now on. You like it?"

The horse looked back at the door.

"You're welcome."

He laid the MP5SD across his lap and the pack next to him, and closed his eyes. Keo leaned against the corner and tried to get some sleep, knowing full well it wasn't going to happen for a while.

It took two hours before he got sleepy, then another hour before he drifted off.

He dreamt of Emma, but it could have just been memories of their last night together when she asked him to stay. He hadn't answered, even though he knew it had taken a lot for her to put herself out like that.

"Don't leave tonight," she had said. *"Stay with me. Stay with us."*

But he had left anyway. Because even though he tried not to be, sometimes he couldn't help but default to being his old asshole self.

FOURTEEN

Crunch-crunch.

Crunch-crunch.

Keo opened his eyes for the second time that night, and this time he stayed awake even as his hands tightened around the submachine gun resting in his lap. His eyes slowly adjusted to the darkness before glancing down at the neon hands of his watch:

2:51 a.m.

The sounds were coming from behind him and slightly to the left, which meant...

The window. The one with the big dresser blocking it. Someone—or some*thing*, more likely—was moving around on the other side.

Crunch-crunch.

Keo looked across the pitch-black room at the horse, lying in the middle of the room sprawled out on its side where Keo had last seen it before he closed his eyes and drifted off to sleep. For a big animal, it was being surprisingly quiet, and if not for the absolutely still world around him at the moment, he might not have even noticed it was there.

Ninja horse, Keo thought, when he heard it again:

Crunch-crunch.

He glanced over at the dresser. It was still in place over the window and didn't seem to have moved since the last time he checked on it. Of course he was looking at it from the side, so his angle was a little askew. It could have very well inched slightly in either direction, and he might not know since he hadn't paid super close attention to its positioning. He only knew it was completely covering the window, and that had been good enough.

He calmly checked that the MP5SD's fire selector was on semiautomatic (there was no point in wasting bullets if he didn't have to, not when one would do just as well as a dozen against a ghoul) before slowly, quietly sliding his legs underneath him and then pushing up, up along the length of the wall.

A slight jab of pain from his right thigh, a reminder of the bullet graze from earlier today—No, yesterday, now.

He ignored it and kept pushing up on both feet.

Once fully on his feet, Keo took a tentative step toward the window. Then another, and another, until he was standing almost right next to it.

Crunch-crunch.

There was definitely something out there, something stepping on brittle leaves that covered the yard. He'd made the same noises when he was walking through the place yesterday. Whoever—or *what*ever—was out there wasn't being very shy about their presence.

Keo was fully loaded with silver rounds, and he had the

knife with its silver-coated blade as a backup. He hoped he didn't need it. He was pretty decent in hand-to-hand combat, but it was a last resort he'd rather avoid if at all possible, especially if there was more than one ghoul out there—

Voices. He could hear voices outside.

Human voices.

Of course they're human voices. Ghouls don't talk, idiot.

Well, that wasn't entirely true. He had met a few ghouls that could talk—even hung around one in particular for a few days, but those were a special breed. The usual run-of-the-mill ghouls, with black eyes, could make guttural noises that could possibly pass for screams, but they didn't actually form words, if they even remembered how. The ones that could talk had blue eyes. Stark, pulsating blue eyes that you never forgot once you looked into them.

He shivered just thinking about it.

But Keo was sure he wasn't hearing a blue-eyed ghoul talking on the other side of the cabin walls right now. It helped that the speakers didn't appear to be whispering but talking almost in a normal voice. There was none of the *hiss* that usually accompanied the blue-eyed ghouls when they spoke. Then again, it had been years since Keo was in a room with one of them, and maybe his memory was a little hazy.

No. They're humans. Gotta be.

Which meant what, exactly? The first and easiest explanation was that Buck's people had found him, had tracked him from the outskirts of Princeville where he had left Lewis in the truck and all the way here. He hadn't exactly been careful about leaving behind tracks—in fact, it had never occurred to him to *be* careful—so any decent pair of eyes could have followed him all the way to his current hiding spot.

Crunch-crunch as whoever was out there moved back to the window.

Keo stood perfectly still, the submachine gun in front of him, and listened very carefully as voices passed by his position moving from right to left, coming closer toward the barricaded hole in the wall.

"How many?" someone asked. Male.

"I don't know," someone else answered. Also male. "It's too dark in there. I couldn't see shit."

"Did you go inside?"

"You fucking kidding me? Do I look stupid to you?"

The first guy chuckled. "Is that a trick question?"

"Blow me."

"Maybe tomorrow." Then, "You have a flashlight. Why didn't you use it?"

"Might spook them."

"That's the point."

"It's too easy. I'd rather have some fun first."

"Ugh, you and fun," the first one said.

"Fun's what makes this all worth it."

"Let's get this over with. I'm tired."

"You're always tired. Must be all that sodium."

"Better than eating dirt."

"I hear that."

Crunch-crunch as the voices faded, this time moving away from Keo and the window.

What were the chances they would keep going and leave the house behind?

With your luck? About one in a few million.

He leaned sideways toward the dresser, listening for more conversation, but the two men seemed to have finished saying everything they had to say. Instead, he heard silence except for the *hoots* of an owl nearby and crickets in the grass.

Keo checked the horse. It was still asleep, oblivious to what was happening.

Some ninja horse.

He was marveling at just how well the horse could sleep and envying it when the first *BAM!* exploded from the window and made him jerk slightly back from the wall in shock.

The dresser wobbled and moved back a full two or three inches, and even as it was settling back down there was another *BAM!*, and this time the furniture began toppling backward from the blow, moving almost in slow-motion before it *crashed!* against the floor.

The horse jumped to its feet at the loud *crash!* It whinnied loudly as it whirled around, seeking out the cause. It moved impossibly fast for such a large animal, and Keo had a mental image of it kicking him by accident and putting a horseshoe-size dent in his forehead.

But it didn't. It might have gotten a start, but Horse wasn't out of control.

Keo turned back to the window, and he wasn't sure who looked more shocked at what they were seeing: Horse inside the room or the man standing outside the window holding a shotgun in his hands while he peered inside.

The man was wearing almost all black, with a heavily frayed bulletproof vest over a long-sleeve sweater. His face was partially covered by a blood-red half-mask that only hid his mouth and nostrils, giving the man an almost demon-like appearance.

"What the fuck?" the man said, his voice slightly muffled. He had directed that comment at the horse since he had no way of seeing Keo standing next to the window, hidden against the wall.

"What is it?" a second male voice said from somewhere outside.

"It's a horse," the first one said, as if he still couldn't quite believe it.

"A horse?"

"It's a fucking horse!"

That "fucking horse" snorted and scraped one of its front legs on the floorboard, a warning to the half-masked figure outside.

"What's it doing inside?" the second man asked.

"The hell if I know," the first one said. "Sleeping, I guess."

"Sleeping? Inside?"

"I guess?"

"How'd it get inside the house?"

"Through the door, I'd imagine."

"Yeah, but that door was locked from the other side."

"The fuck?"

You have no idea, pal! Keo thought, and was preparing to give the man the (second) surprise of his life by spinning into view when an object sailed through the window in a wide arc before he could act. It bounced on the floor almost in front of Horse and instantly began spewing a thick white cloud.

The thoroughbred immediately realized the danger and let out a loud whinny before it began thrashing around, and Keo thought, *Oh, goddammit, it's going to kill me. It's going to get in an accidental kick and knock my head right off.*

He started backing away, trying to put as much distance between himself and the suddenly wild animal as he could. Keo pulled his shirt over his mouth and nostrils, but he knew it wasn't going to do a damn bit of good because the thick smoke had begun to swallow up the small room. The first wracking cough hit him like a freight train, and soon his eyes were watering, and it wasn't long before his skin began feeling as if it had caught on fire.

"Did you hear that?" a voice said. Keo had lost track of who it was.

"Hear what?" a second voice said.

"I hear coughing." Then, with alarm, "Someone's in there with the horse!"

Keo continued backing up until he bumped into the corner where he had spent most of the night and there was nowhere else to go.

Shit. Shit, shit, shit!

"You sure?" a voice asked.

"You can't hear that?" the other one said.

"I can't hear shit. I can't see shit, either."

Keo's eyes were burning as he looked for a way out. The door was to his right, but it was across the room with Horse in his way. The thoroughbred was spinning in circles and letting out pained whinnying noises. What were the chances he could somehow squeeze around it without getting kicked in the head? Or kicked anywhere else, for that matter? He assumed it was going to hurt regardless of where the animal landed its thousand pound-backed blow.

The window! It was open, and smoke was flooding out of it. It was the only real path out of the room. Except there were at least two people out there. They may or may not be Buckies, but either way they weren't just going to let him climb out—

Fuck it, he thought and ran toward the window.

He saw flashes of movement around him—the horse, then

someone at the window backing up as he approached—but it was all a blur as he dove through the opening.

He landed in a pile and instantly sucked in as much air as he could while simultaneously gasping for breath.

The blow came from behind him, like a rock smashing into the base of his head.

God, he hoped it wasn't a rock. Better yet, he hoped it wasn't whatever the men had used to dislodge the dresser earlier. Compared to that heavy piece of furniture, his skull might as well be papier-mâché.

He slammed face-first into the grass and couldn't muster the energy to pick himself back up. Wetness seeped into his skin (*why was the ground wet?*), and he heard the panicked sounds of the horse somewhere behind him. He felt bad for the animal, but he was in no position to help it or even himself.

"Is he dead?" someone asked.

"I dunno," someone else said.

"You hit him pretty hard."

"Shit, you saw how he shot through that window. Like a friggin' bat outta hell."

"Like Meat Loaf?"

"Yeah, like Meat Loaf," one of them laughed. "Only skinnier."

Jokes, Keo thought. *They got jokes, these assholes.*

He might have offered up a comeback of his own, but every inch of his skin was burning, and the only thing Keo could think of to do was mercifully close his eyes and wait for the bullet.

FIFTEEN

He woke up to a throbbing headache, like a one-hundred-and-twenty-eight-pound cannonball was ricocheting back and forth endlessly inside his skull. But his brain seemed (*seemed!*) intact, and when he opened his eyes, he could see just fine. Well, not really *just* fine, but he could see, and that was the important takeaway. There were some white spots in his vision, sure, but they were easy enough to look past at the two guys sitting across from him while snacking on strips of beef jerky.

Keo sat up with some effort and looked around him.

He was inside the great room of the same cabin, lights from the fireplace separating him and his two captors providing plenty of illumination to see with. The men were well-armed, with gun belts and knives—no, not knives, but machetes; there was a big difference, namely the reach and cutting power—strapped to their hips, and each one had a pump-action shotgun slung over his back. One was in his early thirties, the other younger, about late twenties. They both sported thick facial hair and would have looked identical, except one of them was a redhead.

Keo's hands and legs were free, which confused him. His weapons were gone, but they had left his gun belt with an empty holster. He spotted both the MP5SD, his pistol, and knife in a pile along with his bug-out bag in the corner to his left.

"You got a name?" the older of the two, who wasn't the redhead, asked.

"Yeah," Keo said.

When he didn't keep going, the two men exchanged an amused look before Redhead said, "You being a smartass?"

"Not nearly smart enough," Keo said, and reached back to rub at the bump at the base of his skull.

"Sorry about that. You sort of, uh, came at us out of nowhere, and we weren't sure what to do. You're lucky; we usually shoot first and ask questions later. Does it hurt?"

"What do you think?"

He stared at the two men again. They weren't Buckies, he knew that much. Not only because he couldn't locate a circled M anywhere on their bulletproof vests, but more importantly he wasn't restrained or, worst case, dead.

That knowledge allowed him to relax, if just slightly.

"Which one of you geniuses hit me?" Keo asked.

"Him," Redhead said, indicating his partner.

"Guilty," the other guy said, reaching back and patting his shotgun. "I call her Annie."

"Annie's a real bitch," Keo said.

The guy chuckled. "That she is."

"Your horse got away," Redhead said.

"What?" Keo said.

"Your horse. It got away. Sucker was waiting for me at the front door when I opened it. Quiet as a mouse; I didn't even hear a peep out of it until it nearly took my head off. Last I saw, it vanished into the woods." Then, with a crooked grin, "You always sleep with your horse?"

"It's not my horse."

"No?"

Keo shook his head. "No."

"It looked pretty domesticated to me," Not Redhead said. "You took it from its previous owner?"

"He didn't need it anymore."

"I see."

"Do you?"

Not Redhead grinned. "Yeah, I do. It's a tough world out there." He reached into his pack and took out a see-through bag and tossed it over.

Keo caught it, opened it, and smelled dehydrated jerky. "What is this?"

"Deer," the redhead said.

Keo took out a piece, gave it a try, decided it was good enough, and finished off the stick before dipping in for seconds.

"Mikey, I think he likes it!" Not Redhead chuckled.

"I guess so," his partner said. Then, "I'm Willis. That's Lam."

"Like the Lamb of God, minus the *b* at the end," the guy named Lam said.

"Thanks for the tip," Keo said. "I'm Keo."

"What kind of name is that?"

"John was taken."

"Say what?"

"Exactly."

Willis and Lam exchanged another look, this one more confused than amused. But they shrugged it off.

Definitely not Buckies.

Keo glanced around him while he chewed on another piece of jerky. His watch read 5:11 a.m., which explained why it wasn't nearly as black outside the windows, but it was still dark enough that Willis and Lam shouldn't have been sitting here with a raging fireplace, making themselves into a target for any ghouls passing by. He would have been alarmed if he didn't already know who the two men were, or what they did for a living. The shotgun and the machete gave it away.

"You know who we are, don't you?" the one named Willis asked, one corner of his mouth grinning at Keo.

Keo nodded. "You're slayers."

"That's right. But you thought we were someone else at first, didn't you? Who did you think we were?"

Keo shrugged. "Someone else."

"Given that reaction, I guess it's lucky for you that we came along instead."

"You wouldn't be wrong."

It had been almost two years since he ran into a slayer. The last time was somewhere outside of Wichita City, Kansas. Keo wondered if that old man was still alive.

"What are slayers doing down here?" Keo asked.

"The same thing we do everywhere else," Lam said. "Hunting ghouls."

"We tracked a pretty sizable group headed south from

nearby Olsen," Willis said. "But we lost them somewhere around Winding Creek."

You didn't lose them, we killed them for you, Keo thought. *Me, Jim, and Duncan. But mostly Jim's shotgun.*

"You've been to Winding Creek?" Keo said instead.

"Not yet. We're heading in tomorrow morning," Lam said. "Which is very soon," he added, glancing down at his watch. "Figure they might want to hire us on for a while if we can show them there are ghouls in the area."

Besides the old man outside of Wichita, Keo had seen plenty of guys like Willis and Lam before. Too many of them in the years since Houston, in fact. Slayers were essentially mercenaries that hired their services out to towns to clean out any ghouls in the area. Without fail, they were rough and tumble types, people who couldn't—or didn't want to—stay put in one place for too long. For a time Keo had even hung around a few of them, but the idea of going from place to place searching out ghouls and killing them wasn't something he was interested in doing for a career.

"There's just the two of you?" Keo asked.

"We crossed into Texas with six," Lam said. "But you know how it is. This ain't a job for the faint of heart. One mistake and"—he snapped his fingers—"that's it. Six feet under."

"Or worse," Willis said.

"Or worse," Lam nodded.

"We got some friends following us down here later. It's a big state; we were hoping to find enough jobs to keep us busy for a while. Maybe enough to last us a few years before we moved west."

"Doesn't sound like much of a retirement plan," Keo said.

Willis chuckled. "Beats farming and cleaning up cow shit."

"You're going into Winding Creek in the morning?"

"That's right. You from this area?" Then, after Keo nodded, "What's it like? We thought about going in last night, but you know, it's not always the smartest idea to pop into a new place in the dead of night. People've gotten shot for less."

"You'll see," Keo said, and chewed on another piece of deer jerky.

"Goddammit," Lam said, though Keo didn't think that was a somber *goddammit* but more of an annoyed *goddammit*.

"There goes our meal ticket," Willis said.

Yup. Definitely more annoyed than somber.

And he thought *he* didn't play well with others. Lam and Willis had come here looking for a job. Instead, they had followed Keo into Winding Creek only to find a lot of blood in the streets, empty buildings, and not a single survivor to offer them employment.

They stood in the town square an hour after sunup, with plenty of light to see everything that needed to be seen. The place looked much different than when Keo was last here less than twenty-four hours ago. Then again, at the time he had only seen the very spot he was currently standing on from a window almost a block away. It was a moodier atmosphere up close, and the already decaying bodies only added to that.

"Jesus Christ. Who did this?" Lam asked.

"You ever heard of a town called Fenton?" Keo asked.

Lam and Willis exchanged a look.

"What?" Keo said.

"On the way down here," Willis said. "But we didn't go inside."

"Any reason why not?"

"They didn't exactly have their welcome mats out."

"Meaning?"

"There were guard towers and machine gun nests along the roads into town. The place looked more like a military outpost."

"Given their artillery, it didn't look like they'd need our services," Lam said.

"How big is Fenton?" Keo asked.

Willis shrugged. "Pretty big, from what I saw. And growing."

"Growing how?"

"They were putting up new buildings. Looked like a real boom town."

What the hell does a booming town need women and kids for? Keo thought, remembering everything Wendy and Lewis had told him.

"You gonna tell us what happened here?" Lam asked.

Keo did, and the two slayers listened quietly.

When he was done, they exchanged another look, before Willis finally said, "Damn glad we stayed out of Fenton."

"How many people did you see up there?" Keo asked.

"Like I said, we didn't go inside," Lam said, "but there was a lot of activity. They have a thriving farming community, too. And plenty of livestock. It didn't look like they would need to raid other towns for supplies."

"And gas," Willis said. "They had plenty of gas. You could hear machinery running everywhere, and there was a line of cars going in and out. You know what a technical is?" And when Keo nodded, "They had a lot of those, too."

"Where are they getting the gas?" Keo asked.

He remembered all those vehicles inside Princeville that Buck's people were using. They were also using horses, but they seemed to have plenty of fuel to burn. There was a reason Keo mostly walked everywhere; the same for the slayers. Fuel, at least the ones that were still usable after all these years, were rare commodities.

"Hell if we know," Willis said. "But they had plenty of it, though. You could smell gasoline in the air around the place from all that construction they were doing."

"It looked like they were building an army," Lam said. "Or a bigger army, anyway, 'cause it looked like they had a good chunk of that already. We've been across a dozen states, killing ghouls since The Walk Out, but I'll be damn if that wasn't the closest I ever came to seeing someone assembling a real honest to goodness armed forces. The only thing they were missing was air power."

A burgeoning army. Technicals out the ass. And plenty of gas.

So what the hell does Buck need with the women and children?

"Anything left?" Willis was asking as he looked around. "In the buildings and houses?"

Keo shook his head. "I didn't have a lot of time to look around when I was here yesterday. Too busy trying not to get shot. But you boys feel free to check."

"Hell, we're already here," Lam said, though he didn't sound all that enthusiastic. "Might as well make it worthwhile." Then, "What about the bodies?"

"What about them?" Willis asked.

"Should we bury them?"

"Man, it'd take weeks. Let the animals have them. They gotta eat, too." He looked over at Keo as if just realizing he was still there. "You knew them, right?"

Keo didn't respond right away. If Emma and Megan had been one of the bodies instead of just the men and women they'd stumbled across since entering the city limits, it might have been a different answer. But it wasn't, and he had to find Jonah. He had to find Emma and Megan, and spending even a few more hours here burying all these bodies wasn't going to help him achieve that.

"You're right; animals gotta eat, too," Keo finally said. "Besides, if they don't, something else will be by to take them."

Keo didn't have to say what that *something else* was because Lam and Willis already knew. It was their occupation, after all.

"Let's get this over with and get outta here," Lam said. "This place's already starting to give me the creeps."

They headed toward the main warehouse where most of Winding Creek's goods were stored—it was the largest building by far and hard to miss—while Keo went in the opposite direction.

It had occurred to him while walking back to town that although he did have a map of the area at his cabin, he would have a better chance of not just identifying but locating whatever *Jonah* was from a map inside Winding Creek. After all, if Lewis had told the truth and he sent Emma and Megan along with the other survivors to whatever this Jonah was, then the women already knew of its existence. And if they knew, maybe it was common knowledge with the other townspeople, too. Say, like with its only two lawmen.

Keo found the sheriff's office near city hall and stepped around the dried blood splatters on the walkway. There were bullet holes in the walls and one of the windows was shattered, and through the still-open door, Keo spotted a wild dog at work on a body lying prone on its stomach. He recognized Duncan right away by the 1911 still holstered at his hip.

The dog looked up as Keo neared and bared its teeth at him, but when Keo stood still and watched it back, the animal decided he wasn't a danger and went back to eating. Keo's stomach turned slightly at the sight, but he reminded himself that he'd seen a lot worse and stepped around Duncan to get to the big desk at the back.

The jail cell at the far end, along with the gun rack on the wall, were empty. There were stray cartridges on the floor, probably dropped when the building was being looted, but there were no signs of Jim.

Keo went to the desk and opened the drawers one by one before finding what he was looking for in the very bottom drawer—a stack of maps. He took them out when he heard a growl and looked up to find the dog again, giving him the evil eye.

"Go ahead, keep eating, I'm not gonna stop you."

The dog seemed to bristle at being spoken to, but after a few seconds, it returned to Duncan's dead body and there was only the sound of sharp teeth rendering flesh.

Keo got the hell out of there as fast as he could, then found a bench far from the blood and bodies and went through his haul.

He spent the first ten or so minutes scouring each map

looking for a town called Jonah. Failing that, he started hunting for roads called Jonah. When that didn't turn up anything either, his next hour was spent looking for anything called Jonah—*anything* at all—but the closest he came was a small stream called Jonas Lake somewhere near a city called Conroe just outside of Houston.

He was still searching for a clue—*any* clue—when Lam slammed a wooden crate on the bench across from him and began sifting through it. Keo recognized the box—it was one of Mark's. Keo had seen it plenty of times when the baker showed up at Emma's place with a fresh supply of bread.

In the bright morning sun, and with Lam sitting down across from him, Keo glimpsed the teeth marks along the sides of Lam's neck, and as the man took off his fingerless gloves to scratch an itch, there were more similar markings around his wrists. Both Lam and Willis had been wearing long-sleeve shirts, and the collars of Willis's jackets were high up enough that Keo hadn't noticed the bites before last night or this morning. And that was exactly what they were—bite marks made by ghoul teeth.

He had met others like Lam (and probably Willis, too). Not as slayers, but as survivors of The Purge. The ghouls didn't always turn the ones they bit; sometimes they kept them alive as sustenance, drawing blood from them night after night. The lucky ones, it was said, were the ones that stopped being useful and were either finally turned or allowed to drift away.

Keo looked back down at the map before Lam could catch him staring. "Found anything good?"

"They left behind a lot of stuff, mostly things they probably didn't think were worth taking," Lam said. He pulled out a half-empty bottle of water, a pair of socks, and a can of sardines. "I don't blame them; they got their pick of the place, so why bother with the leftovers?"

"You've seen this before? Towns being raided like this?"

"Too many times to count." Lam took out a can of SPAM, then produced a titanium scork from his pocket and began eating. "It happens throughout history. The strong take advantage of the weak." He shrugged. "I like to think what me and the other slayers do as being the complete opposite."

"Someone's gotta do it," Keo said.

"Damn right. And if we can get a hot meal and a bath out of it? Hell, I consider it a fair trade."

"I wouldn't disagree. I've met plenty of slayers. You've always been standup guys."

Lam grinned. "What can I say? We get to kill ghouls, and every now and then there's a pretty farm girl who shows us how much she appreciates what we do. It's win-win."

Keo chuckled. "I don't think I could do it, though. No offense."

"None taken. It's not everyone's cup of tea." He looked around. Then, "We found horse stalls. A lot of them."

"They took the horses."

"What about the livestock?"

"I don't know. Probably those, too. If not, then they've wandered off. Or something else got them."

"Right. Something else."

Keo sneaked another curious look at Lam as the man scorked a big chunk of SPAM into his mouth. Most slayers he'd met were either adrenaline junkies or people looking for a little revenge. Or a lot of revenge, in the case of one old man. The Purge had left them permanently scarred, emotionally and physically, and not all of them had been able to adjust to life post-Purge. Keo often thought of it as a form of post-traumatic stress disorder. They had been fighting the creatures for so long that they didn't know how to stop.

"One thing's for sure," Lam was saying, "there aren't a lot of ghouls around the area. They would have taken care of the bodies last night if there were."

"Have you noticed a decreasing number of them out there?"

"They're definitely getting harder to find. Why do you think Willis and me were out there looking for them in the middle of the night when we stumbled into you? The ones we've found have been pretty weak; as dangerous as an old lady with osteoporosis."

Keo remembered the ones at the abandoned house that he, Jim, and Duncan had killed. Then there was the lone creature that had broken into his cabin the night before.

"Some would say that's a good thing," Keo said.

"Some would, but not when killing them's your occupation," Lam grunted, and took another bite out of the SPAM.

Keo looked back down at the maps spread in front of him. "I can't find it. This Jonah. You ever run across a place called that?"

"Jonah?" Lam shook his head. "I've been to a lot of places —big and small—but never heard of a city or town called Jonah."

"It's supposed to be farther down south, maybe along the coastline."

Lam thought about it before shaking his head again. "Doesn't ring any bells. Sorry."

They both heard the loud *boom!* of a shotgun blast and glanced across the town center at one of the apartment buildings. Not just any building, Keo saw, but the same one he'd been in yesterday when he found Wendy. The gunshot had come from the second floor where Wendy's body would still be.

"The fuck?" Lam said. He opened his pack and took out a two-way radio, then keyed it. "You shoot yourself in the foot again?"

The radio squawked, and Keo heard Willis's voice. "Fucking dogs, man."

"Dogs? As in plural?"

"Three of them. A whole pack. They scurried after I blasted the alpha."

"What were they doing up there?"

"There's a line of bodies in the second-floor hallway. They look paramilitary, but guns are gone."

The slayer looked over at Keo. "You wouldn't happen to know anything about that, would you?"

"Maybe I do, maybe I don't," Keo said.

The redhead chuckled before saying back into the radio, "Get what you can, and let's get outta here. I don't wanna stay any longer than I have to. The place gives me the creeps."

"Roger that," Willis said.

Lam put the radio away. "What's next for you? If you can't find this Jonah?"

"Head south," Keo said, folding and then shoving maps into his pack. "Best-case scenario, I stumble into this Jonah guy —assuming it's a guy. Or someone who knows where a Jonah-something is."

"Worst case?"

"I get some exercise and breathe in some nice ocean breeze."

"Doesn't sound too bad."

"What about you two?"

"Probably head west. Maybe even go into Houston."

"Houston? Are you serious?"

"Come on, it can't be as bad as we've heard."

"It's not; it's worse."

"Bullshit."

Keo shrugged. "It's your funeral. Just make sure to keep that pretty flesh of yours all nicely covered up. There are some very hungry people—and I use the term loosely—waiting in there for nice boys like you to waltz through the place."

"Whatever, man. We can handle whatever Houston throws at us. Besides, Willis and me are kind of history whores. We always thought we'd swing by the city eventually, maybe take a tour of where the Battle of Houston took place. You know, the *real* battle grounds?"

"You know about that?" Keo asked.

Lam gave him a noncommittal shrug. "I've met a few people who say the real fight wasn't on the streets but *under* it. I guess we'll find out when we get there. It's only been five years. There should still be signs of what really happened that caused The Walk Out."

"A tour, huh?" Keo said.

"What? You don't want to know how it happened? How a handful of humans took on and killed King Ghoul in his own nest? It's history, man. Probably the most important history in human existence, as far as I'm concerned."

Keo zipped up his pack before slinging it on. "I got enough history for a lifetime. I'll pass on this one."

"You know what they say about history."

"That it's boring?"

"Yeah, that too. And also, 'Those who don't remember it are doomed to repeat it.'"

"Fuck history; I got a submachine gun." Keo stuck out his hand and Lam shook it. "Good luck to the both of you."

"You too, man. Hope you find Jonah whatever—or whoever—that turns out to be."

Yeah, me too, for Emma and Megan's sake...

SIXTEEN

"Hope you find Jonah, whatever—or whoever—that turns out to be."

Truer words were never spoken, and they reminded Keo he was doing something he had promised himself he wasn't going to do ever again: Get involved in other people's business.

Remember the last time? Song Island? Black Tide Island?

What's with all the islands? What happens if Jonah turns out to be another island?

With your luck, there's a better-than-average chance of that being true.

Wasn't that why he had stayed in the cabin outside of town by himself? And why he never spent the entire night at Emma's? It was one reason—the *best* reason, as far as he was concerned—but there were others. Getting involved in other people's business usually ended up with him on the wrong end of a lot of guns.

There used to be a time when he actually got paid to stick his nose in other people's business. But of course all that changed when the world went kaput, monsters turned out to be real, and it was every man for himself. Then there was a woman, then another woman, and more women...

What was it with him and women?

And yet here he was, wandering through the woods heading south with no idea of where he was going, when the smart move would have been to turn west—or east or north, anywhere but south—and kept going. He could easily avoid the Buckies by leaving the state altogether. After all, Fenton was just one city in a big ass state.

So why was he still heading southeast?

Because that was where Jonah (whoever or whatever that turned out to be) was, and where Emma and Megan went, and regardless of what he tried to tell himself—or how much he chastised himself—he just couldn't turn away now without making sure mother and daughter were okay. Maybe it was the softy in him (*You went soft a long time ago, pal*), but he just *had to be sure.*

Besides, to do anything else would be an asshole move, and Keo was not an asshole. At least, he was trying very hard not to be one.

Keo figured that sooner or later he'd run into the Gulf of Mexico, and once he did that he could continue south along the coastline. It wasn't exactly the best plan, but in the absence of anything even approaching an idea of where he was going—

Snap!

He darted forward, then right until he was behind one of two large trees. The MP5SD was already in his hands and Keo was sliding around the gnarled surface of the trunk, essentially going in a circle, when he spotted his pursuer.

It walked toward him, dragging its reins behind it like it

had all the time in the world. The soft, slightly damp ground meant it didn't make a lot of noise, and it was only because of a dry twig snapping that Keo had heard the animal at all.

Damn horse really is a ninja.

As soon as Keo fully rounded the tree trunk, the thoroughbred stopped moving and looked across the twenty meters or so at him.

"You again," Keo said, lowering his weapon.

Horse took that as a positive sign and walked over at its own leisurely pace.

"What's the matter? Can't find someone else to bother, so you had to keep looking for me? How did you find me again, anyway?"

It might have sniffed the air.

"Hey, it's a free country; do what you want."

Keo turned and resumed going southeast.

He didn't look back for the longest time, but when he finally did, the horse was still back there, though it had made up ten meters since the last time Keo checked.

Keo hadn't been walking long enough to get tired and need a ride, so he continued on foot. He didn't stop again until around noon to eat a bag of MRE from his supplies. He found a spot next to a tree with plenty of shade to enjoy his warm lasagna, but not before removing the animal's saddle.

"You're welcome," Keo said.

The horse snorted its approval, then immediately began grazing on the plentiful grass nearby. He could imagine the thoroughbred out here for a long time, with plenty of feed to go around and no real dangers. Five years ago, nighttime would have been Horse's most dangerous hours, but that was true for just about everything whether they walked on two or four legs and couldn't take flight or, in a pinch, scamper up a tree for safety.

The horse eased its way over before stopping to chew on a stalk of grass about ten feet in front of Keo.

"By the way, where were you last night? You just took off after I got my head bashed in, didn't you? Some guard horse you turned out to be."

It looked over at him—briefly, before returning to its feeding.

"Feel free to apologize anytime."

Keo was a city boy—had been all his life—and although he'd learned enough about what made horses tick since, they were still mysteries to him, and in a lot of ways Keo preferred it that way. He liked walking wherever he could when possible, because it kept him in shape; these days, being more physically capable than the next guy could save your life.

When he was done eating, Keo pulled off his pants and took a few minutes to clean and redress the graze on his thigh. The horse stopped its meal momentarily to sniff the air when Keo applied some ointment to the wound.

"What?" Keo said. Then, when the horse went back to its meal, "That's right, go back to eating. You seem to be really good at that."

The pain had numbed over, and he hardly felt it anymore even after all the walking he'd done this morning, but maybe that had a little something to do with getting bashed in the head by the butt of a shotgun. After that, a little tingle from his thigh was barely worth acknowledging.

He was pulling his pants back on when the animal suddenly went very stiff just before its head snapped up and it looked behind them. Keo took the cue and snatched up his submachine gun before slipping behind the cover of the tree he'd been sitting against. The horse remained silent next to him, unmoving, eyes focused on something behind them.

But there was nothing back there that Keo could see, hear, or feel.

He slowed down his breathing anyway to help with his senses, but there was still just the chirping of birds in the trees above him and the *scratch-scratch* of four-legged creatures scurrying along some branches nearby.

"What?" Keo whispered to the horse. "You hear something or not?"

Horse turned its head to look at him.

"Well?"

Keo swore the thoroughbred might have shrugged its shoulders before it went back to grazing. But that was impossible, because horses didn't shrug.

Or did they?

"Make up your mind, Horse. This is no time for games."

He remained standing, gun at the ready, for the next five minutes, paying just as much attention to the (nonchalant) way Horse chewed on its lunch as he did to his evergreen environment. Birds. Squirrels. Something that might have been a hawk flying past the crowns of the trees above him.

After a while, Keo came out of his alert stance.

"You smelled something?" he asked Horse. "Heard something? Felt something, maybe?"

The animal ignored him.

"If I have a heart attack, it'll be your fault, you know that, right? Not that you'd care."

Keo picked up the saddle and put it back on the horse before grabbing his pack and starting off again. He didn't have to look back to know Horse was keeping up because he could hear the squishy *thump-thump* of its hooves against the soft ground. He wasn't sure if it was being loud on purpose, for his benefit.

Weird horse.

He knew he was headed in the right direction when he could feel the change in the air—it started to get breezier, and he could almost taste the salt on his tongue. Keo thought Horse would begin to wander off when it realized where Keo was headed, but the animal continued to follow on his heels anyway.

"You know that's saltwater out there, right?"

The horse didn't respond but didn't break off, either.

"Just remember you're a horse, Horse. You don't drink saltwater."

A few minutes later, they reached the tree line and the end of the wooded area after what seemed like a few days of walking, though it had been less than four-something hours. They stepped out into a large wide-open field overgrown with grass that reached all the way up to Keo's waist.

The breeze was heavier out here, causing the stalks of grass to sway side to side, and it was easy to imagine the whole thing as one big, massive rug. He could see the coastline in the distance—maybe less than a mile—and hear the echoes of ocean waves bashing against a beach.

And there, finally, the first manmade structures he'd seen in a long time jutting up from the ground about where the beach would be. It was a group of buildings clumped tightly together. He counted six, but there could have been more, because all he could really see were seemingly connected shadows.

"What do you see?" he asked Horse. "You got better eyes than me, don't you? Super eyes? You know, I used to know someone with super eyes. He's gone now, though..."

When was the last time he thought of Frank? It had been a while, actually. Frank wasn't his real name, but only a few people knew that.

"Well?"

The horse dipped its head and brushed at the grass with its muzzle.

"Not the answer I was looking for. You're no help at all."

Keo looked back at the buildings. He was too far away to make out what he was looking at exactly, especially with the sun in the background silhouetting everything out there. It could have been a town (*Jonah Town?*) or a leftover seaside bed-and-breakfast, for all he knew. (*Jonah's Bed-and-Breakfast, maybe?*)

"Now remember, no swimming. Understand?"

Horse sniffed the air but didn't acknowledge him. Or, at least, Keo didn't think it did.

I'm talking to a horse like it's a real person. Jesus, if anyone sees this, I might die of embarrassment.

Keo unslung the MP5SD and held it in front of him as he began walking across the field. The thickly massed blades of grass made the crossing slow going, not that Keo was in any hurry. There was plenty of daylight left, and there didn't seem to be any activity in the area. There wasn't even anything that looked like a road, which made him wonder how anyone went back and forth from the buildings. Was there a spur road he couldn't see from his position?

That was, of course, assuming he wasn't looking at a ghost town, and Jonah-whatever could still be out there, somewhere else. The other possibility was that Lewis had lied to him, which was entirely possible. But why would a dying man lie? The only reason Keo could think of was if he still hadn't trusted Keo.

But I have such a trusting face.

Kinda.

He pushed the doubts into the back of his mind. He'd find out the answer soon enough, so there was no point in rehashing it.

Horse kept pace next to him and seemed to have less trouble moving through the unending waves of grass than Keo. For Keo, parts of the field were so heavy with sunburnt blades of brown-green stalks that it was almost like trudging his way (slowly) through thick mud—one that went all the way up to his waist.

"So here's the deal," Keo said to the animal. "My legs are just fine for now, but sooner or later I'm gonna want a ride if you insist on coming along. Deal? Consider it the price of my company."

The horse stopped moving and lifted its head.

Keo stopped, too, and turned to look at it in its large brown eyes. "I'm just saying, why walk when there's a perfectly good saddle on your back. Know what I mean?"

The animal let out a series of short snorts and took a step back, then another one, just before a gush of wind told Keo why the horse was suddenly so alarmed: *Sweat and body odor in the air.*

He spun back around, lifting the H&K in the same fluid motion, just as some kind of creature lunged out of the ground, its body wearing a layer of grass that covered it from head to toe.

And it was *pointing a rifle at him.*

SEVENTEEN

It wasn't a creature. Or a monster. It was a man wearing a ghillie suit covered in the exact same grass that swarmed the fields around him, and he had a camo-painted rifle in his hands pointed at Keo from less than twenty meters away.

This is not good.

The camouflage was good, and Keo might have walked right past the ambusher if the wind hadn't blown in the right direction at just the right time. Even then, the horse had caught it first, but Keo liked to think he would have also, eventually.

Yeah, let's go with that.

In the second or so it took the man to reveal himself and lift his rifle, Keo had already pushed through the shock and was about to pull the trigger (*Not fast enough, pal!*) when he saw movement out of the corners of both eyes and two more ghillie suits sprung out of the ground to his left and right. The two new figures flanked the first, which meant they had all been lying there this entire time while he stupidly walked right at them.

It took Keo just a half-second to pick up the sun glinting off the other two rifles, both of which were also aimed, predictably, at him.

Aw, man, this is so not fair.

He didn't know how long he stood there, the submachine gun pointed at the first ambusher, but no one said a word or moved for the longest time. He could hear Horse shuffling his legs behind him, and the animal might have let out a warning whinny or two.

Stupid horse, this is where you run.

Except the animal didn't, and continued to hold its position behind Keo. He didn't know what to make of that, not that he really had the time to try to figure it out with three rifles pointed at him. All it would take was one pull of the trigger and he was a dead man. Oh, sure, he could probably get one of them—two, if he was *really* fortunate—but he was definitely not going to get all three before at least one of them put a round through him.

Bad. This is very, very bad.

Three rifles and three guys in ghillie suits, though there was a good possibility one of them was a woman. The one on his right. She was smaller than the other two by a good foot, though the varied heights of their suits might have been throwing him off. Not that it mattered, really. A woman or a kid or a donkey, it was still another person with their weapon pointed at his head.

Finally, after what seemed like minutes but was probably less than a few seconds, Keo said, "Looks like we're at an impasse."

The man in the center exchanged a quick look with the one to his right (Keo's left) before doing the same to the one on his left (the possible woman). Keo couldn't really read their reaction from twenty meters away; the fact that all three ambushers' faces were covered in black and brown paint didn't help. They had really gone all out with the whole "blending into the environment" part; he had to give them that.

"How you figure that?" the man in the center said. He had a deep voice. "There are three of us and only one of you. That doesn't sound like an impasse to me, son. Sounds more like a 'You're royally screwed.'"

The man's got a point.

"That's not true," Keo said anyway. He kept the MP5SD pointed at Deep Voice even though he could see all three of them without having to move his head thanks to their forced early reveal. "There's Horse."

"Your horse?" the one to Deep Voice's right said. He sounded much younger than his companion.

You hit puberty yet, kid? Keo wanted to ask him but said instead, "That's three against two," and thought, *Man, do I even buy that? Do they? How long before they shoot me in the face?*

Damn, I don't want to get shot in the face...or anywhere else, for that matter.

"Your horse," the second man said, as if just to be sure.

"Yeah, Horse," Keo nodded.

"Are you for real?" the woman (*Aha, I was right!*) to Keo's right said. "His name is Horse?"

"He didn't exactly come with a name tag," Keo said.

"But you call your horse Horse."

"It's a horse. I don't think it cares what I call it."

"Good point, Holly Golightly."

"I don't know who that is."

"Don't you?"

"Nope."

"Too bad, cause it's a killer reference."

"Speaking of which, I'd appreciate not getting shot by you and your dad here."

The woman chuckled. "He's not my dad."

"Grandpa?"

Deep Voice grunted. "Enough."

"Why?" Keo said. "I was having a nice conversation with your not-daughter."

The man ignored him and said, "Put down your weapon."

"Can't do that."

"You don't have a choice."

"That's not true. I can choose *not* to lower my weapon."

"Then we're going to kill you," the younger man said. He regripped his rifle, though Keo wasn't sure if that was for effect or if he was just a little bit nervous.

Which one makes me feel better?

Oh, right; neither.

Now that he'd had some time to get a better look at his ambushers, Keo was pretty sure his biggest threat was Deep Voice in the middle. The man was armed with a bolt-action rifle with a large scope on top like his two companions. They really did look like a father and his children out for a little hunting trip.

So kill the old man first. Gotcha.

Either Deep Voice suspected what Keo was thinking, or he got lucky when he said, "It won't be the first time these two have killed someone. Even if you somehow get me, they'll get you for sure."

"And your horse, too," Young Guy said, and once again regripped his rifle. It looked like a nervous gesture to Keo that time.

Shoot the old man, then take out the girl, and then *Mr. Nervous.*

Good plan. Now all you have to do is make sure you don't die while pulling it off.

"Leave Horse out of this," Keo said. "Don't make me sic PETA on your ass, kid."

"Kid?" Young Guy said. He sounded incredulous, which was a little amusing. Then again, Keo might have just thought it was amusing because he was trying very hard not to accept just how up a creek he was at the moment.

"What are you, fifteen?" Keo asked.

"Old enough to shoot you dead," the kid said.

"A lot of people thought they were old enough to shoot me dead. I'm still here, and they're not. What does that tell you?"

"That you're stubborn?" the woman asked.

"That's one way to look at it."

"What's another?"

"Persistent."

"Not quite the word I'd use, but sure, if it makes you feel better."

"You know what would really make me feel better?"

"I'm all ears."

"Not being shot."

She might have smirked. "You've been shot before?"

"Yes. And it's not fun, let me tell you. So I'm very anxious to avoid it happening again. Maybe you can tell your little brother here to calm down before that happens."

"I'm not her little brother," the young man said.

"Little cousin?" Keo said.

"Dammit, enough," Deep Voice said. He sounded annoyed now.

What do you gotta be so annoyed about? I'm the one about to get murdered out here in this friggin' field of nightmares.

"Put down your weapon, and we'll take you alive," Deep Voice said.

"And then what?" Keo asked.

"Then you'll come with us."

"Where to?"

The man made a backward nodding motion—just barely, since he did it while keeping his eyes (and weapon) on Keo the entire time.

"What, the ocean?" Keo said. "No thanks. I didn't bring my swimming trunks."

"You're a real piece of work," the woman said. Keo couldn't tell if she was amused or irritated. "You're this close to getting shot to hell, and you're making jokes. I don't know whether to be impressed or feel bad about your total lack of awareness for the current situation."

"I won't tell you again," Deep Voice said. "Lower your weapon."

"I can't," Keo said, and thought, *Because if I do you'll kill me, and there's still a mother and daughter out there I have to find.*

"You don't have a choice."

"I thought we already went over this. I have plenty of choices. Okay, maybe 'plenty' isn't the right word. I have *some* choices. I can lower my weapon like you want, or I can *not* lower my weapon."

"You wanna die, is that it?" Young Guy asked. Keo didn't have to wonder what he was feeling—it was all irritation. "You must have some kind of death wish, man."

"Not at all."

"Sure feels like it to me."

"Hey, you're the ones who ambushed *me*. I was just going for a walk with my horse, the two of us minding our own business. The way I see it, you three should be apologizing to me."

"Say what?" Young Guy said.

"But I'll overlook that part." Before they could say anything, he quickly added, "In fact, here's my proposal: We all lower our weapons, say 'Nice to see ya,' and go our separate ways. How about that?"

"Can't," Deep Voice said, shaking his head.

"Why not?"

"You already saw us."

"Saw you? I can barely tell what you look like. Those are some excellent paint jobs, by the way."

"Doesn't change the fact you know what you know."

"I know what I know? What does that even mean?"

"You know what he means," Young Guy said.

"I truly don't," Keo said.

"We don't have any choice, either," the man in the middle said. He sounded almost...regretful?

Not as regretful as I'm going to be when we all start shooting.

"These are dangerous times," the man continued. "Even if you're not who we think you are, you need to be vetted."

"I don't have rabies or anything," Keo said.

"Rabies?"

"Yeah. No rabies. So I don't need a vet."

The woman smirked. "I've decided: I'm mostly impressed with you."

"Glad to hear it," Keo said. "Who do you think I am, anyway?"

"We know who you are," Young Guy said.

"So enlighten me."

"That vest gave you away."

"*That vest?*" Keo thought.

Then, *Shit. The vest. The same vest I took off the dead Bucky and have been wearing since Princeville.*

That vest, you idiot. They think I'm one of Buck's men. One of the guys from Fenton. No wonder they're not going to let me go. I wouldn't, either, after what those assholes did to Winding Creek.

So what did that make these three?

"The enemy of my enemy is someone I don't want to shoot me in the face." Or something like that.

"I found this vest," Keo said. "It's not mine."

"Bullshit," Young Guy said, and fidgeted slightly.

"Swear to God."

"How did that happen?" Deep Voice asked.

"Lots of things are just lying around these days. It's not that hard and definitely isn't a reason for the three of you to shoot me for it."

"Nice story, bro," the woman said. She might have been grinning, but it was hard to tell with all that goop on her face. "Got another one?"

"I knew a guy in Afghanistan who got kicked to death by a donkey," Keo said.

"Just shoot him, Carl," the kid said. He took one hand off his rifle and swiped at a bead of sweat. "We're wasting our time. Let's just shoot him and get this over with. There could be more of them out there."

"There isn't," Keo said.

"Bullshit again. You could just be stalling us."

"I'm not."

"And I say *bullshit*."

The kid's going to shoot me. He's going to lose it and shoot me. Crap.

"Easy, Floyd, easy," the man named Carl, a.k.a Deep Voice, said.

"Yeah, Floyd, easy now," Keo said. "No one has to die. Least of all me."

"Shut the hell up," Floyd snapped.

Keo grinned. "I'm just trying to be friendly."

"This is your idea of friendly?" the woman asked.

"Again, I wasn't the one lying around on the ground waiting to ambush someone. I'm just an innocent traveler."

"An innocent traveler with a horse named Horse."

"That's it exactly. You've got it."

"Your horse is awfully well-behaved. It hasn't even tried to take off."

"What's it doing back there, anyway?"

"Huh?"

"Horse. What's it doing back there? I can't actually see, since I'm afraid you guys might shoot me if I turn my head even just a little bit. Especially Mr. Nervous over here."

"It's..." The woman's eyes darted away from Keo for a second before coming back to him. "It's grazing. I guess it's hungry."

"It's always hungry. That horse eats like a horse."

"Carl," Floyd said, "this is taking forever. Let's just shoot him."

"Whoa, whoa, let's not, Carl," Keo said. Then, focusing on Carl, "I get the feeling you think I'm someone I'm not. Why don't you tell me who that is, and I'll do my very best to convince you that you're wrong."

Carl chuckled. "You'd just lie to get out of this."

"Not true. People say I have a very honest face."

"Not with that scar," Floyd snickered.

"Ouch."

The woman chuckled. "First time someone told you that?"

"Yes, actually," Keo said. "I'm a very big people person—"

The *pop!* of a gunshot interrupted the rest of Keo's speech, and he was already dropping to the ground when Carl's head snapped back as a spray of blood flicked into the air.

Someone shouted Carl's name—it could have been the woman to Keo's right or the young man to his left, but at that very second Keo couldn't distinguish their two voices and didn't care to try—just before the field around him was filled with bullets and the *pop-pop-pop* of automatic rifle fire filled the world like cascading thunder.

His nostrils were instantly swamped with the smell of burning foliage as rounds sliced through the stalks of grass around him and dirt flicked at his face and eyes and just for good measure, the rest of his body. Keo was only aware of moving, rolling away from the spot where he had dropped because that was where the shooters had last seen him and where they would be pouring their lead. It was the smartest thing he could have done, because mere seconds after the first volley, even more bullets began digging into the patch of ground where he had been not more than a few seconds earlier.

Roll, baby, roll!

Somewhere behind him, he thought he heard Horse letting out a loud (and almost angry?) squeal.

Run, you stupid horse, run!

He had no time to look up and back to make sure the animal did the sensible thing because he had rolled onto his stomach and was now too busy crawling forward and angling to his right.

The gunfire kept coming, the *pop-pop-pop* seemingly louder now than before, which either meant the shooters (and there was definitely more than one, he was 100% certain of that) were moving in for the kill or—

Silence, as the last gunshot faded, before disappearing completely.

Keo rolled onto his back and lifted his head just high enough (*Not too high, you idiot!*) to look past the swaying edges of grass in front of him.

A group of men walked out of the tree line, reloading their rifles as they did so. There were at least five of them that he could see, wearing civilian clothes with black assault vests over their shirts. The sun blinked off a white circle with the letter *M* on the closest shooter's ammo pouch.

Buckies.

EIGHTEEN

Buckies.

The same guys that Carl, Floyd, and the young woman thought he was one of. Maybe that was also the reason why whoever had taken the first shot had gone for Carl instead of him, even though Keo was standing right in front of the other man. Did the Buckies think he was one of them? There was a very good chance of that. After all, he was wearing one of their vests. What were the chances the Buckies thought they were even *saving* him?

Sorry, Carl, but better you than me, pal.

Keo remained where he was, on his back, with his head only partially lifted off the sunbaked ground under him. Thank God for the tall stalks of grass camouflaging his position. He spent a few seconds trying to gauge how far he had rolled, then crawled in the time between when the shooting began and stopped.

But he had to have put enough distance between him and his three ambushers because the Buckies were now about

twenty meters away. There were five of them, three with bala-
clavas pulled over their faces while the other two sported ball
caps. They were moving in formation—or a pretty good
facsimile of one, anyway—as they approached the spot where
Carl and the others had fallen.

Or, at least, Keo assumed that was their destination: the
last known location of Carl, Floyd, and whatever the girl's
name was. Not that any of their names meant a lick, because
chances were they were all dead. The Buckies must have
unloaded two magazines apiece downrange. *At least.* Keo
knew for a fact Carl was a goner. The way his head had
snapped back after the first gunshot, even before he saw the
flicker of blood, was all the evidence Keo needed.

That left two possible survivors—his new buddy Floyd and
the girl. But even that was a stretch. There had been enough
bullets buzzing in the air that Keo was shocked he had gotten
away unscathed.

It had to be the assault vest he was wearing that had
saved his life. The same vest that had almost gotten him
killed by Carl and company. He was sure of it now. (*Probably.*) The circled *M* was visible in the front and, more importantly, in the back where the shooters would have spotted it
all the way from the tree line through any kind of optics. He
wouldn't be surprised if whoever had taken out Carl was
using a high-powered scope. Something like that would easily
have identified the *M* on the back of the vest Keo was
wearing.

But if that explained why he had gotten out of there
without catching a bullet, it didn't really excuse the huge
number of rounds that had been flying in his general vicinity
earlier. All it would have taken was one stray round and it was

officially a case of friendly fire. That was, of course, assuming the Buckies were purposefully trying to avoid hitting him.

Either/or, he thought, because he was still alive and right now nothing else mattered in the slightest. It was a little selfish (*A little?*), but a little selfishness went a long way these days when it came to staying alive.

He watched the Buckies continue pushing forward, all five men slightly bent at the waist to lower their profile. They were taking their time, opting for caution over speed. Keo had to admit, he was impressed with their patience, and it really did look as if they had some real training in their back pockets. That, more than anything, convinced him he was looking at a group of people who had, once upon a time, been in an army. If not Uncle Sam's, then a very good version of one.

Gee, I wonder what that M stands for?

Or should I say, who.

A gust of wind swept across the land, lowering Keo's cover just slightly enough to make him nervous. He quickly lowered himself back down to compensate, but soon the grass was back to regular heights and he could lift his head and reacquire the approaching men.

They had been spreading out to cover more ground ever since they left their tree line cover. The closest one was about ten meters in front of Keo and getting closer, though the man didn't know it. They were sweeping the fields around them, a couple even occasionally glancing back at the woods behind them just in case.

"You see them?" one of them said. He was wearing a red handkerchief around his right elbow and was exactly in the middle of the five-men team. Red Handkerchief carried a dull green M40 rifle that Keo had seen plenty of Marines favoring.

There was no doubt in Keo's mind this was the guy who had taken out Carl. It would have been child's play, given how wide open and still Carl had been while he went back and forth with Keo.

I guess it's kinda my fault, when you get right down to it. Sorry, Carl.

"Saw them go down," the one next to Red Handkerchief said. He was one of the three sporting a balaclava, and his voice sounded slightly muffled as a result. He gripped an AR-15 tightly with two fingerless gloves.

"All of them?" Red Handkerchief asked.

"Yeah. Maybe."

"Shit. That's not good."

"So what?"

"The fourth guy. The one with his back to us."

"You sure he was one of us?"

"Yeah, yeah, I saw the *M*."

"Could have been anything. Maybe his name starts with an *M*."

"It wasn't anything. It was an *M* in a white circle."

"So he was one of ours."

"That's what I'm saying."

"What's he doing out here ahead of us, then?"

"Hell if I know. But if anyone asks, we never saw him."

"Hey, I'm good with that." Then, to the other three, "You guys hear that? No one tell Buck what happened. There was never a fourth guy out here."

The other three nodded, and a couple of them chuckled, and Keo thought, *Now that's no way to treat friendly fire, boys. For shame.*

Red Handkerchief suddenly stopped, then pointed with

his rifle. "There. I see a body. Go check it out."

"Why me?" Fingerless Gloves, who like the other four had also stopped, asked.

"You're closer."

"Not by much."

"Still closer."

Fingerless Gloves smirked. "Shoot it if it even twitches."

"I got ya back," Red Handkerchief said.

Fingerless Gloves moved toward the spot, and he had taken exactly two steps when there was a *bang!* and the man's head snapped back almost identical to the way Carl's had done just minutes ago.

Even as Fingerless Gloves was collapsing, a figure in a ghillie suit (*Floyd? Unnamed lady?*) popped out of the ground in front of the remaining four men, about five meters from the spot where Fingerless Gloves had been headed. The sudden reappearance startled Red Handkerchief (*Don't you just hate it when they pop out of the ground like that?*) and the remaining three. The Buckies were still recovering when Ghillie Suit fired a second time from the handgun it was gripping in both hands, and a second Bucky dropped.

But that was all the victims Ghillie Suit was going to get, because the remaining three were already aiming—

Two out of five ain't bad, Keo thought even as he sat up and lifted his weapon and shot the closest Bucky, who had wandered so close to Keo's position that Keo didn't even have to aim to hit the man once in the thigh, then again in the chest when the man spun in his direction, giving Keo a much better second shot.

Red Handkerchief had fired about the same time Keo did, and Keo saw the ghillie-suited figure falling out of the corner of his right eye even as he was scrambling up to his knees to get a better look at the remaining two.

The Buckies hadn't heard Keo killing their comrade, because the H&K barely made any noise thanks to its built-in suppressor. By the time they did notice something was happening to their right side, Keo was already on his knees.

He shot Red Handkerchief almost exactly in the middle of the man's turning face, and as the Bucky went down, exposing the last remaining vested man, Keo flicked his MP5SD to full-auto to compensate for the longer distance and squeezed the trigger. He didn't let go until the man had disappeared, as if the ground had swallowed him up.

Keo hopped to his feet and swept the area, looking for someone to shoot. None of the Buckies got back up, and Ghillie Suit was nowhere to be found. Keo had seen the elaborate costume go down when Red Handkerchief fired, so he or she was either dead or wounded. The former was for the best because it meant one less threat for Keo to worry about, just in case they hadn't figured out that Keo had just saved their life.

He hurried over to the closest Bucky just to make sure he wasn't cheating and was wearing a bulletproof vest. The man was lying on his stomach and didn't move when Keo reached him, but Keo put an extra round into the back of his head anyway just to be sure.

Better safe than sorry.

He moved to the other four, checking them one by one— and making sure they didn't get back up like the first one— before he jogged over to where he had last seen Carl and company, not far from where Fingerless Gloves had fallen.

He located two bodies easily, lying close to one another, the ground and grass around them ripped to shreds by gunfire.

Carl was on his back, sporting an almost perfectly placed bullet hole in his forehead. The second body was lying face-down on the ground, and Keo reached for the shoulder to turn it over to see if it was Floyd or the girl—

"Don't you fucking touch him," a voice said.

Keo froze in mid-reach. The voice had come from his right, and it was definitely a woman.

Floyd and Carl it is, then.

"Don't shoot," Keo said.

He resisted every instinct to turn his head even slightly. What were the chances she *didn't* have a weapon pointed at him right now and was just bluffing?

Don't press your luck, idiot.

"Give me one good reason," the woman said.

"I saved your life."

"The hell you did."

"Actually, yeah, I did. Or did you think those other three fellows fell down and died out of fright when you pulled your pop-out-of-the-ground gag on them?"

The woman didn't answer.

A second of silence, then five...

"You're hurt," Keo said. "I can help."

"Why would you help me?" the woman asked. "You're one of them."

"Like I told Carl, I'm not. I stole this vest."

"You stole it?"

"Well, not technically. The original owner was dead."

"What happened to him?"

"I cut his throat."

Again, silence.

Keo's legs had become slightly wobbly, and he swore his

face was starting to itch for some reason. He wanted desperately to pull his hand back from it mid-reach or at least change up his stance to lighten the strain on his body.

"We good?" Keo asked.

Another second, followed by another five...

"Yeah," the woman finally said.

Keo breathed a sigh of relief and straightened up, looking over.

She was also standing up gingerly, an act that seemed to take a lot out of her, while putting away a handgun.

Yup. This close to her blowing my head off.

She peered at him from behind her painted face. "Who the hell are you?"

"Keo," he said.

"What?"

"My name. It's Keo."

"What a stupid name," the woman said. She bent down, stopped temporarily, and seemed to regather herself before finishing the move and picking her rifle up from the ground. "I'm Sherry."

"Nice to meet you, Sherry," Keo said. He glanced south toward the group of buildings in the distance. "So, can I ask you a question?"

Sherry blinked at him and grimaced, and he noticed she was holding her side with one hand. "I guess you've earned at least one question."

"That place over there. What's it called?"

"Jonah's," Sherry said.

Keo grinned.

"What are you so happy about?" Sherry asked, narrowing her eyes suspiciously at him.

NINETEEN

Sherry was bleeding from at least two bullet wounds, but only one had the potential to kill her if it wasn't taken care of as soon as possible. The other one was a graze along her left leg that she had suffered during the first volley that killed Carl and Keo's best friend, Floyd.

"I should look at that," Keo said.

"What?" Sherry said as she picked up both Carl and Floyd's rifles.

"Your wounds."

"I'm fine."

"You're bleeding."

"I'm fine."

"You don't look fine. You can barely stand."

Sherry ignored him and said, "You coming or not?" and walked off with the two extra rifles cradled in her arms.

One, two, Keo thought as he watched Sherry walk off.

Or tried to.

She managed ten feet before she collapsed, dropping the

rifles before slamming into the ground next to them on her back.

Keo walked over to where she lay and stood above her. She blinked up at him while gasping for breath, her hands clutching her bleeding right side. All ten of her digits and generous portions of her palms were covered in fresh blood.

"You still fine?" Keo asked.

She clenched her teeth. "Go to hell, Keo. What kind of name is that, anyway?"

"Wendell was taken."

"Come again?"

"Only with the pretty ones."

Keo crouched next to her and got a better look at her wound. There was already a lot of blood on the ground beneath her, which meant she was bleeding on both sides.

"Looks like a through and through," Keo said.

"What does that mean?"

"It means you're going to bleed to death pretty soon if I don't clog it up."

She grimaced. "Can you do that?"

"What? Clog it up? Sure. You got a sponge?"

She narrowed her eyes. "Fuck off."

He chuckled. "Lucky you, I brought a first aid kit with me."

"Yeah, lucky me."

She lay still as Keo unslung his pack and took out the kit.

"You've done this before," she said as he used a bottle of warm water to wipe away at the blood around her waist to get a better look at the gaping hole.

"Once or twice. This is going to hurt, by the way."

"And what, getting shot didn't?"

"This is going to hurt more because you know it's coming."

"That makes no sense."

"Trust me, it makes perfect sense."

"Oh, shut up and just do it."

"I'm going to have to ruin your fancy ghillie suit to get at it."

"Just *do it already*."

Keo decided that he liked her, so he did his best to keep her pain to a minimum as he cut away a section of the ghillie suit, then cleaned and dressed her wound. She grunted, then gritted her teeth to keep from crying out at least three times. Finally, he made her sit up so he could wrap her waist with gauze tape.

When he was done, he took out his bottle of painkillers and shook out two white pills. "You're going to need these."

"What are they?" she asked.

"For the pain."

"It's not that bad."

"I'm not so much worried about you as I am about me. This'll look better if you walked me to Jonah's than if I were to carry you. For that, you'll need these for the pain."

"You afraid of getting shot, Keo?" she grinned, before taking the pills and swallowing them with the leftover water from the bottle he'd used to clean her wound.

"Hell yeah," Keo said, and stood up.

He looked toward the buildings in the distance. He had a feeling someone over there could see him back just fine. What were the chances that same someone had him in the crosshairs of their scope right this moment? He was, as far as he could tell, about a mile away, but there were plenty of rifles that could shoot a man dead from that distance.

"Wait here," Keo said, and walked back to where Red Handkerchief had fallen. He picked up the man's M40 rifle, then went through his pouches for extra ammo for the weapon.

"What are you doing?" Sherry called from behind him.

"Sniper rifle," Keo said, walking back to her.

She was on her feet again, trying mightily to keep from toppling over even as sweat covered her face.

"This thing's good at eight hundred meters," Keo said. "That's almost half a mile."

"Can you use that?" Sherry asked.

"Couldn't be that hard. This scope's so big a housewife could use it."

"At eight hundred yards?"

"Maybe four hundred..."

Sherry looked down at the rifles she'd dropped—Carl's and Floyd's, as well as her own—then back at him.

"You don't need the other two," Keo said.

"I can't just leave them out here."

"Someone else can come back for them later." He picked up her bolt-action and slung it, then offered her his hand. "Come on."

He thought she was going to argue, but instead she relented and moved in closer so he could wrap one arm around her body, careful not to jostle her bandaged waist, and they started the long walk back to the silhouetted buildings in the distance.

"So, no backup?" Keo asked.

"You mean, why didn't anyone from Jonah's rush out here to help us when the shooting began?"

"Before, during, or after, yeah."

"You were right; if you'd walked toward the town alone,

especially in that vest, they would have shot you down like a dog before you even got close."

"Maybe I should take the vest off..."

"That might be a good idea."

They stopped, and Keo spent a minute doing just that, shoving the spare magazines into his pack instead.

They were about to start moving again when Sherry said, "You must have trained him pretty well."

"Who?"

He followed her gaze back toward the tree line.

Horse, walking toward them. It didn't look hurt and seemed to be taking its sweet time as it skirted around the dead Buckies.

"That's one sneaky horse," Sherry said.

"Too sneaky. I was thinking about putting a bell around its neck, just so I'll know where it is at all times."

"I guess it's learned to be quiet."

"It would have had to, to survive all these years."

He wrapped his arm around Sherry's body, and they started walking again.

It didn't take Horse long to reach them, and when it did, the animal downshifted into a slow walk to his left. Keo looked over at it, checking for visible signs of injury, but Horse had escaped the firefight unscathed.

"And where were you?" Keo asked the thoroughbred. "Just took off again like last time, didn't you? Thanks for nothing."

It glanced over at him, stared for a few seconds, before turning away again.

"What did he say?" Sherry asked.

"Huh?" Keo said.

"The horse. What did he say?"

"About what?"

"When you asked where it went?"

"How should I know? I don't speak horse."

"Then why—" Sherry started, but stopped herself and shook her head instead. "You're an idiot."

He chuckled. "So you're not impressed with me anymore?"

"That ship's sailed."

"My loss, I'm sure." Keo glanced back at the tree line (*"Just in case,"* as someone he knew liked to say) before looking forward at Jonah's. "What were the Buckies doing here?"

"The what?"

"That's what I call them. Buckies."

"Why?"

"Their leader. His name's Buck."

"And that's why you call them Buckies?"

Keo shrugged. "In absence of an actual name, yeah. What do you call them?"

"Killers. Murderers. Scumbags. A hundred other names I could think of."

"So, not friends, then?"

Sherry shook her head before giving him another one of her suspicious looks. "You said you killed the guy who was wearing that vest you had on. Which means you've run into them before. Where?"

"Winding Creek."

"You were there? During the attack yesterday?"

Keo nodded. "That's why I'm here. I'm looking for two people who might have escaped down here."

"What are their names?"

"Emma and Megan. Ring any bells?"

Sherry thought about it for a moment before shaking her head. "I don't recognize the names, but there's a lot of people at Jonah's. We've been taking in refugees from a lot of places the last couple of weeks. Those...Buckies have been busy."

"Refugees?"

"Winding Creek wasn't the first town those fuckers visited," Sherry said, her face darkening noticeably. "It's war out there, Keo. And this is just the beginning."

Oh, great. Just what I need. Another war where no one's paying me anything to fight.

My career's really gone down the toilet these days...

Jonah's was exactly six very large buildings resting on large poles where the beach met the fields of grass. The stilt construction was par for the course for structures next to an ocean that could swallow them up without a moment's notice. Keo was pretty sure he could make out figures moving around on some of the second-floor decks despite the sun in his eyes. There might have also been people on the roofs of a few of the houses, but he couldn't be certain because if there were, they were lying on their stomachs to lower their profile.

With Sherry in tow, Keo's almost-mile trip took almost an hour of slow walking and occasionally stopping to let Sherry catch her breath. The horse remained with them the entire time, seemingly content to walk very slowly beside him. The thoroughbred sniffed the air occasionally, as if trying to determine if there was any danger in front of them.

"You guys have sentries?" Keo asked.

"Yeah," Sherry said. "We were supposed to be the early

warning system. Me, Carl, and Floyd. There are probably two or three snipers with their scopes on you right now."

Tell me something I don't already know.

"You knew the Buckies were going to show up sooner or later," he said. It wasn't a question.

"They first came almost a week ago."

"What did they want?"

"You saw what they're doing out there. Do you even have to ask?"

"The refugees you took in."

"Yeah."

"But you didn't give them up."

"We told them they weren't here, but I doubt if they believed us. And after what just happened, it's pretty clear they didn't."

"You think they're going to send more?"

"I think they're going to realize their men are dead when they don't report in."

"And then what?"

"That'll be up to Jonah."

"Your fearless leader?"

"Kind of."

"Kind of?" Keo thought. It was an odd response. Was he or wasn't he?

The buildings continued to grow in front of them, and Keo could make out movement on the ground and underneath the houses as well as along the second-floor decks that wrapped around the four sides of the structures. He was pretty sure he could make out three people lying on rooftops now, the sun glinting off the barrels of their weapons.

"How did you find this place?" he asked. "It's not on any map I've looked at. There isn't even a road leading to it."

"It's a new development. Two of the houses were still being finished when we arrived. I don't think any of them have even been lived in. There was supposed to be a road leading to it that curls around the woods, but they never finished that, either."

They were within fifty meters of the buildings when Keo stopped. There were trucks parked underneath the structures and along gravel parking lots that linked the houses. Keo counted thirty or so visible faces peering back at him and probably a lot more indoors that he couldn't see.

Horse stood patiently to his left, occasionally snorting the air whenever a particularly strong breeze washed over them.

"Remember, don't drink the water," Keo said to the animal.

"I'm pretty sure he's not dumb enough to drink the water," Sherry said.

"You can't be too sure. He is just a horse, after all."

"Some horses are smarter than people."

"Yeah, but can they shoot a gun?"

Sherry gave him a look that said she wasn't sure if she should answer or not. When he chuckled, she rolled her eyes and looked forward just as a Jeep rumbled through the grass toward them. Keo counted two in the front seats and two more in the back, the barrels of their rifles jutting in the air, but no mounted machine gun.

"Don't touch your guns," Sherry said.

"Trigger happy?" Keo asked.

"I wouldn't say that. Mostly...anxious. We've been hearing nothing but horror stories about your friends the Buckies."

Keo reached over to put a hand on Horse's reins to steady

the animal. The horse turned its head to look at him, maybe to ask what he thought he was doing, but it seemed to understand and went back to watching the approaching Jeep.

The vehicle stopped in front of them, and the two in the back immediately hopped out. All four were wearing civilian clothes, and the two that had leapt out pointed their weapons at Keo.

"Don't shoot," Sherry said. "He's...a friend."

"Try to sound a little more enthusiastic, why don't ya," Keo said.

The driver stayed inside the Jeep, but his front passenger climbed out, and together with the other two carefully approached Keo and Sherry. They were all wearing gun belts (Keo assumed the driver was as well), but the third man was only carrying a 1911 pistol in one hand. The man looked around at the fields behind Keo and Sherry, as if expecting some kind of ambush. When nothing happened, he fixed them with a look before spending a few extra seconds on Keo's face.

Keo got a good look at the guy in return: Thirties, five-foot-something even with boots on, and dark black eyes. Keo had seen plenty of alpha males before, guys who called the shots even if they didn't look the part, but Shorty, well, fell short.

And yet he seemed to be in charge by the way the others fanned around him. "What happened out there, Sherry?" he asked.

"Fenton's men," Sherry said. "They killed Carl and Floyd."

The man nodded at Keo. "Who's this guy?"

"This is Keo," Sherry said. "Keo, this is Jonah."

"Of Jonah's fame?" Keo asked.

"I don't know about fame," the guy named Jonah said. He

nodded at the two men with rifles, and they slung their weapons and hurried over to take Sherry from Keo, then walked her over to the Jeep.

"How many were there?" Jonah asked.

"Five," Sherry said. "I'd be lying out there with Carl and Floyd if it wasn't for Keo. He saved my life."

"Thank you," Jonah said to Keo, and stuck out his hand.

Keo shook it. Up close, the guy was almost a foot shorter than him.

"He's looking for someone," Sherry said as she settled into the Jeep's front passenger seat.

"Someones," Keo said. "A woman named Emma and her daughter, Megan. They would have fled down here from Winding Creek sometime yesterday morning."

Jonah shook his head. "The names don't ring any bells."

"You didn't even think about it."

"I don't have to. I'm good with names." He holstered his pistol. "Besides, there were only ten people from Winding Creek yesterday, and there's no Emma or Megan among them. Sorry."

"Just ten?" Keo asked.

The numbers didn't add up. There are about twenty missing heads from Winding Creek," Wagner had said to him back in Princeville.

"*So how do you know twenty got away?*" Keo had asked him.

"'*Cause we know how many were in that town, and the count doesn't add up,*" Wagner had answered.

So if twenty got away, why are there only ten people here? Keo thought to himself now.

"More might have gotten out during the attack, I don't

know, but only ten showed up here yesterday," Jonah said. "Sorry."

Keo nodded somberly. "Yeah, me too."

"You're from Winding Creek?"

"Sort of."

"'Sort of?'"

"It's a long story."

"I'm sure it is," Jonah said, and nodded at the driver before climbing into the back of the Jeep. He looked back at Keo. "Come on; maybe it's your lucky day and I'm wrong, and your friends might have made it and I got their names mixed up. It's been known to happen."

The Jeep made a wide U-turn and drove back toward the buildings.

Luck, Keo thought as he climbed onto Horse. *What's that?*

TWENTY

As expected, luck was not on Keo's side, and among the ten Winding Creek "refugees," Emma and Megan weren't two of them. In some ways, not finding both mother and daughter was better than finding one but not the other. Of course, that could have just been Keo trying to see the positive of a shitty outcome.

The survivors were all women except for one man, someone named Breckin, whom Keo didn't know. They were being housed in one of the buildings that were half-finished, which had since been converted into a big dorm, with cots for sleeping and a communal eating area. There were fifteen other people there, all refugees from two other towns that had been raided by Buck and his people. After seeing how well-armed and trained the Buckies were, Keo had to admit that twenty-five survivors were more than he had expected.

Fortunately, one of the Winding Creek women was someone Keo did know—Christine, who lived just two houses down from Emma. She had somehow made it out with her daughter, Jordan, but one look at her face when Keo asked about her husband Gerry told him everything.

They left Jordan and the others and walked out onto the outside deck, where two guys with AR rifles stood guard. They both had binoculars and were keeping a vigilant eye on the wide-open field behind them—all one mile or so of it—with the wall of trees in the distance. The outside deck wrapped around the house like a ring, allowing them to keep watch on every side, though at the moment the only one that mattered was north.

Keo spotted four boats moored on the beach—a couple of fishing vessels and two rowboats. They looked beaten and faded but in one piece. Keo wasn't a math whiz by any stretch of the imagination, but there were way more people in Jonah's than there were boats to accommodate them.

I guess escape by sea's out of the question. For the majority of the people here, anyway.

He didn't have to glance at his watch to know night was coming. He could see it in the fading sunlight over the Gulf of Mexico and the slowly darkening sand. A shadow moved over him and Christine as they leaned against the railing as the sentry on the rooftop changed up his position.

"I don't know what happened to them," Christine said. "It was so chaotic. Everyone was running, and there was so much shooting." She paused and gripped the wooden railing. "We wouldn't have made it out if it wasn't for Lewis."

"He was sure they had both gotten out," Keo said.

"Then they probably did. I don't think he would lie about that."

"He wouldn't. He didn't have any reasons to."

"They probably got out after we did. It was so chaotic..."

She paused again. "They might still be on their way here. It's only been a day."

A lot of things can happen in a day, Keo thought, but he said instead, "But if they didn't come here, you have any ideas where else they might have gone?"

Christine shook her head. "I'm sorry, Keo, I don't. I wouldn't even think to come here if Lewis hadn't told us to." She might have trembled slightly. "God, why did they do that? Why did they just come into town and kill everyone?"

Not everyone, Keo thought, remembering what Wendy had told him.

"The babies. They took all the babies."

"How long have you guys been trading with Jonah's?" he asked Christine. "How did Lewis know about this place?"

"Lewis and Vince left Winding Creek a year after The Walk Out, but they came back every now and then, just to catch up. I hadn't seen them for two years before they showed back up yesterday. I guess that's how they know about trading with Jonah's."

"And you can't think of any other place Emma might have taken Megan?"

"I'm sorry, Keo. I don't know."

Keo nodded and gave her his best attempt at a reassuring smile. "It'll be dark soon, so I won't be going anywhere until tomorrow. If you remember anything—anything at all—don't hesitate to let me know. And ask the others, too."

Christine nodded. "I will. Maybe someone will know something." She hesitated, and he could see her struggling with something.

"What is it?" he asked.

"Who else made it? It can't just be the ten of us, can it?

Out of the whole town? It can't be just the ten of us left, can it, Keo?"

He remembered Wendy again, her husband Rick lying dead in their living room, and all the bodies the Buckies had left behind for the animals (*and other things*) to take care of.

"A lot of other people could have made it out," he said, hoping it was at least semi-convincing. "They could have gone somewhere else instead of coming here, just like Emma and Megan."

While Keo was busy talking with Christine, Jonah had sent his men back out into the fields to recover Carl and Floyd's bodies. They also returned with the Buckies' gear and weapons but had left the dead men out there.

Keo found Jonah a good five-minutes' walk from the settlement. Sherry was also there, along with two others that were digging graves for Carl and Floyd, far enough from the beach and water that they wouldn't be washed away. There were already four other graves there, but none that looked too recent.

Sherry had cleaned the paint off her face and was wearing new clothes. Her waist was heavily bandaged, but she didn't look like she was in pain as she watched the graves being dug, only looking away when Keo showed up.

"Did you find your friends?" she asked.

Keo shook his head. "They're not here."

"They didn't make it?"

"I think they did. Someone assured me they did."

"But they're not here," Jonah said.

"No," Keo said.

"You think they might have gotten lost on the way over?" Sherry asked.

"I don't know," Keo said. "Christine didn't see them, and neither did anyone else on the way over." Keo looked off into the fields. "This place isn't exactly a hop, skip, and a jump away from Winding Creek. There's a lot of miles to cover."

"A lot of things could happen out there. Especially these last few weeks."

"How long ago did the others show up?"

"The ones from Dresden was two weeks ago," Jonah said. "That's when we got wind of what was happening. The guys from Juno were just six days earlier."

"Why exactly did they all come here?" Keo asked.

Jonah shrugged, and from his expression, Keo thought he had probably been asking himself that question for a while, too. "Your guess is as good as mine," the man said. "It's not like we ever put out a sign that said, 'Come here if you're in trouble.'" He looked over at Carl and Floyd's bodies, both wrapped in blankets, waiting nearby on the ground. "We're just trying to get by. We trade for what we need, and truth be told, I haven't left this area in three years, so if you're asking me why people are coming here seeking shelter, I don't have a clue."

"What about you?" Keo asked Sherry.

She shook her head. "I haven't left this place in four years. Neither had Carl and Floyd. We came here together looking for a place to get lost, to start over on our own terms, and that's what we found. There's nothing for us out there."

Jonah walked over to Keo, then kept going. Keo took the hint and followed him, leaving Sherry and the others still digging behind them.

They headed back toward the houses along the beach, and Jonah didn't say anything until they were far enough from Sherry and the others that they couldn't be overheard. Keo found that intriguing. What was it Jonah had to say that he didn't want the others to know?

"You know who they are, don't you?" Jonah finally said.

"Who are we talking about?" Keo asked.

"The guys you call Buckies. The ones from Fenton, with the circled *M* on their vests."

Keo shrugged. "Maybe."

"You're not going to tell me?"

"I could be wrong."

"You could also be right."

"Mom always says it's better to keep silent when you might be right than to speak up when you might be wrong."

"That's never stopped me before," Jonah chuckled.

"You've been out there," Keo said. It wasn't a question.

"Who hasn't?"

"You were a collaborator."

He thought Jonah might have bristled. "Everyone I've met used to work for the ghouls. Carl, Sherry, Floyd. Everyone from your town."

Not my town, Keo thought but didn't say it.

"What does the word 'collaborator' even mean anymore?" Jonah continued.

"True, but there are degrees," Keo said. "You wore a uniform."

"I won't lie; I did. What about you?"

"I wasn't."

"Wore a uniform?"

"A collaborator."

"Then you'd be the first saint I've come across in a long time."

Keo smiled. "No one's ever accused me of being a saint."

"What about your mom?"

"She's called me a lot of things, but never a saint, either."

Jonah finally stopped walking halfway to the houses. Keo did likewise next to him and watched the waves pouring over the sands from the black sea.

"But the past is the past," Jonah said. "No point in reliving it. I learned that a long time ago." That seemed to bring back some memories, and Jonah made a face at the darkening ocean. "Gotta keep on keeping on, as someone once said."

"Considering what's happening out there beyond this little paradise of yours, apparently not everyone thinks the same."

"That would appear to be the case."

"How long have you been here?"

"Five years." He nodded down the beach. "I almost died about five miles from here, in this little abandoned marina. There was just me and a lot of bodies."

"Sounds familiar."

Jonah grinned. "Which part?"

"All of it."

"I guess we have a lot in common." Jonah paused. Then, "Anyway. After I miraculously *didn't* die, I walked up the beach and found this little slice of paradise, as you called it. I wasn't looking for company, but then people started showing up. Before you know it, we'd made ourselves a little community." He sighed, then pursed his lips and looked back at the fields behind them. "I guess it's true what they say; all good things must eventually come to an end."

"What did the Buckies want?" Keo asked. "Sherry said they came here last week."

"The refugees," Jonah said.

"And that's it?"

Jonah shrugged. "That's all I know. That's all I *want* to know."

"You're not curious? Why they're raiding the towns? It can't just be for the supplies."

"You're talking about them taking the women and children?"

Keo nodded. "You know about that, too."

"The refugees mentioned it. They were concentrating on killing the men but rounding up the women and children."

"So what's that all about?"

"I don't know. Neither did the ones that made it here. They don't have a clue. But it's obvious, isn't it?"

"What's that?"

"The Answer. Whatever it is, it's in Fenton."

"Someone told me a guy named Copenhagen runs the place."

"That's what I hear, too."

"You never traded with them?"

"Once or twice, but I've never met the man himself or sent people to Fenton. It's too far north, and we can get everything we need from Winding Creek, Dresden, Juno, and a half-dozen other places that's a hell of a lot closer."

"What do you know about them? The Buckies?"

"Not much..."

"But you know something."

Jonah nodded. "I know their type. They're mercenaries. Paramilitary. Whatever you want to call them. Fenton's not the only one using them, either. Dresden had their own smaller group. Your friends the Buckies wiped them out first."

"So I take it you didn't always have guys with rifles on rooftops?" Keo asked, looking up the beach at one such figure crouched on top of one of the buildings now.

"Not even close." Jonah grunted. "Funny thing is, five years ago I would be running around out there with those guys. But things change."

"You turned a new leaf."

"Not quite. More like I adjusted."

Keo watched some kids and a couple of adults washing themselves in the ocean water. "Why did you let them stay? You had to know what kind of trouble they were bringing with them."

Jonah followed his gaze. "There was just six people from Dresden at first. I mean, six people, and half of them could barely walk. I don't know how I could have turned them away. I guess I could have, but it didn't seem...right."

"And then more showed up..."

The shorter man sighed. "And then the others showed up, yeah. That was when I knew I had screwed up, but by then it was too late. I might have been the de facto leader of this place because I was here first, but there were thirty-eight others who also called it home, and there was no way they were going to turn down women and children who had been through hell and back."

Keo glanced over at the black wall of trees in the distance. He wondered how many Buckies were already in there right now looking back at him, waiting to attack. Or maybe they had come searching for their friends and found their bodies instead and were now returning to report in to Buck.

"They're coming," Jonah said next to him. "Tomorrow, the day after, or the week after. But they're coming. Maybe I could have talked my way out of it before today, but not after you killed five of their people."

"In my defense, I only killed three," Keo said. "Sherry took out the other two."

"You say po-tay-to, I say po-tah-to."

"What are you going to do when they do show up? I doubt they'll be in a talking mood."

"I have no idea. Try to talk my way out of it anyway, I guess."

"You good at that? Talking your way out of trouble?"

Jonah shrugged. "I used to be, but I'm a little out of practice."

"They're gonna want answers."

"That's the best-case scenario."

"What's the worst case?"

"They don't even give me the chance to lie to their faces," Jonah said.

Keo chuckled. He decided that he liked Short Stuff, even if the man was right and they were, probably, all doomed when the Buckies eventually showed up.

It's a good thing I won't be here tomorrow, Keo thought, but decided to keep that part to himself.

TWENTY-ONE

Jonah stayed in one of the houses near the middle of the six buildings, flanked by three on one side and two on the other. He shared it with five others, all of whom were currently outside patrolling the grounds at the moment.

"I spent the first seven months here by myself, trying to finish up this house," Jonah said. "It took forever. Then the others showed up. After that, it only took a month, if that."

"Why this one?" Keo asked.

Jonah shrugged. "It was the least finished. I guess it was symbolic; me finishing it, starting over."

"Where'd you get the parts?"

"Everything we needed was in piles outside, just sitting there waiting for someone to punch in a time card and finish the construction. Turns out that was me. Never in a million years did I think I'd be spending my time hammering in nails and liking it. I guess you end up doing a lot of things you never planned on these days."

Ain't that the truth, brother, Keo thought as he leaned

against the deck railing and looked across the pitch-dark field at the solid black wall of woods on the other side.

"Ghoul problems?" Keo asked.

"Not out here," Jonah said. "Not this close to the ocean. You know about that, I assume?"

"That the only thing the little critters fear more than sunlight and silver is large bodies of salt water?"

"Uh huh. Saw one of them come close a few years back, but that was it. Only the really desperate ones would even think about trying their luck with us all the way out here."

Or the really hungry ones, Keo thought, remembering the one he had killed in his cabin.

There was constant ambient noise around him, crickets filling the air in front and the ocean waves pounding the beach at the back. A pair of sentries walked by below, talking quietly among themselves. Jonah had also put four men on each side of the beach in case of a surprise night attack. Overall, it was a decent perimeter defense and convinced Keo that Shorty knew what he was doing. Mostly, anyway.

I guess no one's getting a lot of sleep tonight.

He looked back at the trees. There was something foreboding about it, and he couldn't shake the feeling there were people in there watching him back. If there were, they'd be getting a pretty clear look at him with an LED lantern hanging almost directly above him. The lights were solar-powered and hung from the edges of each one of the six buildings.

Talk about a spotlight, Keo thought, before taking a couple of steps back from the railing until he was partially hidden in the shadows.

"What's the matter?" Jonah asked when he came back out

onto the deck and handed Keo an unlabeled bottle of beer. "You look spooked."

"Just being careful," Keo said. He took the bottle and was surprised to find it cool to the touch. "You got a working fridge in there?"

"Nah. We keep a cooler full of them in the ocean. I fished these out earlier."

Jonah had already taken off the cap, so Keo took a sip. The beer had lost most of its flavor and body, but it was still better than drinking bottled water. He watched Jonah lean against the railing, at about the same spot he had been earlier, and thought about telling the man he probably shouldn't expose himself so readily, but decided he was just being paranoid.

"It was nice while it lasted," Jonah said, taking a sip from his beer.

"You sound like you've already given this place up."

"I'm a pragmatist, and I know what these Buckies are capable of."

"Are we talking about personal experience?"

Jonah grunted. "Maybe."

"What else did you hear about this Copenhagen guy?"

"Not much, but anyone who could hire these old chums of ours to do the dirty work isn't someone to fuck with. It takes a lot of balls to be in charge." He paused to take another sip before lowering the bottle and staring off into the night. "Decisions have to be made, and sometimes men sacrificed for the greater good. It takes a toll on you, grinds you down. The only way it doesn't is if you don't have anything for it to grind down in the first place."

"Is it safe to say you weren't just a foot soldier in the day?"

"Not quite."

"So what happened?"

"Ran into people who were tougher than me. Smarter, too."

"Ain't that always the case?" Keo took another sip from the beer. It wasn't the best thing he'd ever tasted, but it was cool enough that it didn't taste too bad. "So if you've already given this place up, where are you guys going?"

Jonah looked back at him. "Why should I tell you? You're leaving us tomorrow anyway, aren't you?"

"Who said anything about leaving?"

"Oh, come on. You came here looking for two very specific people. You got some information from the Winding Creek refugees, and now you're going to go back out there to continue the search. It's a no-brainer."

I guess he's making up for the lack of height with some smarts, Keo thought, and said, "Maybe."

"I have a plan and let's leave it at that."

"It's always nice to have a plan," Keo said, and thought, *I wish I had one right now. Wouldn't that be nice?*

"I like having options," Jonah said. "You never know when the world will try to kick you in the nuts. When that happens, I like being able to pivot. I find that it's a good way to keep from dying unnecessarily."

"Has that always worked for you?"

"So far..." He paused, then, "By the way, where's your horse?"

"My horse?"

"Yeah. I saw it walking around on the beach earlier. I don't see it anywhere down there."

Keo shrugged. "I have no idea. It's not actually my horse."

"No?"

"For some reason, it keeps following me—"

Keo didn't hear it, but there was no confusing *what* it was when something chopped into the wooden railing about six inches from Jonah's chest, spitting wood into the air before *zipping* past Keo's waist and punching into the wall behind him with an echoing *thunk!*

"Sniper!" Keo shouted, and spun toward the door.

He didn't hear the next three shots, but he saw them landing—two embedding into the wall to his left before the third shattered a window just as Keo raced past it. The beer bottle flew out of his hand sometime between the second and third shot, but Keo wasn't paying enough attention to be sure where it landed.

"Fuck all!" Jonah shouted behind him.

"Fuck all?" Keo thought even as he leapt through the open door and slammed into the floorboards inside the house.

There was another LED lantern on a table nearby that partially lit up the room, though not enough to cover all of the spaces. Keo was rolling over onto his back and into a patch of shadow just in time to see Jonah slipping inside after him. The man grabbed the door and swung it shut as two more rounds smacked into it from the other side—*thunk! thunk!*—but didn't penetrate.

Jonah ducked as he jumped over Keo, then slid to the floor and crawled over to a nearby wall far from any of the windows. Keo thought that was a fine idea—the sniper couldn't hit what they couldn't see—and crawled over to the table where he had laid down his MP5SD, reached for it, then went over to join Jonah.

Keo had just reached Jonah's position when a radio

squawked and an alarmed voice said through tiny speakers, "What was that? Did someone shout something?"

Jonah unclipped the two-way from his hip and keyed it. "It's me. There are snipers in the field. I repeat: There are snipers in the field."

Keo had to admit, he was impressed with Shorty's calmness. The man didn't scream into the radio or shout incoherently.

He's definitely been through this before.

"Should we return fire?" someone else asked through the radio.

"Not unless you can see them," Jonah said. "You'll just make yourselves into a target. Until then, stay low. That goes for everyone."

"Roger that," someone answered.

"Are you hurt?" a female voice asked. Keo recognized Sherry.

"No, got indoors with everything still intact," Jonah said, patting himself down just to be sure. "Yeah. I'm good."

"Keo?"

"He's fine, too."

"Nice of her to ask," Keo smiled.

"Well, you did save her life out there," Jonah said. Then, into the radio, "Landry, Max—you guys see anything?"

"Who's Landry and Max?" Keo asked.

Jonah looked up at the ceiling.

The rooftop sentries.

"I got nothing," a male voice answered. Jonah mouthed the word *Max* at Keo, before Max added, "I'm not seeing anything out there, Jonah."

"Are you using your night-vision?" Jonah asked.

"Yeah, yeah, of course. I'm still seeing squat. If he's out there, I don't see him. But there's a mile of grass. He could be anywhere."

"What about you, Landry?"

He waited for a reply.

Five seconds, then ten.

Uh oh, Keo thought, when Jonah said into the radio, "Landry. Are you there? Landry, answer me, goddammit."

But whoever Landry was, he never answered.

"Shit," Jonah whispered. Then, calmly into the radio, "Max. Can you see him?"

"He's down," Max said. "He's down, Jonah. Landry's down."

"Where?"

"On the roof. He's still on the roof, but he's not moving..."

Jonah exchanged a look with Keo, and even in the semi-darkness Keo could tell the man was trying to figure out what to do or say next. Keo wanted to help the poor guy out, but all he could think about was running out there, looking for Horse, and escaping through the beach. And he could do just that without ever having to see a single Bucky. The bad guys were probably shooting from the woods (which was possible but not likely—it was a damn mile, after all) or they were already staked out in the fields (which was much more likely), but the beach would be cleared. All Keo had to do was find Horse and point him either south or north and keep going along the sand.

Unless, of course, the Buckies had people watching both beach directions, too. What were the chances of that? It would almost entirely depend on how many they had brought this time.

Five this morning. Maybe five again tonight.

Or more...

Keo was still thinking about his options when Jonah keyed the radio and said into it, "Baker, I want you to wake everyone up."

"Got it," someone answered.

"Stratton," Jonah said, "take a group to bolster the guards on our south. Jerry, I want you to do the same on our north—"

"Fuck!" someone shouted through the radio just before a rifle fired—the *pop-pop-pop* filling the world outside in a rush of gunfire. Someone was unloading an entire magazine and didn't stop until they had run empty.

Jonah waited until the last shots faded before he keyed his radio. "What was that? What just happened?"

"They shot Barnes," another man answered through the radio. "Goddammit, they got Barnes. Shot him through the head. *Jesus.*"

"Where are they?"

"I don't know. I can't see them."

"Anyone else?" Jonah asked.

"I don't see anything out there," someone else answered.

"I can't see anything from my building, either," Sherry said.

"Okay, okay." Jonah seemed to take a breath. Then, "Stay out of the open. They can't shoot what they can't see. Watch your spots, and if you see anything moving out there, let them have it. But don't expose yourself if you don't have to. Got it?"

"Roger that," Sherry said.

A few others responded in the affirmative.

"Where was Barnes?" Keo asked.

Jonah put his radio down. "What?"

"Barnes."

"South end."

"And Landry was on the north end?"

Jonah nodded. "Yeah. So?"

"Someone took a shot at us in the middle."

"What's your point, Keo?"

"My point is, there are at least two of them out there, with the possibility of three or more. They have the south and north ends covered, along with the center."

It took a few seconds, but Jonah finally got it. "Oh, crap. They've got us cut off from any routes of escape. Even through the beaches."

"Looks that way," Keo nodded, and thought, *There goes my out.* "Even if there's just three of them out there, they can pick us off if we try to make a run for it in any direction. They might not get all of us, but they'll get enough."

"Goddammit. Got any more good news for me?"

"Yeah. I dropped my beer."

Jonah gave him an *"Are you serious?"* look before chuckling. "I'll get you another one when this is over."

"I gotta wait for this to be over?"

"Hey, life's full of sacrifices, buddy."

"I guess so," Keo said, and laid his submachine gun in his lap and leaned back against the wall.

"I didn't hear it," Jonah said. "The first shot or the others. I heard them *hit,* but I didn't hear the actual shots."

"They're using suppressors," Keo said. "My guess is they're already in the fields. Probably spent the last few hours crawling through it from the woods. There could be a few hundred of them out there, for all we know. It wouldn't be hard in that pitch darkness."

Jonah sighed. "I guess it was too much to hope they might

wait a few more days before they made their move. Most of our emergency supplies are already in moving crates."

"When was moving day supposed to be?"

"I was going to make the announcement tomorrow morning."

Jonah looked toward the closest window, which was also the one that had been shot out. Moonlight and chilly air filtered inside, and Keo pulled his shirt's collar up and over his neck for warmth. There were just the crickets in front of them and the surf behind them again.

"How many of your people know what they're doing out there?" Keo asked.

"Meaning?"

"Meaning, how many have killed before?"

Jonah shook his head. "I don't know. It's not like I gave everyone an interview before I let them join us."

"You said they were all collaborators. How many wore uniforms like you?"

"Most of them."

"But not all."

"Like I said—"

"Right, you didn't ask."

"No, I didn't. What's your point?"

"The Buckies," Keo said. "The ones that were at Winding Creek and the ones out here this afternoon. They're not amateurs. They've had some training. I mean, real training. Not the collaborator's idea of training."

"Makes sense, seeing how easily they took the towns," Jonah said. He looked over at Keo. "And you're telling me you don't know who they are? Or what that *M* of theirs stands for?"

"Not a clue," Keo lied.

Jonah narrowed his eyes at him, clearly not believing Keo, but before he could push further, the *pop-pop-pop* of automatic rifle fire exploded outside again. The gunfire came from nearby, to Keo's left.

Then someone else joined in, and the shooting continued for ten seconds before the last shot finally faded, and there was just the crickets and the waves again.

"What happened?" Jonah said into his radio.

"It was me," someone answered.

"Jameson?"

"Yeah," the voice said. "Sorry, I thought I saw someone in the grass."

"Did you?"

"I... I'm not sure."

"I shot, too," someone else said through the radio.

"Did *you* get anyone?"

"No, I don't think so. I thought I saw something moving out there, but I don't—I don't know."

Jonah shook his head and gave Keo an exasperated look. Then, into the radio, "All right, all right. No one fires unless they're absolutely sure. You're just giving away your position every time you do. As long as we stay out of the open, they'll have to come get us. When they do that, *then* shoot the hell out of them."

"Copy that," Sherry said. "Everyone, calm down. Just... calm down."

Jonah put the radio away. "Does that answer your question?"

Keo smiled. "Hey, at least they're not shooting at each other."

"Yeah, there's that, I guess." He glanced back at the window for a moment. Then, "You got any ideas?"

I got a few thousand ideas, but all of them involve me running away on horseback, Keo thought, but he said instead, "I'll let you know in about an hour."

"Why an hour?" Jonah asked.

"Because the first thing that immediately pops to mind is absolutely idiotic, and it's going to take me at least that long to even convince myself to do it."

TWENTY-TWO

It actually took him two hours to convince himself, and it was five past midnight when Keo told Jonah about it.

Shorty laughed when he was finished. "You're insane. But it's your life, man. You wanna do it, it's your call. I'm not gonna stop you."

"You could at least try," Keo had said.

"I stopped trying to make people do something they don't wanna do a long time ago. All it gets you is a bullet."

"You saying I want to do this?"

"I'm saying this is probably not your first time doing something this stupid."

Keo had sighed, and thought, *He's got a point.*

He didn't blame Jonah for thinking that way, and the truth was he thought it was kind of crazy, too, but it wasn't like he had any choice. The snipers were proof that the Buckies had set their sights on Jonah's and everyone inside it. By morning there would either be more snipers out there or the entire Bucky Nation. Either way, Keo liked his chances better if he knew exactly how many were out there, and if the number was manageable, then cut it down to give the people at Jonah's a fighting chance in the morning.

He got everything he needed from Jonah's well-stocked supplies. The MP5SD fit into the waterproof bag, and a strip of rawhide rope was enough to keep it in place. He added a second bag for spare magazines and a knife, and a third for clothes, socks, and a pair of sneakers. He had considered dropping a handgun in there, but he was already going to be carrying too much weight and the submachine gun had to do. And besides, if everything went according to plan, he could always acquire a pistol later.

Yeah, if everything goes according to plan.

Positive thoughts, positive thoughts...

Sherry warned him that the water was going to be cold, but he had no idea until he dipped a testing toe into it and immediately pulled his entire foot back.

"I told you," Sherry said.

"Yeah, yeah," Keo said.

"Maybe you should wait for morning."

"It'll be too late in the morning."

"You don't know that."

"I don't know a lot of things, but I do know the best defense is always a good offense."

They stood on the sand, in the darkest part of the beach that Keo could find. The fact that no one had shot him in the last minute or so was proof he had chosen the spot wisely. Sherry didn't share his confidence and kept looking around them at the darkened corners of the shoreline. For someone who had been shot very recently, she looked pretty okay, though of course he didn't discount the wonders of the meds he'd given her, then the others she'd gotten once Jonah's people fixed her up properly.

She turned back to him now. "God, this feels like such a bad idea."

"It's the only one I can think of," Keo said. "Can't just stay put and wait for them to surround us. And that's exactly what those snipers are out there for—to keep us pinned. If they had enough men, they would have attacked by now."

"So you're going to do what, go out there and kill them?"

"Best case? Yeah. Worst case, I can find out how many are actually out there and adjust accordingly. Right now, we're just guessing."

She sighed. "What if you drown?"

"I'm a very good swimmer."

"How good?"

"Really good."

She didn't look convinced, but maybe it had something to do with him standing in nothing but his boxers while shivering against the chilly night air. Or he could have just read her wrong. It was a little difficult to see much of her in the darkness, even standing just a few feet away.

"When was the last time you swam in an ocean like this?" she asked.

"A few years ago."

"A few years ago?"

"I haven't exactly been around large bodies of water lately, Sherry, so the opportunities were slim." He stared at the black Gulf of Mexico, its breeze and cold water washing against his bare legs. "But it's not something you forget."

"Should you really be naked? Or mostly naked? It's really cold in there."

"I'll warm up once I'm inside."

She shook her head. "I thought you were nuts before this afternoon when you tried to talk your way out of getting shot, but this..."

"I don't see another way. Do you?"

Sherry gave him a resigned look before shaking her head. "I guess there's nothing left to say, except good luck."

He shook her hand and glanced over at Jonah's building. The man himself was leaning over the railing on the side deck watching them. Or, at least, Keo thought that was him. It could have been a human-size pole, given the lack of details.

He turned back to Sherry. "See you in the morning."

"I hope so," Sherry said. Then, almost hesitantly, "Hey, thanks."

"For what?"

"For saving my life yesterday, idiot."

Keo smiled. "Didn't think you were ever going to admit it."

"I can be a little stubborn, too."

"I'll see you in the morning, Sherry," Keo said, and tightened the straps around his body.

"Yeah, see you in the morning," Sherry said, but he could hear the doubt in her voice.

He didn't blame her. Keo had nothing but doubts about the plan.

Think positive thoughts. Think positive thoughts...

He took the first step into the water. A shock of electricity rushed through him as the cold ocean licked at his ankles.

This is such a bad idea, he thought, but instead of turning around, he continued forward.

The water reached up along his legs to his knees, then over

the bandage along his right thigh, before sloshing around his waist.

He held his breath, thought, *This is such a bad, bad idea in so, so many ways*, before vanishing under the surface.

It was cold, but he'd been in colder waters before. A lot colder. The middle-of-December type of cold in San Diego's Mission Beach. Not that that was much comfort as he went out a hundred meters just to be safe, before turning and starting north. He kept the shoreline within sight out of the corner of his left eye at all times, using the lights coming from the houses as a guide so he wouldn't stray too far.

His legs were starting to ache, but that was not unexpected; he hadn't gone swimming in such a long time, and his body was having to remember how to do it. By the second one-hundred-meter mark (this time northward) he was doing full strides and barely felt the waves rippling against the side of his body.

He wasn't entirely sure how long it took, but eventually he located the beach again, and after running up the slanted floor, went into a quick crouch and looked around. The lack of gunfire was the best thing he could have hoped for, and he allowed his eyes to adjust to the new darkness while catching his breath. The months of living in the cabin by himself, with daily treks into Winding Creek, had kept him lean, so Keo wasn't *too* fatigued.

Jonah's was visible to his left farther down the shoreline. He could just barely make out the shapes of a couple of buildings, mostly thanks to the LED lanterns that hung off the second-floor decks. The snipers would probably stay as close to the structures as they possibly could without coming into danger themselves in order to keep an eye on the residents. What were the chances they would anticipate someone *swimming* out of there?

Or maybe the better question was, what were the chances the snipers would anticipate someone being *stupid* enough to swim out of there?

His breathing had slowed down when Keo unslung one of his bags and ripped it open with his fingers, then took out the MP5SD. In his experience, the H&K would have worked just fine after being submerged in water, but he hadn't wanted to take the chance, especially since it was his only gun. He pushed up to his feet and hurried up the beach and toward the field on the other side. He didn't stop until he was surrounded by grass.

It took him five minutes to change into his dry clothes— cargo pants, T-shirt, and thermal sweater. He slipped the sheathed knife behind his waist and took out the night-vision binoculars that Jonah had lent him. Keo scoured the area just to be sure he was still alone, even though he was pretty sure he was. After all, someone would have shot him by now if he wasn't.

Good thoughts. Think good thoughts.

He let the binoculars dangle off his neck and got up again, then started moving up the field. It would have been nice to have night-vision goggles so he could see in the dark without having to hold the glasses to his eyes, but Jonah didn't have any to give him.

Beggars can't be choosers.

He took his time, grateful that he had at least four hours

before morning sunlight. That was plenty. He didn't make a lot of noise as he pushed through the endless sea of sod, thanks to the lightweight running shoes he'd chosen over the heavier, thicker boots.

With hours to spare, Keo felt no urgency and stopped multiple times to get a better sense of his position in relation to Jonah's while making sure he wasn't putting himself into the line of fire unnecessarily. Eventually he reached the tree lines and slipped inside. With the cover of the woods finally, he was able to start making his way back toward Jonah's, all the while looking, listening, and *feeling* for evidence of Buckies in the area.

What were the odds that Buck—or whoever was calling the shots out there, this Copenhagen guy, maybe—wasn't coming at all? Maybe the snipers, however many there actually were, were just here to cause trouble. Then again, they had killed five Buckies yesterday. True, it was really just him and Sherry, but Buck wouldn't see it that way. Keo wondered if a *"But they shot first"* defense would work.

Probably not.

His hair was almost completely dry by the time Keo finally stopped and went into a crouch with the MP5SD gripped tightly in front of him. He spent five minutes—then just for good measure, another ten—listening to everything around him.

The wind whistling through the trees, the flutter of branches above him, and creatures big and small on the ground. But no sounds of movement by something big enough to qualify as human. Or voices. No threats.

He faced the tree line ten meters in front of him and eased toward it. The snipers would be out there on the other side, though not close enough to hear him coming. They would have crawled their way through the brush toward Jonah's to get a better field of fire on its inhabitants. How close? That would depend on how good they were and what kind of optics they were carrying.

He sat down again, and surrounded by the sounds of the woods, found himself thinking about what he was doing. He glanced behind him, into the thick army of trees. Somewhere out there was Emma and Megan. Maybe in trouble, needing his help. Instead, he was wasting his time out here dealing with snipers that had Jonah's in their crosshairs.

What the hell am I doing?

What did he really owe Jonah and Sherry and the others? Nothing. Nothing at all. He'd come here to find Emma and Megan, but they weren't here. There was no one in Jonah's that mattered to him. There was Christine, but did he really know her that well? They'd had dinner a few times, but that was it. As for the rest...

You gave Jonah and Sherry your word. So what's that worth?

He'd lied before. Gave his word and then went back on it. Six years ago, he would have done it without batting an eye.

But that was then...

Back when you were smarter.

Remember?

He sighed and turned back toward the shoreline.

He checked his watch. He had made better time than he thought—

A brush of air against the back of his neck!

Keo spun, the submachine gun swinging up, his heart hammering in his chest.

Nothing. There was nothing behind—

The hairs along his arms stood up straight and the smell came out of nowhere, striking every part of his body like a physical force, coming from—

Above!

No, no, no, no! his mind screamed as he looked up and saw it—*glowing blue eyes piercing the darkness above him.*

It plummeted out of the sky like a reverse bat out of hell and landed with almost no sound in front of him, and Keo thought, *Oh, fuck me.*

He was trying to squeeze the trigger on the MP5SD (*The head! Shoot it in the head! It's the only way to kill the blue-eyed ones!*) when the creature moved, its hands a blur as it grabbed his throat with five long, bony fingers, the contact sending a jolt of electricity across Keo's entire body. Razor-sharp bone joints pressed against his skin, digging into his flesh and threatening to slice their way to the muscles underneath.

It effortlessly slammed him backward and into a tree trunk, knocking the breath out of Keo's lungs before it ripped the submachine gun out of his hands and tossed it away like an adult taking away a child's toys.

His mind was still trying to process what had happened, what *was* happening, and failing badly. The sight of it—here, now—made him hesitate, made him doubt everything he thought he knew.

It was rangy and stood much taller than him, its skeletal frame a different shade of black than the ones he'd killed back at his cabin, then later with Jim and Duncan at the bungalow. There was an innate intelligence in its eyes—deep blue, like twin throbbing stars—that peered back at him as if it could see through him and into his soul. Moonlight gleamed off its dome-shaped head, and sections of its hairless dark black skin seemed to ripple with every slight movement it made.

Keo had seen its kind before. He had fought one and almost died because of it. He had even become friends—or as much of "friends" as you could get with an undead thing— once upon a time.

He shivered now, every inch of him recoiling from being so close to it, and something he hadn't felt in a long time—fear, overwhelming fear—seized every single one of his bones.

It held him against the tree as if he were nothing more than a gnat to be disposed of at its whim. Keo could barely breathe because it was choking the life out of him, even though it didn't seem to be exerting any pressure at all. It stood casually, looking at him from one angle, then another, as if trying to decide if it knew him or not.

He had forgotten just how inhuman they appeared up close, even more so than the black-eyed ones, despite the blue eyes' ability to *almost* pass for human. Maybe that was why they were so much more *in*human. It was a hard concept to grasp even to his own mind, but that kind of contradicting logic wasn't anything new when it came to the blue-eyed ghouls.

And they were so different from the black eyes. Deadlier, smarter, and much, much tougher to kill. It had been years since he'd heard of someone running across one of them after The Walk Out. They had gone into hiding, back into the shadows. A slayer he had spent a few days with around Dallas had mentioned hunting one down, but that had been the last known sighting. It was easy to think they were all gone, that somehow The Walk Out had vanquished them, too.

But Keo always knew better. He had never fully believed

that they weren't still out there, plotting, waiting, biding their time.

And here it was. God, *here it was.*

Finally, it pulled its head back slightly but didn't relinquish any pressure around Keo's neck. His windpipe threatened to break against its fingers—bony fingers that shouldn't have been so strong, and the fact that they were, impossibly so, was so inconsistent with how the creature looked. Frail and desiccated, and yet so unnaturally *powerful.*

Its eyes pulsated, the things it called lips—little more than thin razor wires—forming something that could pass for a smile.

"You," it said, its voice coming out as a whispery hiss that dug deep, deep into the very center of Keo's being. "I know you. I've seen your face before. I recognize your *stink.*"

TWENTY-THREE

Stink? Look who's talking!

But Keo couldn't deliver that witty comeback, because he could *barely breathe*. He wouldn't be surprised if his face was already purple, or blue, or black. Or maybe all three colors at once. (Was that even possible?) He hadn't managed a full breath in over—

How long had it been? Seconds? Minutes? It could have been an eternity for all the (lack of) awareness he currently possessed. It didn't help that every one of his senses was frayed, threatening to overload and explode, from the monster's mere presence.

It radiated an odor that was beyond words—a rotting smell, like a physical thing trying to choke Keo from the inside out. The intensity of its very *being*, the unnatural balance of heat and cold that radiated from every fabric of its dark, pruned black skin caressed Keo's face and other parts of his exposed body.

He wanted to retch, but he couldn't do anything even remotely close. Instead, he struggled against it, trying to kick out with his legs, but he had no power down there. He flailed at the creature's arm instead.

"What's the matter?" it hissed. "Don't have anything clever to say?"

Hey, if you want a conversation, stop choking me!

He couldn't shout that out, either. In fact, he was pretty sure he was about to pass out from not being able to breathe.

The submachine gun. Where the hell did it go?

There, behind the monster, the smooth, round contours of its suppressor glinting against a stray path of moonlight that managed to pierce the plentiful tree crowns above them. There was just enough light for Keo to see with, to be *terrified* by.

The H&K. So close, and yet so far. He would never get to it in a million years, not unless he could escape from the creature's grip. And that was impossible. Keo imagined this was what it must feel like to be in the grasp of the Jaws of Life—

The knife!

It was still behind his waist, in its sheath. All he had to do was reach it.

Oh, is that all?

"Say something," the creature hissed. "Tell me a joke, funny man. Make me laugh."

Maybe next time! Keo thought as he dropped his right hand and reached behind his back. *Got it!*

His fingers were wrapping around the handle of the combat knife, the words *The brain! Plunge it into its brain! It's the only way to kill it!* booming in his head when the ghoul smirked at him—or did something with its lips that almost resembled a smirk.

"It won't be that easy, clever little meat," it hissed, before it threw him across the woods.

Keo would have opened his mouth to scream if his brain had caught up to what had just happened—that the creature had flung him away with hardly any effort—but he was still processing it when he smashed into a tree, snapping branches against his back, before falling inelegantly down to the soft earth.

He managed to somehow roll onto his back despite the pain (Jesus, was his spine broken? It felt like every joint in his body had come loose from the impact and subsequent fall), then onto his side, before frantically scrambling back up to his feet. All the while, his mind screamed, *Get up, get up now or you're going to die!*

"*Or worse,*" a voice said in the back of his mind.

But what could be worse than death?

Oh, there were plenty of things, and he had seen them all. *Plenty* of things.

The knife. He had held onto it during the "flight," thank God. It was a nine-inch stainless steel blade with a black matte handle.

Good enough, good enough.

Even if it wasn't good enough, it would have to do because it was all he had.

The monster stalked toward him. It didn't so much as move as it slithered through the night, a snake on two feet. He might have had trouble seeing its taut, black skin against the heavy patches of shadows in the lightless forest if not for its throbbing eyes gazing back at him. They drew him in, demanded his attention, and he couldn't look away even if he wanted to—and God, he didn't want to. He couldn't *afford* to.

If it was even a little bit afraid of the knife in his hand, there was nothing on its inhuman face to show it. Maybe it knew he was having a hard time catching his breath, and maybe it could hear his heart hammering behind his chest. Or possibly the damn thing could smell the fear wafting out from every inch of him.

"You were there," it said. "At the very end. In the tunnel. You were there with the rest of the meat sacks."

"*There?*" Keo thought.

It didn't take long for him to understand.

Houston. It's talking about Houston.

Under *Houston, to be exact.*

"Yeah, I was there," Keo said, the words coming out with some difficulty. He might have actually croaked some sounds that he thought were words. In fact, there was a very good chance he was choking on his own bile right this minute.

His mind spun, and he almost lost his balance. Keo backpedaled once, then again before he bumped into the trunk of the tree he'd crashed into. One of the branches he'd broken loose *snapped* under his feet.

He pushed through the pain, through the heavy fog in his head. "I saw the big guy go down. I heard him squealing like a little girl, too."

He watched for clues that he was getting through to it, but the creature's face was placid. He knew for a fact that the blue eyes were very different from their black-eyed counterparts—they weren't just more intelligent, but they had emotions. Stories about how they would toy with their victims just for the fun of it were legion, whereas the black eyes just wanted to feed.

"No, you didn't," the creature hissed. "But you were there. With the others. You were close enough, at the end. I'll find them, too, and I'll make them all pay. Every last one of them, no matter how long it takes."

"Yeah, good luck with that."

"You're going to help me. You're going to tell me where they are."

"Only if you say please."

"But first I'm going to punish you. Because you killed one of us. I saw it, through his eyes. You and the woman, in the barn..."

The woman? Keo thought. Then, understanding, *Keep her out of this, you piece of shit!*

He changed up his grip on the knife.

God, he wished he had a gun. Why the hell didn't he bring one, extra weight be damn? Probably because he wasn't 100% sold on his swimming ability after such a long hiatus.

Should have risked it anyway. Now here you are, with a knife against something that can move faster than you can blink. Should have brought the gun.

Or two guns.

Or five...

The creature was still taking its sweet time walking to him, like it knew every step it took only increased Keo's anxiety and made him question every decision he had made since the attack on Winding Creek. And there were so, so many questionable decisions in just the last few days alone.

Keo briefly considered making a run for it but dismissed the idea almost right away. There was nowhere to go. At least, nowhere he could *make* before the ghoul caught up to him.

The blue eyes were so much faster and smarter. Their speed alone limited his options.

So he didn't move. At least this way he could see the monster coming, and that gave him a chance. It wasn't a big one, but being able to look the ghoul in the eyes meant he could react in time.

Yeah, keep telling yourself that, pal.

"What do you have to say for yourself?" it hissed.

"I've killed a lot of your kind," Keo said. "You're going to have to narrow it down."

"No, not a lot. Just one."

Shit. It really does know. What else does this thing know, and do I really want to find out?

"Whatever you say, ugly," Keo said instead, and thought, *Jesus. I'm trading barbs with a ghoul. This is insane.*

He almost laughed. Which part about tonight wasn't insane? Was it when he decided to go for a midnight swim in nothing but his boxers? Or was it the part where he bumped into Blue Eyes?

What the hell was it doing in here? How long has it been here? Was it...waiting for someone?

The creature's lips were curving into something that might have been a grin. It wasn't quite successful, but he was certain that was the intention. "I'm going to play with you," it hissed. "You'll beg me to kill you, to end it, but I won't."

"Sounds like you got it all planned out."

"It'll be fun," it continued, as if he hadn't said anything. "For me, at least. But for you, it'll be an everlasting nightmare—"

It didn't finish, and instead suddenly stopped and turned its head, and Keo glimpsed a large brown wall (*Wall?*) bursting through a large bush and piercing his peripheral vision like a missile. The ghoul lifted its hands, turning fully, when something smashed into its chest, and the bony blue-eyed figure seemed to crumple against the impact just before it lifted into the air and sailed backward.

Holy shit!

The ghoul demolished a tree branch—then another—before crashing back down to earth more than twenty meters away, just as—

Horse!

It stood where the monster had been seconds ago, raking the ground with one of its front legs while snorting in the air like it was getting ready for round two. It stopped only for a second to glance over at Keo before turning its attention back to—

Blue Eyes was already on its feet, and Keo thought, *The gun, you idiot, the gun!*

He ran for it, even as the creature raced across the open grounds, though Keo couldn't tell what its target was—him or the thoroughbred. He decided it didn't matter and dove the last five or so yards for the submachine gun, reaching out with both hands—

Got it!

He hit the ground in a tuck and roll (*Hollywood, eat your heart out!*) and snapped back up into a kneeling position. The creature had launched itself into the air, aiming right for Horse, who refused to move.

Keo squeezed the trigger.

He would have worried about his shots being overheard by the snipers he'd been trying to sneak up on if not for the built-in suppressor that made each gunshot sound barely above a coughing noise. Not quite silent, and there was just enough of an echo to make him nervous, but it was nowhere near the loud gunshots that would have attracted the attention of everyone within a mile (or five) radius.

The first few rounds missed, but the next two or three didn't, and the ghoul jerked back while in midair as bullets struck it in the chest—they went right through its flimsy skin and slammed into branches in the background—and it fell down. Not that it stayed that way—and not that Keo expected it to die the way the black eyes had, instantaneously after being shot with silver bullets. The blue eyes were different—faster, smarter, and *harder to kill.*

The head! Go for the head and take out the brain!

It was the only way to kill them, something Keo and just about anyone who had ever encountered one of the blue-eyed freaks had learned a long time ago. But shooting something that could move *so goddamn fast* wasn't the easiest thing in the world, especially when it was flying through the air, so he had aimed for the biggest part of the monster instead.

Now that the creature was on the ground and wasn't moving nearly as fast, Keo aimed for its head and fired—*and hit it in the cheek.* The silver round dug out a big chunk of the monster's face, and thick, coagulated black blood splattered the sod at its feet.

It twisted slightly when it was shot, and Keo's second bullet grazed off its forehead.

Dammit!

The ghoul seemed to smirk at him before it turned and fled, and Keo jumped up to his feet, switched back to full auto—

Oh no you don't, you ugly bastard!

—and emptied the rest of the magazine after it.

The creature launched itself into the air, jumping onto branches and using them to ricochet onto another tree, each time going higher and higher like some kind of goddamn bouncing ball. Keo continued shooting after it, striking it in the back a couple of times, but the monster kept going—up and up and *up*—until it had vanished completely into the darkened tree crowns above them.

*Sonofa*bitch.

Keo quickly reloaded. It took two seconds, and each one was excruciating. He kept expecting the creature to pounce and never allowed his eyes to remain at one spot for longer than half a heartbeat, but the only sounds came from the weapon in his hands as he reloaded.

There, done!

He thought about pursuing Blue Eyes, but one look at the dark patch of shadows in front of him, and Keo gave up on that notion. He'd hurt the creature, gotten it at least five or six times (*maybe*), but he'd seen them heal from much worse wounds. Five or six bullets, even ones made of silver, had barely slowed this one down.

Yeah, no thanks.

He looked over at Horse instead and found the animal staring back at him. "Remember what I said about putting a bell around your neck? Yeah, let's not do that."

The thoroughbred snorted, then nonchalantly lowered its head to start grazing.

Keo walked over to the animal, every part of him aching. But aches were better than feeling nothing at all, which was what he would be doing if Horse hadn't saved his bacon. A horse! How was he going to tell people that a horse (even a ninja one) had saved his life?

His throat was still sore, and he imagined there was some bruising around his neck. He rubbed at it now, trying to massage away some of the pain. It didn't help, but he could breathe and swallow, and that was good enough for now.

"I distracted him, you know," Keo said. "That's how you managed to sneak up on him. It was definitely not because you move like a friggin' ninja. It was absolutely a team effort. Admit it."

Horse ignored him and continued to eat.

"What are you doing here, anyway? They just let you walk out of Jonah's? Is that—"

The horse lifted its head suddenly and sniffed the air, and Keo turned, following the animal's gaze before spinning around in a full 360 degrees.

But there was nothing out there.

Nothing that looked like a ghoul, anyway.

Just trees. And branches.

And more trees.

"Well?" Keo whispered. He kept his eyes on the darkness around and above him, but mostly he kept tabs on Horse's responses. The animal definitely had better senses than him. "You smell it? Is it still out there? Let me know if it's still out there. It's kind of important."

Keo didn't relax until the thoroughbred went back to grazing.

He sighed and came out of his shooting stance. "Jesus, I think you just gave me a stroke—"

The *snap!* of a dry twig from behind him made Keo turn toward the source, his forefinger tightening against the trigger of the submachine gun, the thoughts *Shoot for the head. That's the only way to kill them; shoot for the head!* racing through his mind.

But instead of a blue-eyed ghoul, there was a soft human voice, whispering out from behind a tree. "Keo. Don't shoot."

TWENTY-FOUR

The face peered out hesitantly from behind the scarred trunk of a large elm tree, and even with limited light, his eyes had adjusted enough to the night to make out a human face. The eyes that looked back at him were green and filled with humanity. There was dirt on her face, dried mud along her forehead and above her lips.

She didn't look as if she had eaten in a few days when she stepped out into the open and smiled at him. "Don't shoot, Keo."

"Jesus," Keo said, and came out of his shooting stance. "*Wonsungi.*"

The girl raced across the clearing and jumped into his arms. Keo wasn't ready for it, even though he figured out what she was doing when she was halfway to him. She still caught him by surprise, and he just barely managed to adapt at the last second or else she would have sent both of them to the ground.

She wasn't openly bawling, but she was sobbing against

him. For such a small girl, she had deceptively strong arms, and if he didn't know she was ten years old, Keo might have thought she was a full-blown teenager.

He kept his eyes on the woods around them while she clung to him, unsure exactly how long this was supposed to go on. She didn't seem willing to let go anytime soon, and Keo didn't like the idea of prying her off like some unwanted annoyance. The girl was clearly traumatized, and it didn't escape him that it was just her, with no signs of Emma anywhere.

Horse stood nearby watching them, but that curiosity lasted only for a few seconds before he went back to dining on the plentiful grass.

After a while, Keo figured enough time had gone by that he started pulling back slightly, then set her down to get a better look at her. She was wearing baggy pants and a sweater, with plenty of dirt and mud covering both articles of clothing. Her hair was a mess, leaves poking out of them like they were growing out of her head. Her eyes were bruised, but only because she had been crying.

"Where's your mother?" Keo asked.

She shook her head and struggled to answer, then unraveled her arms from around him and wiped at her eyes and cheeks. "She's gone."

"Gone where?"

The girl shook her head. "They took her."

"Who?"

"The men..."

"The same ones that attacked the town?"

She nodded. "I think so."

"Were they wearing assault vests?" Then, when she gave him a questioning look (*Right. How would she know what an assault vest was?*), he kneeled, and using his knife, carved a circle with the letter *M* in the middle into the dirt. "Did they have this on their clothes?"

That resulted in an enthusiastic nod. "Uh huh."

Buckies. Of course it'd be Buckies. Who else would it be?

"Where did they get your mother?" he asked.

"Yesterday, while we were coming here."

"You were on your way to Jonah's?"

Another nod. "There were five of us, but we got split up. Mom and me went one way, and they went another. I heard shooting, the screaming..."

"How did they track you?"

"I don't know. They were just there."

"But you got away?"

"I ran. Mom told me to run, so I ran."

Keo looked around them again just to make sure they were still alone before he turned back to her. "This was yesterday? In the daytime?"

"Uh huh."

"How many men took her?"

"I don't know..."

"A dozen?"

"Maybe."

"More?"

"Maybe..."

The more questions he asked, the more confused she looked.

She's a kid, and she's scared. Stop with the Twenty Questions, you idiot.

Keo pursed a smile at her and nodded. "Okay. That's good enough for now."

He stood back up, but before he could say or do anything, the girl grabbed him around the waist and didn't seem as if she was ever going to let go.

"Don't leave me, Keo," she said, her voice barely above a whisper.

"Why would I?" Keo sighed. "I'm not going to leave you. Okay?"

She craned her head to look up at him, tears streaming down her cheeks. He'd never seen her cry before, and the sight broke his heart. "You promise?"

"I promise," Keo said.

"Say it again."

"What?"

"Mom says if you say it twice, it's a real promise."

Keo smiled. "Okay, *wonsungi*. I promise. Again. Good?"

She nodded and went back to smearing tears against his clothes.

Keo sighed, then glanced back at the tree line. Jonah's was on the other side, along with the snipers between here and there. How many snipers? That was the question.

He checked his watch. Three hours until morning.

He patted Megan on the back, not quite sure what he was supposed to do in this situation. It wasn't like he'd ever had to take care of a kid before. They usually avoided him, and vice versa.

"All right, kid," Keo said quietly. "Everything's going to be okay. You're safe now. You're safe now..."

Depending on how he wanted to look at it, the situation had either turned out very well or gone sideways on him. The upside was that he had found Megan (*One out of two ain't bad,* he thought, especially considering the week he'd been having), but her presence also made carrying out the original plan difficult. How was he going to take out two (maybe three, or possibly more) snipers with a ten-year-old kid in tow?

Who says you have to keep your promise to Jonah's? You came here looking for Emma and Megan. Well, you found one of them.

He was tempted to go with that. After all, what did he owe Jonah or Sherry and the others, really? If anything, he'd already done his part by saving Sherry from the Buckies earlier. Even if he hadn't shown up, Jonah's would still have had to deal with Buck's boys. So really, when he thought about it logically, there was no reason for him to stay.

So why are you still here?

Good question...

He was weighing his choices as he led Megan away from the spot where he had tangled with Blue Eyes and went farther back into the woods, away from the tree line and the snipers on the other side. He'd gotten lucky that his fight with the creature hadn't alerted the Buckies—*if* they had been close enough to the woods to overhear, anyway—but Keo was still trying to figure out what the hell the monster was doing out here.

Had the ghoul been stalking the snipers? Or was there another reason it was sitting in the tree just...waiting.

Was it waiting? And if so, for what? Or who?

Keo kneeled next to a large bush while Megan crouched in front of him. She had been carrying some berries in her pockets that she had picked while heading south with her mother, and was eating those now. The horse stood next to them, chewing leaves from a low-hanging branch. Keo felt better with the thoroughbred nearby; it had proven it possessed the survival instincts to make it out here by itself, and the animal definitely had a better sense of smell and hearing than he or Megan did.

Ninja horse to the rescue. I can dig it.

He spent a few minutes watching Megan eating her berries one by one. She wasn't wolfing them down but cherishing each and every one as if afraid they would run out. She didn't look as malnourished now as when he had first spotted her, which made sense since it had only between two days since the attack on Winding Creek, and Emma would have done everything possible to keep her fed until they were forcibly separated yesterday.

"Where were you when you guys ran across the Buckies?" Keo asked. He kept his voice as low as possible while still allowing Megan to hear.

The girl matched his pitch with her answers. "About five miles from here."

"On the road?"

"Uh huh."

"And you walked all the way here by yourself?"

She nodded. "Mom said that if we got separated for me to keep going south until I found the ocean. So that's what I did."

"You didn't know about Jonah's?"

"What's Jonah's?"

"Never mind. Did you see anyone else on the way here? Anyone at all?"

She shook her head. "No one. Just you."

"And you were out here at night this whole time by yourself?"

"I climbed up and hid in the trees when it started to get dark. They can't climb. The ghouls."

Some of them can, Keo thought, remembering the sight of Blue Eyes perched on the tree branch above him. *Some of them can...*

He asked instead, "Why did you risk coming down while it's still dark?"

"I would have stayed up until morning if I hadn't heard people talking. Ghouls don't talk."

Some of them can, he thought again, but said, "That's how you found me."

"Uh huh. But there was just you." She gave him a quizzical look. "Who were you talking to, Keo?"

Keo thought about telling her the truth (*"See, there was this blue-eyed ghoul, and apparently it knows I was in Houston, and it knows I took part in killing one of its kind, so it's really pissed off at me right now, and I'm pretty sure it's still out there, somewhere, waiting for me to let my guard down to gets its revenge."*) but decided it probably wasn't the best idea.

"Him," he said instead, nodding at the horse next to them.

"The horse?" Megan said.

"Yeah. His name's Horse."

She made a face. "What kind of name is that?"

"It's a great name. Unfortunately, Horse doesn't talk much."

"Of course not, Keo. He's a horse."

"Yeah, I know."

She looked at him curiously, as if trying to decide if he was messing with her.

Keo smiled. "Anyway. You said there were others with you and your mom while you guys were coming here. How many were there?"

"Kevin, his dad, and Jules and her mom. And I think someone else that I don't know, but I'm not sure..."

Keo didn't know who Kevin was, but the only male Winding Creek survivor at Jonah's was Breckin, and none of the other women with Christine were named Jules. That told him that like Emma, the others never made it to their destination. Which meant it was a miracle Megan had—in the dark, no less.

She's way tougher than she looks. You'd be proud, Emma.

Keo checked his watch again. Two hours and twenty-four minutes until morning.

"What are you doing out here at night?" Megan asked.

"Looking for you and your mom," Keo said.

"You were looking for us?"

He was amused by the surprise in her voice. "Of course. What else—"

She threw herself at him, and like the last time, she almost bowled him over. He just barely managed to stay partially upright while hugging her back.

"Mom said you'd come looking for us," Megan said. She sounded somewhere between sobbing and laughing. "She said you wouldn't abandon us. I wasn't sure. But I should have been. I should have known you wouldn't abandon us, Keo."

"Of course not, *wonsungi*. You know better than that," Keo said and patted her on the back while thinking to himself, *Jesus, can you get any more awkward? You suck at this.*

She pulled away and wiped at her eyes. She was trying to

smile and talk at the same time. "Are you going to go look for her? For Mom?"

"Yeah," Keo nodded. "After I make sure you're okay, I'm going after her next."

"What about the ones who took her?"

"I'll take care of them, too."

"They had guns, Keo."

"I have guns, too, *wonsungi*."

"You'll be okay? Can you get help?"

He thought it was cute that she was concerned for his welfare. When was the last time someone actually gave a damn about whether he lived or died? Really, *really* cared?

"Yeah, I'll be okay," Keo said. "Don't you worry. I'll get her back."

"You swear?"

"Only on Saturdays, but never on Sundays."

She gave him a confused look.

"I mean, yes, I swear," Keo smiled.

"I knew you liked her," Megan said, smiling back at him.

"Of course I like your mom. Did you think I didn't?"

She shrugged. "I wasn't sure."

"Did I ever do anything to make you think otherwise?"

"Well, you never stayed over..."

I guess she noticed that, too.

"I always meant to," Keo said.

"You did?"

"Yes."

"Will you stay now? When we get Mom back?"

It's a trick. Don't hang yourself, dummy, Keo thought, but he smiled again anyway and said, "Yeah. I will."

She pursed her lips, fighting back a scream of joy. Instead, she lunged at him again, and this time he was ready for it and embraced her back.

Better. You're definitely getting better at this.

Next to them, Horse looked on curiously.

TWENTY-FIVE

He didn't push Megan for specifics about how the Buckies not only found, but captured, Emma and the others on the road, mostly because whatever details she knew weren't going to help him find her. How it happened didn't matter, because he already knew where they had taken her—the same place they were taking the others: Fenton.

What the hell is going on in that place?

Besides, Keo had no interest in further traumatizing the girl by making her relive yesterday. He was already thinking about the job ahead of him, trying to help her get her through it.

"See the world. Kill some people. Make some money. And console a kid about her abducted mother?"

Yeah, that wasn't exactly on his list of expertise, and he wasn't looking forward to trying his hand at it. At all.

Instead, he occupied his mind with the Buckies and Fenton and just what was going on in that place. That question and others swirled around in Keo's head as he made his way back to the tree line with thirty minutes left before night finally gave way to morning.

Too many questions and not a lot of answers made his head hurt. He knew one thing: the attack on Winding Creek was one clue in a larger puzzle. Jonah had told him as much, with the Buckies having already attacked two other towns. And those were only the places he knew about, because there were survivors. How many more were out there? How long had this been going on? And maybe, most importantly, *what the hell is going on in Fenton?*

In his travels since Houston, Keo had gone through hundreds of small towns, some with only a handful of people and others with as many as a few thousand. There were definitely more places like Winding Creek out there—communities that were lightly protected, with people who thought the worst was over and that their long nightmare was finally at an end. How wrong they were.

Hell, he could have taken Winding Creek with a couple of guys. Once you took out Jim and Duncan, what kind of resistance was left?

Easy pickings, every single one of them.

He felt bad for the townspeople of Winding Creek and Dresden, and the third town that Jonah had mentioned. What was it? He couldn't remember. Something with a J. But sympathy only went so far, because at the moment there was really only one concern on his mind: finding Emma.

He had come up with a way to achieve that goal and had thought of it while Megan was telling her story about how they had run into the Buckies on the road. It was going to take some doing, but then what else was new?

If it were easy, any ol' Dick, Jane, and Tom could do it.

So he sat near a few meters from where the woods met the fields and waited for morning. He could feel dusk creeping up on him like a physical creature. It wasn't exactly the best feeling, mostly because Keo was also still thinking about his encounter with the blue-eyed ghoul. He spent most of his time listening for snapping twigs and footsteps, and glanced behind and above and, every now and then, just for good measure, below him whenever he thought he felt the air shift, no matter how slightly.

He didn't like leaving Megan behind, but it was better than dragging her along for this. Besides, she had Horse to look after her. The thoroughbred was a tough cookie and was old enough to have survived The Purge, then the years after that. It was a survivor, all right, and it wasn't afraid of very much. If Keo had any doubts about that, seeing it jump out of nowhere and blindside Blue Eyes erased them.

That is one tough hombre.

Besides, things were going to get hairy real fast, and the last thing he needed was to worry about Megan getting caught in a crossfire. He could picture himself having to tell Emma why he had dragged her little girl into a gun battle, and failing badly.

He blinked as a thin ray of sunlight hit his eyes. It had pierced through the thick tree crowns above him.

Already?

Keo glanced at his watch again.

I guess morning's early today.

He relaxed his stance and changed up his grip on the MP5SD. The presence of sunlight meant no ghouls—at least not where there was light, like the area around him now. He could also stop worrying about Megan and Horse and concentrate on the task at hand.

Keo got up, and, bent slightly over at the waist, moved closer toward the tree line. It didn't take long before he could see the sunburnt green and brown carpet on the other side. And there, in the distance, Jonah's six buildings silhouetted against the shoreline. There was still enough dusk that the thick stalks of grass looked more like ocean waves swaying back and forth.

He held the binoculars up to his eyes, switched off night vision, and scanned the horizon. It wasn't going to be very easy to find a pair (or more) of snipers in all that waist-high grass. Even an idiot would know to dress properly for the environment, and with nearly a mile's worth of land from here to the beach, Keo wasn't all that confident about his chances of locating the enemy position. Or positions, which was more likely.

The only upside was that he hadn't encountered an entire army waiting to attack Jonah's. That much was clear after his run-in with Blue Eyes and the information Megan had given him. He might have been using a silenced weapon, but he had moved around loudly enough in the woods that anyone nearby would have surely heard him. Of course, he could have been wrong and there might be Buckies in other parts of the woods. It was a hell of a big place, after all, and you could get lost in it if you weren't careful.

Now that's not very positive thinking, pal.

He continued scanning the horizon, concentrating on the acres between him and Jonah's, and only extending his search to where the houses ended on both sides. That limited his searching perimeter enough that if anything popped up between him and the beach—

He saw it before he heard it—a gray object in the sky coming from beyond the shoreline. It appeared above Jonah's and slashed overhead, flying just low enough that he could see its belly and the Sidewinder missiles attached underneath its wings.

Now that's *something you don't see every day.*

It was a plane, and not just any plane, but an A-10 Thunderbolt II. But like most people who had been on a battlefield, Keo knew it by its nickname, the Warthog.

The aircraft streaked past the field before disappearing above Keo's head and beyond the woods—

Movement out of the corner of Keo's left eye, this one coming from the ground in front of him. He looked down just as a head, mimicking a curious gopher, popped out of all that green about a quarter of a mile in front of him. The man was looking after the Warthog, and as soon as the A-10 vanished, the figure lowered his profile and attempted to re-blend back into its surroundings.

Gotcha.

Keo zeroed in on the man—or, at least, he assumed it was a man (*What a chauvinist!*)—as his target produced his own pair of binoculars and peered forward at Jonah's. The figure was kneeling, rising just slightly above the grass line to see past it. As Keo had expected, the man was wearing appropriate clothes—green and brown and gray—that helped him to blend in with his environment. Keo might not have ever caught him if he hadn't risen just a bit too high to look after the Warthog.

The figure didn't expose himself for very long before he sank back into the grass.

Keo waited, still looking through the binoculars for the other two (assuming there were two more out there), but they never made themselves known.

At least I found one.

With the location still fresh in his mind, Keo lowered his binoculars and lifted the MP5SD and began jogging in that direction. He wasn't too worried about making noise, not while he was still almost four hundred meters away from his target.

As he got closer, he was hit by heavy winds coming inland from the ocean. There was enough grass slapping against each other to wash over sounds of his movements, which he was pretty sure were minimal to begin with. With the appearance of dawn, the animals around him had also come alive, adding more to Keo's cover.

At the three-hundred-meter mark, his target still hadn't reappeared, and Keo had to convince himself he was going in the right direction. It would have been a hell of a thing if he had gone off track somewhere in the last hundred meters—

Think positive! Think positive!

He sighed and kept moving.

Two hundred and fifty meters...

The sun was casting a massive orange glow across the entire field now, and Keo thought if anyone looked out from Jonah's, they would surely have spotted him. But would they know it was him and not just some random Bucky? Jonah and Sherry would have told the sentries about him being out here by now. Not that he was afraid of being sniped from the buildings. The best shooter Jonah had was Carl, and he was already underground with Floyd.

For the next fifty or so meters, Keo recalled his conversation with Jonah, just before he went down to the beach with Sherry:

"*Don't shoot me,*" he had told Shorty.

"*I can't shoot that far anyway,*" the man had said.

"*No, Jonah, I mean, tell your men not to shoot me.*"

Jonah had chuckled. "*I'll see what I can do.*"

"*I'm serious. I don't want to get shot by your guys. This is already going to be hard; I don't need to dodge bullets coming from your houses, too.*"

"*You've done this before?*" Jonah had then asked.

"*What? Go swimming after midnight?*"

"*No, running into a field that's probably filled with bad guys intent on murdering you.*"

Keo had grinned.

"*What's so funny?*" Shorty had said.

"*A bad guy with a gun,*" Keo had said. "*That's what people used to call me.*"

Jonah had grinned back. "*Yeah? You and me both, brother.*"

He was thinking about Jonah, about what Short Stuff had been five years ago—or even six years ago—as he made the two-hundred-meter mark. The guy didn't look like a cop, and although he wasn't too short for the Army, Keo couldn't quite picture him humping around in a uniform. Maybe *a* uniform, but definitely not while serving Uncle Sam.

Keo pushed Jonah out of his mind when he realized he was already starting to breathe hard. He blamed it on the lack of food and little sleep. It was hard to catch a nap when you were hiding in dark woods with a scared ten-year-old girl and a constantly eating horse, while you knew for goddamn certain there was a blue-eyed ghoul somewhere out there, maybe waiting, just waiting for you to close your eyes in order to pounce.

Think positive!

At the hundred and fifty meters mark, Keo was feeling good again. He had gotten a second wind and his legs weren't nearly as weak as they had been in the previous fifty, which was definitely very good—

A human head popped out of the ground about forty meters in front and slightly to the right of him. It was *not* the same head he had seen earlier through the binoculars from the tree line, because this one wasn't quite as elaborately covered in camouflage. Keo knew because he saw the man's face when he turned around, as if he was searching for something.

I guess I wasn't as quiet as I thought!

Keo saw the whites of the man's eyes at the same time he was spotted, and the man might have opened his mouth to say something when Keo lifted the MP5SD and, slowing down just enough to increase his aim, put the first round squarely into the man's face. Thank God for the optic on the submachine gun, because it made the thirty or so meters that separated them a piece of cake.

The gunshot was little more than a *pfft!* and the noise was already fading into the crisp morning air even before the head disappeared.

And we're off!

Keo was lowering his weapon to continue running at full speed when *a second head* appeared, except this one didn't stop at just the head—a torso followed as the man spun around in Keo's direction, revealing a black assault vest with a white circled *M* in the middle. The Bucky was gripping a rifle, and he was lifting it when Keo shot him in the neck. A spray of blood arced through the air and splashed the moving grass around him.

Oh, fuck me, Keo thought when three more heads, followed very quickly by the rest of the men attached to them, jumped out of the ground near the same spot where the two he had shot had been hiding.

He had two options—and only two options: Get down and hide, or run straight at them.

It was a no-brainer. At least, it was for Keo.

Why? Because you're the world's dumbest man?

Something like that, he thought as he switched the fire selector on the H&K to full auto and, running full speed toward the Buckies, squeezed the trigger and prayed.

TWENTY-SIX

Of course there would be a small army hiding in the fields.

Of course it wouldn't just be two (or, at worst, three) snipers waiting for him.

Of course this wasn't going to be easy.

Of course he was probably going to die trying to help a group of people he didn't know from Adam (with the exception of Christine, of course) until twenty-four hours ago, because that was what had become of Keo's life these days.

For some reason—and it hit him out of the blue—as he was charging toward the three Buckies even as they were still rising up from their cover and were swinging their weapons in his direction, Keo thought of her.

Not Emma. He was surprised it wasn't Emma.

Instead, he thought of *her*.

It had been five years since he'd last seen or even talked to her. He'd heard stories about what she was doing now, how she was raising an army of her own with the purpose of saving the world from itself. It was a mighty feat, but if anyone could do it, it was her.

And he was imagining the look on her face when someone told her what had become of him, how he had run straight into a fight he had no skin in, only to get himself killed.

"That's Keo for ya," she would probably say. *"Always doing something stupid even when he knows better."*

I definitely should have known better, he thought as he sprayed half the magazine at the three figures even as they began firing in his direction almost simultaneously. Or two of them were, anyway, because the third took two rounds to the chest and was falling when his comrades opened up.

Bullets *zip-zip-zipped* around Keo as he launched himself with wild abandon and landed sideways on the ground. The impact jarred enough of his senses that he barely noticed the stabbing pain coming from his left side. He was bleeding, he knew that much, but didn't have time to fully acknowledge it because there were still two men out there trying to kill him and he had to *keep moving.*

Two? You better hope there's just two nearby!

The truth was there could have been more. Not just in the spot where he had knocked off the first two, but somewhere nearby. What were the chances there were just five and that was it? What were the chances he wasn't nearly as shit out of luck as he had originally thought?

About as good a chance as you getting out of this alive, pal!

He sighed and struggled up onto his knees, blades of grass swiping at his face and shoulders and arms as he scrambled pathetically against the soft, wet dirt. The *pop-pop-pop* of fully automatic rifle fire shattered the early morning around him. He could smell burning foliage almost right away as bullets pierced through the vulnerable wall of grass to his left and right and above.

Above? Yup, above, too!

Keo lunged forward, away from the exploding ground, and rolled once, twice—a half dozen times (*maybe?*) before finding his knees under him and pushing his head up just enough to see two men in black assault vests racing forward but *not* at his current position. They were making a beeline for where he had begun his crazy rolling spree.

Twenty meters and closing in *fast*.

One was frantically reloading while the other peered through his gun's red dot sight at the spot to Keo's left, far from his current position. The man must have caught Keo moving out of the corner of his eye, because he swung his weapon over—

Keo shot him once in the thigh, even though he was aiming for the chest. Then, when the man stumbled, Keo put a second 9mm round into his gut. The Bucky vanished into the grass even as his partner spun in Keo's direction, while at the same time pulling back his rifle's charging handle. He was lifting his weapon when Keo shot him twice in the chest and watched him, too, collapse out of view.

He had a moment of triumph (five against one and he was still alive!), but it only lasted for a second or two before a loud *crack!* thundered, and he twisted even as searing pain erupted from somewhere along his temple.

He dropped to the ground as a second *crack!* exploded, and a large-caliber round sliced stalks of grass in half two inches from where he had landed on his stomach. Keo rolled away from the spot even as the sniper fired again—and again—

but the man was aiming at the same location while Keo was getting farther away.

Rolling, rolling, rolling! he thought and wanted to laugh out loud, but there was too much pain to push anything through his lips but haggard grunting.

He finally stopped moving when he couldn't make himself complete a new roll, and lay flat on his back staring up at the sun while sucking in one large breath after another. He reached up and felt along his right temple and brought his hand back covered in blood. It stung and it *hurt*, but it wasn't life-threatening. At least, not the "my brain is leaking out" type of threatening wound, even if it did feel as if his skull was about to shatter at any second.

Keo wiped the blood on his pants and looked down at his left side. Now *that* one looked bad. It was a through and through, and he was definitely leaking out of two holes made by the same bullet.

Not good. Not good at all.

It took him a moment—a minute? Two?—before he realized the shooting had stopped. The sniper (*snipers?*) had either gone back into their holes, or they couldn't locate him anymore. But the lack of bullets flying in his general vicinity didn't mean there wouldn't be bullets flying later when he tried to get up.

And he had to get up. He had to look for help. He hadn't thought ahead to bring a first aid kit with him, and everything he had, he had on him. Which wasn't much. There was the knife and the last magazine for the MP5SD.

Shit, he thought as he swapped out the almost-empty mag and put a fresh (final) one into the H&K. Another reason he should have risked the extra weight and brought a handgun along. Instead he was now down to thirty rounds and done.

Shoulda, woulda, coulda.

He wasn't entirely out of luck, though. There were five dead bodies with plenty of ammo for him to salvage. There were two dead Buckies nearby, and all he had to do was find the strength to roll over to them—or just one of them—and take what he needed. He'd seen one of them carrying an AK-47 and the other had an AR-15. Either rifle would be perfectly acceptable, especially once he ran out of bullets for the submachine gun. And if he was lucky, maybe one of them would be carrying a first aid kit on them.

If he was lucky.

If he didn't die before he reached them.

If there weren't Buckies moving toward his position now to finish the job.

Keo lay perfectly still and listened (it was much easier than trying to move), but the only sounds that came to him were the back and forth of grass swaying in the fields and the winds rushing from the nearby shoreline. He couldn't hear anything that indicated footsteps or voices, and though the first sniper bullet had nearly taken his head off, they didn't have to be close to have gotten off a good shot.

So who were the guys he'd encountered? Maybe the snipers' support staff. Normally snipers worked either alone or with a spotter; but then, these weren't your everyday snipers. Maybe Buck's boys had their own way of operating.

Who the hell cares. You're bleeding to death, remember?

Oh, right.

He finally managed to make himself roll over onto his good side, flinching and gritting his teeth to keep from screaming out the entire time, and got his bearings. The two dead Buckies were somewhere in front of him. Ten meters or so, give or take. It was definitely makeable even if he had to crawl his way over, which was probably the only possible approach in his current condition. Sure, it would hurt like a bastard, but it was better than exposing his head and getting it shot off—

Crack! as a bolt-action rifle fired, but this one sounded from much farther away.

Jonah's. Did that come from Jonah's?

Keo stopped moving and listened.

One minute...

Two...

Suddenly a burst of automatic rifle fire—*pop-pop-pop!*—that was quickly followed by two slow, purposeful *cracks!* from the same high-powered bolt-action rifle. The fact that nothing was exploding around him was proof whoever was shooting wasn't targeting him or anywhere in his general direction.

Keo moved to his knees, feeling woozy with every inch he managed, and finally pushed his head above the tree line.

There, a figure—no, not one, but *two*—racing across the open field nearly a quarter of a mile from his location. That would put them almost halfway to Jonah's, and they looked like ants as they ran at full-speed not at the town but away from it. The two men were far enough apart that the gunfire coming from Jonah's had to be split between the two of them, which Keo guessed was the plan.

A torrent of *pop-pop-pops* originated from Jonah's, bullets raining down on the fleeing figures and kicking up dirt around them. But nothing was hitting and the two men continued moving, running as fast as they could, from the looks of it. Keo thought about picking them off with his MP5SD, but they were well beyond his range even with a decent scope.

Another *crack!* just before one of the retreating figures stumbled and fell. The other one stopped for a moment to look back—just a second, if even that—before he did the smart thing and turned around and kept running, moving even faster now, if that was possible.

The gunfire from Jonah's continued, rounds chasing the lone fleeing sniper, but he had put too much distance for the automatic rifles. The bolt-action fired twice—*crack! crack!*—but neither shot hit their target, and the man kept going.

Run, little rabbit, run, Keo thought. He had to admit, the guy had definitely earned his freedom.

Keo lay back down on the wet (*Why is it so wet? Oh right, my blood*) and looked up at the bright sun hanging above him. The throbbing from his temple was getting a lot worse, and he was likely bleeding to death if the continually growing wetness under him was any indication.

He told himself to start crawling toward those dead Buckies to raid them for first aid kits, but he didn't have the strength to put the thoughts into action. Instead, he continued staring up at the sun as it rose higher and higher above him, and decided that he really liked the idea of living this close to the ocean. Maybe that was why Jonah and Sherry and the others hadn't wanted to leave this place when they stumbled across it, and it took the impending threat of Buck's army to get them to do so.

A house on the beach next to the ocean. What could be better?

Keo closed his eyes, and he must have been dreaming,

because he swore something was licking at his face while someone—a female voice—was calling out his name.

"Keo. Keo."

Screaming his name, actually.

"Keo! Wake up!"

He opened his eyes and saw a small head with dirty brown hair dangling off the sides hovering over him, replacing the sun.

"Don't die, Keo. Don't die."

"Die?" he said. Or whispered. But he was definitely sure he had said it.

Maybe.

"Yeah, don't die," Megan said. "You still gotta find Mom. Okay? You can't die yet. You gotta find Mom first."

"What are you doing out here? I told you to hide..."

"I saw you get shot, and you didn't get back up."

"Oh. Good reason."

He closed his eyes again. The pounding pain from his temple hadn't eased up even a little bit, and the wetness under him had increased. He was probably going to drown soon, from the feel of it. Can you drown on your own blood? There was a first time for everything.

"Keo, come on," Megan said. Her voice sounded very soft and far away. Either that, or his hearing was slipping. "Come on!"

"Come on?" Where are we going?

He was on his feet. Somehow. He didn't know how exactly, but he was back on his feet and—

He was falling again.

No, not falling, but lying down on his stomach, then being pushed across hard leather by someone from behind.

"Come on, Horse, come on!" a voice said. Megan? Was that still Megan?

Then he was moving, somehow.

The field flashed by in front of him. *Under* him. Wind rushed against his face and body, and red drops *drip-drip-dripped* to the ground as he traveled across it.

Blood. That's my blood.

He didn't know how long they walked (*Ran? Jogged?*) but he was aware of them going faster and faster, before finally slowing down again.

"Don't shoot!" someone screamed. "Please don't shoot!"

Then someone was shouting, "Jesus, get them in here!"

Somehow, fields of grass gave way to sand pebbles and voices gave way to the calm, soothing waves of the Gulf of Mexico.

A house on the beach next to the ocean. That's the way to live.

That's the way to live, all right...

TWENTY-SEVEN

Cars. Engines. People shouting.

What happened to the waves?

He struggled to open his eyes. He blamed it on the headache, like someone (or an army of someones) was banging away with a drum set, but the problem was they had no clue about how to play the drums.

Someone needs a lesson. Or two. Or a few hundred.

When he finally did manage to fully open his eyes and keep it that way for more than a few seconds, he found Sherry leaning against a railing next to him. There was wind and sunshine on his face, and he was outside. He assumed it was the deck of one of the houses in Jonah's, though how he got here was a mystery. He wasn't bleeding to death, which was all he really cared about.

Not bleeding to death is good. Definitely very good.

Or, at least, he didn't think he was bleeding to death. The comfortable mattress (was it a mattress?) he was lying on didn't feel the slightest bit damp. There was still natural sunlight around him, so he hadn't slept through the day. Unless, of course, he had and was waking up days later, which would not have been ideal given what was out there—or more specifically, what was incoming.

Buckies. A whole mess of Buckies.

Sherry must have heard him stirring, because she glanced over. "Look at you, still alive. Jonah and I took bets on when you'd wake up."

"Who won?" Keo asked.

"No one. I said tomorrow at the earliest, and he didn't think you would."

"Oh, ye of little faith." He paused. Then, "Speaking of Short Round..."

Sherry smiled. "He's busy coordinating the evacuation."

He thought about trying to sit up, to test how badly off he was after his little stunt in the fields, but decided the consequences weren't worth finding out. Besides, he was lying on some kind of soft cot—or a mattress on a pallet. Whatever it was, it was damn soft, and the wind and sun in his face was so soothing.

I'm still at the beach. Definitely still at Jonah's.

"So how long have I been out?" Keo asked.

"A few hours," Sherry said.

"What time is it?"

"We're coming on noon. You're lucky to be alive, Keo. You were bleeding like a stuck pig when the girl brought you over. But fortunately, we got to you in time." She seemed to wince. "I wouldn't move too much, if I were you. That bullet hole in your side's not going to disappear anytime soon."

"You're up and walking around."

"I was shot yesterday. Big difference. Besides, I don't have any choice."

"And I do?"

"You have plenty of choices. One of them is to stay down until you're healed. We have some sedatives that will help with that."

"No," Keo said. "I'll sleep when I'm dead."

She frowned. "That might not be a long way off."

"Hey, jokes are my territory." Then, "You said the girl brought me back here?"

"I think her name is Megan? She got you up on that horse of yours and led it over here. Brave kid. She told us you were going to go back out there to look for her mother after you got better."

Keo sighed, and this time did try to sit up, despite his better judgment. He managed it just barely, thanks to the wall on his left providing support. He turned around on the bed and slid his feet off the cot. He was shirtless and his side had been bandaged, and when he touched his temple, he found more gauze up there.

The pain continued to throb, except this time it was coming from below and above his torso, simultaneously trying to see which one was going to kill him first. Moving any part of his body was like being punched in the gut, repeatedly.

It could have been worse. You could be dead right now.

"I saw a plane," Keo said.

"The Warthog?" Sherry said.

He nodded. "You know what it is?"

"They come through here every now and then. Carl was in the military; he recognized what they were."

"They?"

"There's a fleet of them out there, somewhere. Jonah says he started seeing them years ago when that whole Battle of Houston thing was happening. He thinks they might have taken part in it, launched from an island somewhere out in the Gulf of Mexico."

Jonah's right, Keo thought, and said, "Where was the one from this morning going?"

"Don't know. None of them have ever stopped to chat with us."

"Never?"

She shook her head. "I guess they're doing their own thing."

"I guess so." Keo sighed again and leaned back against the wall. He took a breath, found it easy enough, and took another one. "Who shot the snipers?"

"I did," Sherry said. She nodded at a bolt-action rifle leaning against the railing next to her. It looked familiar. "I've never shot that far and well in my life. I think he was up there guiding my aim."

"He?"

"Carl. That's his rifle."

"Ah."

"I take it you're not a believer?"

"Depends on what you're talking about."

"You know what I'm talking about."

"Six years ago, I would have said no without having to think about it. But I've seen a lot of things since then..."

"Exactly," Sherry said. "How can you still not believe after everything you've seen out there? After everything that's happened?"

"I've been accused of being a little stubborn before."

"A little?"

He smirked. "But you do, apparently. Believe, I mean."

"Yes."

"Did you always?"

"No. Not always." She turned around and leaned against the railing. "But like you said, Keo, the things I've seen out there..."

There was a loud banging sound, then car doors slamming below them.

"What's going on?" Keo asked.

"We're leaving. Guys are loading up the trucks as we speak."

Keo clenched his teeth and stood up. It was a mistake, and pain rippled across his body.

"You really shouldn't be up," Sherry said, looking back at him.

"I'll be fine."

He forced himself to walk gingerly over to her. Every step was a knife shooting through his side, a reinforcement of Sherry's comment.

But Keo kept stubbornly going forward anyway. "I've been in worse shape."

"I believe you."

He finally reached the railing and grabbed onto it for support, and looked down.

There was a full-blown evacuation going on below them. Jonah's men were in constant motion, transferring boxes, bundles, and everything else they could carry from the other buildings over to the vehicles. Keo hadn't counted when he was here earlier, but there had to be over two dozen cars down there. Christine and the refugees were also around helping with the moving.

Keo glanced behind him, into the building he was standing on. There was furniture and beds but no people. Megan also wasn't back there.

"Living quarters," Sherry said. "Everyone took their emergency personal items. The only thing left to carry down is you."

He snorted and turned back to the activity below. "Where's Megan?"

"She's walking Horse around on the beach." Sherry chuckled. "One of the sentries saw it running off about ten or so minutes after you went swimming. Jonah and I were wondering if it knew you'd left it behind." She glanced at Keo when she said that last part.

Keo shrugged. "It's a weird horse."

And it saved my life, he thought, remembering how the thoroughbred had burst out of the bush and headbutted the blue-eyed ghoul. *Great. I owe my life to a horse. How the hell am I going to pay that off?*

He looked past the hustle and bustle below and at the empty fields beyond. There were no signs of Buckies and no hints that anything had happened, or that he had almost died out there. There was just a lot of grass rippling against the wind.

But that calmness wasn't going to last forever. Sooner or later, Buck was going to show up, and after what had happened yesterday, then this morning, Keo didn't think he was going to be in any mood to negotiate.

He checked his watch: 11:45 a.m.

"How long has this been going on?" he asked.

"Right after you got back," Sherry said. "We're almost done."

"Then what?"

"Then we're gone," Jonah said as he climbed up the stairs to join them on the deck. His shirt was damp with sweat, and he wiped at his face with a rag. "I hate to abandon this place, but it's better than sitting here and waiting for your Bucky pals to come back. This time they might bring more than just eight guys."

"Was that how many were out there this morning?"

"Five regular guys and three snipers," Sherry said.

"You were right," Jonah said to Keo. "If you hadn't gone out there and done what you did, they could have pinned us down here for days waiting for their reinforcements to show up. Then all our asses would have been cooked."

"I saw two of them making a run for it," Keo said.

"One got away," Sherry said.

I guess Carl's heavenly aiming assist was a little off.

Jonah leaned against the railing next to him and looked down at the ongoing evacuation. He shook his head and sighed. "I'm really going to hate leaving this place. But dammit, it isn't worth dying for."

"Where are you guys going?" Keo asked.

"There are a few places farther down the shoreline that could make for a decent replacement. It won't be the same, but, well, we started from scratch before, and we can do it again."

"Here," Sherry said. When Keo looked over, she handed him the same bottle of painkillers he'd given her earlier. "Thought you'd need it back. We refilled it for you."

"Hallelujah." Keo took the bottle, shook out two white pills, and downed them in one swallow. "You doing okay?"

"I got my own refills this morning." She took a similarly small and unlabeled bottle out of her pocket and jingled it. "Thanks for asking."

"I guess getting shot isn't anything new to you, huh?" Jonah asked him.

Keo smirked. "I'm still around. That's all that matters."

"I hear that."

"How long before you guys take off?"

"Thirty minutes, give or take," Jonah said. "We're loading the nonessentials now. I wanted to wait until I was sure we had extra space."

"Even with all the refugees?"

"We have eleven trucks, two sedans, two motorcycles, and a Jeep." Jonah nodded. "We got plenty of space. For you and the girl, too."

As if on cue, Keo spotted Megan walking over to the crowd, pulling Horse by the reins behind her. She made a beeline for Christine and the group from Winding Creek.

"Where'd you get all the gas?" Keo asked.

"We put a storage tank underneath one of the houses a while back, filled it with as much fuel as we could find before they went bad," Jonah said. "One of my guys is a former airport mechanic; he's been keeping an eye on it for us until we needed it—like now. Guy's a magician. I wouldn't know the first thing about that stuff. Most of these cars were already here before I showed up. The rest came with everyone else."

"How much fuel is left down there?"

Jonah shook his head. "Not much. We filled up every spare can we have to take with us. Why, you need fuel?"

"Nah. Horse can pretty much eat anything except gasoline."

"So does that mean you're going with?"

Keo shook his head.

Jonah grinned at Sherry. "I told you."

"You're nuts," Sherry said to Keo.

Probably, he thought, but said, "I need you to watch her for me. Megan."

"Me or Sherry?" Jonah asked.

"No offense, man, but she'd be more comfortable with Sherry."

Jonah chuckled. "Hey, I can be pretty good with kids. Don't let the beady eyes fool you."

"I have no doubt." He looked over at Sherry for confirmation. "She knows Christine, but I'd feel better if there was someone watching her who could actually protect her if necessary."

Sherry nodded. "Don't worry about her. She'll be in good hands."

"You sure you don't wanna tag along?" Jonah asked. "We could use a man with your skill set."

"I can't," Keo said.

"Can't, or don't want to?"

Keo didn't answer right away. Instead, he watched Megan standing next to Christine. The girl must have sensed him staring, because she looked up and over, and when she saw him, waved.

Keo smiled and waved back. "I promised her I'd find her mother."

"You can barely stand," Jonah said. "You won't be much good against the Buckies in your current condition. Better if you come with us, get healed up first, then go looking to get yourself killed. I mean, go looking for her mother."

Keo chuckled. "Thanks for the vote of confidence, Jonah."

"No sweat."

"She told us the Buckies got Emma on the way over here," Sherry said.

"Uh huh," Keo nodded.

"You know where she is?" Jonah asked. "I mean, if you're going to go after her, you need to at least know that."

"Doesn't take a genius to figure that one out."

"Fenton."

"Yup. Fenton."

"What the hell are they doing with the women and children in Fenton?" Sherry asked. "Christine and the others told us the same thing; they were taking just the women and children. What is going on in that place?"

Keo shook his head. It was a very good question and wasn't anything he hadn't asked himself over and over again since Winding Creek: *What are they doing with the women and children in Fenton?*

"I don't know," he finally said. "But that's where they took Emma, so that's where I have to go."

"Must be the end of the world fever, making everyone a little nutso," Jonah said. "That's assuming you even make it there. And I'm not talking about the getting-shot-on-the-road type of misfortune. I'm talking more about you falling down and dying with no one around to stop you from bleeding to death."

"He's right," Sherry said. "You really should come with us, Keo. You're in no shape to be going out there on your own. You're in no shape to be doing *anything* on your own right now. At least wait twenty-four hours if you're dead set on doing this."

"I'll be fine," Keo said. "Besides, I won't be alone. I'll take Horse with me."

"You can't even ride in your current condition."

"We'll see about that."

"The man's made up his mind, Sherry," Jonah said. "I can respect that. I think it's pretty dumb, mind you, but I respect his determination to get himself killed."

Sherry didn't look like she was ready to give up, though. "Even if you make it to Fenton, you'll be walking into the lion's den. I've heard about what they did to Dresden, Juno, and Winding Creek. If they find out who you are, you'll never make it out of that place alive, Keo."

Keo watched Megan and Christine below, waiting for their turn to pile into the waiting vehicles.

Finally, he said, "Wouldn't be the first time I did something I wasn't supposed to walk away from. I'll just add this one to the list."

TWENTY-EIGHT

Horse didn't seem to notice that everyone was leaving Jonah's except for them, but then the thoroughbred appeared more occupied with the pair of crabs that had washed up on the beach behind them. Keo kept expecting Buckies to come out of hiding, either running out of the trees or popping up from the surrounding fields to start raining bullets in their direction, but nothing of the sort happened. Instead, Jonah's people disappeared up the shoreline one car at a time, carving a makeshift road along the spot where the grass met the beach.

"Head over there if you're still alive after this," Jonah had said. *"If we're not at one of those places, we'll be at the other ones. Just keep going."*

"You don't sound very optimistic about seeing me again," Keo had said.

Short Stuff had chuckled. *"I've been around a long time, Keo. Seen a lot of things that would make your hairs stand up. I even had a back-and-forth with a couple of guys who managed to do things I didn't think were possible. So I absolutely believe* we'll be seeing you again, but I also wouldn't be surprised if we didn't."

"Take care of Megan for me."

"I thought that was Sherry's job."

"Just in case."

"Just in case," Jonah had nodded.

"Can I ask you a question?"

"Only if I don't have to answer."

"Why are you doing this?" Keo had asked. "Is this about saving these people, or is it about self-preservation?"

Jonah had grinned back at him. "Can't it be a little of both?"

And then they were gone, along with Megan. The girl had waved to him as the truck she was in with Sherry drove off. Keo had put on a forced smile and waved back, but even that took a lot of effort and he had thought, *Maybe this wasn't such a good idea after all.*

But it was too late to change his mind now as he watched the last of the vehicles vanish up the shoreline, sunlight blinking off its roof. He continued to hear the sounds of their engines in the open air for a long time afterward. Until, eventually, even that faded and it was just him and Horse standing on a beach with the Gulf of Mexico batting against the sands behind him.

Keo glanced over at Horse. "You should have gone with them. You know that, right?"

The animal ignored him and continued playing with the two crabs.

"I'm just saying, don't say I didn't give you the chance."

Keo grabbed the saddle horn and gingerly lifted himself up and into the stirrups, then spent a few minutes adjusting the two slung packs to achieve a better balance. Mostly, he just wanted to make sure he wasn't going to black out and fall right back down. The thought of lying on the sand, dying, with no one around to pick him up was a very real possibility.

His temple still throbbed, but the painkillers were helping with that, and also with the continued pain from his side. The stitching was better than anything he could have done himself, and he was lucky to be near Jonah's when he was shot.

Lucky? You wouldn't have been shot if it weren't for them.

"Good point. Very good point."

Horse lifted his head to look back at him.

"Don't mind me, just talking to myself," Keo said, and patted the animal on his mane. "Let's take it slow, huh? Easy does it."

Keo took out the bottle of painkillers and popped two more into his mouth, chasing them down with some warm water this time. He spent an extra few minutes letting the chilly air from the ocean wash across him, then closed and reopened his eyes to see if he was in any danger of toppling off the saddle.

Good enough. Good enough.

He picked up the reins and turned the horse around, then pointed it back toward the woods.

———

Keo didn't completely leave Jonah's behind; at least, not right away. He knew where Fenton was—at least, the general direction, which was north—but he wanted to make sure of something first.

He went back into the woods a mile from the shoreline and found a spot far enough from the area where all the action had taken place last night and earlier this morning and sat down to rest. He considered tying Horse in place, but the thoroughbred didn't look like it had any interest in wandering off. Besides, the animal had proven to him that it was more than capable of taking care of itself, not to mention coming through for him in the clutch. If something happened, Keo didn't want to hamstring the horse's ability to react—or to save his life, again.

I'm putting my life into the hands of a horse. Great.

Well, the horseshoes of a horse, anyway, he thought with a chuckle.

He didn't do much of anything except sit and eat the beef jerky and bread Jonah's cooks had given him before they left. He was starving, and the food was a welcome relief. So was the doing-nothing part, as he sat leaning against a tree and waiting.

One in the afternoon came and went, and nothing.

Keo dozed off and opened his eyes to the sound of car engines in the near distance, just beyond the woods. He got up and moved toward the tree line, MP5SD in front of him, and peered out.

Trucks, six of them, each one with mounted machine guns in the back, were tearing across the field toward Jonah's. There were more men on horseback flanking the vehicles as they waded through the waist-high grass. It looked very much like a small army, and Keo caught the white circled *M* on a couple of their assault vests through his binoculars.

Buckies. Of course, Buckies.

It was a lot of firepower. If there were even just two in the technicals, along with the machine gunner, that would mean nearly thirty men in all, including the twelve on horseback. There were probably more since a few of those trucks had backseats and at least two of the technicals had an extra man hanging in the back.

They stopped about half a mile from Jonah's, the ones on horseback climbing off their saddles and kneeling in the grass for cover. The front passenger on one of the lead trucks stepped out and peered forward with a pair of binoculars. The man was standing on the other side of the vehicles and had his back turned, so Keo couldn't see who it was. It didn't take him very long to realize the place was empty, and if they suspected an ambush, it didn't stop them from continuing on ahead at full speeds.

He glanced back at Horse. "I know what you're thinking: where do they get all the fuel? Am I right?"

Horse ignored him and busied itself with trying to get at the leaves dangling from a nearby branch. If the animal was even the least bit interested in all the vehicles revving their engines out there, he didn't show it.

"Exactly," Keo said, and turned back around.

He watched them from a safe distance, listening for more Buckies that might have lagged behind, possibly even lingered in the woods around him as backup. But he had chosen a good position, far enough away from the center of Jonah's and almost at the other side of the fields.

The Buckies had spread out and were going through the houses one by one. They were much too far for Keo to tell if one of the figures moving back and forth was Buck himself. Would the man finally show up in person after he had lost so many soldiers to Jonah's? It was possible, but Keo didn't discount the possibility the man might have so many underlings that losing a dozen or so wouldn't even faze him.

Around four in the afternoon, smoke drifted into the air as

fire began spreading quickly across the wooden structures along the beach. At the same time, the Buckies fired up their engines and climbed back onto their horses, and half of them retreated through the same fields, while the other half headed up the beach in the direction Jonah's caravan had gone earlier.

Keo wasn't too worried about the Buckies catching up to Jonah's group. They'd gotten a large head start, and using the beach was only temporary. He had to admit, for someone who had been fiddling the last five years away on, essentially, a beach house, ol' Jonah had a pretty good head on his shoulders.

The fire over Jonah's abandoned houses raged for some time, eventually consuming everything by 4:34 p.m. Keo watched it in silence while finishing the bag of jerky and another piece of bread. When he was done, he swallowed down two more painkillers to help with the irritating thrumming in his head. He reached up to make sure he hadn't started bleeding again up there, but his hand came away dry.

"Bullet grazed your temple," Sherry had said. *"You don't know how lucky you are."*

Oh, trust me, I know, he had thought when she'd told him that.

Keo didn't get up until he was absolutely certain Buck (*if* he had actually shown up in person this time) hadn't left any of his flunkies behind to see if anyone would try to fight the fire. The final building had collapsed, and the flames were already starting to die down when Keo swung back onto Horse.

"Time to go. Next stop: Fenton."

His next stop was Fenton, but it wasn't right away. He couldn't afford to show up with an aching side and a still-pounding temple. Instead, he settled for a farm just outside of Winding Creek. The owner was a man named Henry whom Keo had gotten to know—or as much as you could "know" someone that you only saw once a month. Henry liked keeping to himself and only really appeared in town occasionally.

Keo didn't bother going into Winding Creek; he already knew what he'd find in there.

There were no signs of Henry at the bungalow, where he lived with a woman and her two kids, which wasn't surprising. Henry wasn't an idiot, and after the Buckies had laid waste to the nearby town, he would have fled. That is, if he hadn't gotten himself killed before he got the chance.

Henry had a pair of goats and raised chickens, taking the eggs into town whenever he needed something in trade, but all the animals were gone when Keo arrived. The place gave off an abandoned vibe even though it had only been a few days since Winding Creek fell. In a year, the grass would reclaim the yards, and a few years after that, the woods would cover this place and no one who didn't know of its existence before would have any clue it was ever here.

Keo walked Horse slowly through the open front gate, then at the same pace across the yard just in case he was wrong and Henry was still there, watching him carefully with a rifle and his finger on the trigger. The last thing Keo wanted was to get shot (*again*) when he didn't have to. Fortunately (for him, anyway, though not so much for Henry and his family), no one had a bead on him, and Keo reached the front door in one piece.

When he knocked on the thick slab of oak, no one answered. When he tried the latch, it opened without resistance. Keo peered inside, one hand on the MP5SD, the other on the door in case he needed to swing it closed quickly.

The curtains over the windows were pulled open, allowing plenty of natural sunlight in. There was no blood on the floor in the great room, and when Keo stepped inside and checked, there were none in any of the bedrooms, either. There was no evidence at all that there had been a fight of any kind. The place was simply empty.

There was also no lingering smell of rotting garbage in the air. That meant no ghouls had nested in the place after Henry and his family left. Keo liked to think the home's previous owners got away, and the lack of blood helped with that theory.

He found food in the kitchen—too much, which would seem to counter his hope that the family had made it out. If that were the case, wouldn't they have grabbed all or most of the nonperishables they could instead of just leaving them sitting around in the pantries?

Think positive, remember?

Keo unsaddled the horse, then ate his fill of the abandoned food while the thoroughbred wandered around inside the house, going back and forth between the windows, sometimes stopping to look out of one of them. Keo grinned at the mental image of someone out there spotting Horse peering out at them from inside the building.

After stuffing himself, Keo went into the bathroom, and using light from a high window, checked his wounds in the mirror. It was the first time he'd actually seen himself in a few weeks, and it wasn't a pretty picture. He was paler than he remembered, with bags under his eyes. The scar along one side of his face looked obscene and ugly in the low light.

Getting prettier every day, pal.

Keo unwound the gauze around his temple to get a look at the bandage underneath, then removed that to check the stitching. Just some minor bleeding, but otherwise everything was where it should be. For such a small bullet graze, the damn thing was still giving him one hell of a headache. By comparison, the pain from his side had lessened into a dull sensation. He still felt it every time he did anything, like climbing on and off Horse, but there wasn't the continuous pounding like there was coming from his temple.

The stitching was still in place down there, too, and there was no bleeding. He assumed the same was true on the other side, except he couldn't see it without another mirror. It didn't feel damp back there, which was good enough.

Before leaving the bathroom, Keo went through the drawers and medicine cabinet. He found bottles of pills for a variety of ailments and feminine products. Another bad omen that Henry and family hadn't run off unscathed. Of course, they could have and just didn't have time to take the food and everything else with them.

Yeah, let's go with that.

He went back into the living room and locked the front door, pushing the deadbolts into place one after another—there were three in all, evenly spaced from top to bottom. Each bolt *clanked!* into place with the kind of satisfying sound that put Keo's mind at ease. Henry knew how to protect his home, and it would take a tank to break the door down.

When that was done, he looked out the windows to make sure there was no one out there. There were security bars over all the windows, each one fastened securely on the other side.

Henry wasn't a fool, after all, and he had lived through The Purge.

Keo pulled the curtains and went to check out the bedrooms more thoroughly this time. He settled on the kids' room. The mattress was comfortable, and as soon as his head touched the pillow, he was almost instantly asleep.

He dreamt of a woman, but it wasn't Emma.

"Where exactly are you going to go?" she asked.

"I don't know yet," Keo said.

"Will you come back?"

"I don't know that, either."

"What do you know, Keo?"

Just that I have to leave, because I can't stand being this close to you and not acting on it, *he wanted to say but didn't, because it wouldn't have been fair to her. She had so much going on, so much on her plate, and she had already lost so much.*

"I know I'm not good at staying still in one place for too long," he said instead. "Try not to miss me too much."

"That's impossible," she said, and smiled back at him. "You're a hard man to replace."

"You can always find another gun. I hear Peters is pretty handy with a rifle."

"That wasn't what I meant, Keo."

That took him by surprise, and she gave him a look that said she had more to say but for some reason, couldn't bring herself to do it.

He wanted to push her, to make her say it, but he didn't. Maybe he was a little afraid what he would do if she did.

"Doesn't mean I'll be gone forever," he said just as the helicopter touched down nearby and the wind from the rotor blades tried to drown out his voice. "Send me an email if you need to get a hold of me."

"An email?" she said, amused.

"Or snail mail. Either works."

"Or I can just send a Warthog to go out there looking for you."

"That'll work, too," he grinned before turning and running toward the waiting helicopter.

He climbed on, and when he looked back, she had stepped away but was still looking after him.

She waved, and he waved back, and it was the last he saw of her.

He remembered watching her on the helipad, her arms hugging her chest, blond hair blowing around her face as the chopper lifted into the air. He wasn't sure how long she stood there looking after him, because soon he lost sight of her, and then there was just the Gulf of Mexico.

He thought of her now.

The crystal blue of her eyes, the golden color of her hair, the smoothness of her skin against the sun...

TWENTY-NINE

He woke up to scratching noises.

From outside the house.

He lay perfectly still and allowed his eyes to adjust to the darkness, all the while listening to the *scratch-scratch*.

It was coming from behind and slightly to the right of him, where the bedroom's lone window would be. The door in front of him, now that he could make it out, remained closed, and it was still just him inside the room.

Keo didn't have to look at his watch to know it was well past midnight—and pitch dark outside in Henry's yard. It was also eerily silent, which was another clue that *there was something out there.* Not just anything, but something that could scare animals, even the ones that were safe up in the trees. They had gone deathly quiet for fear of attracting attention.

He reached over for the MP5SD leaning against the nightstand next to the bed. The heavy feel of it, with a full magazine loaded with silver rounds, was like the warm blanket he had tossed to the floor before falling asleep. The extra weight of the SIG Sauer on his right hip and the tactical combat knife with the silver-coated blade on his left added to his overall sense of security. He had dozed off with his clothes and boots still on, mostly because he was too exhausted to take them off.

Have silver, will survive the night.

Hopefully.

He couldn't smell it—couldn't smell *them*—but he knew what was out there. Maybe he should have known they would be in the area after what he had seen in Winding Creek: the bodies. That always attracted scavengers. Animals in the daytime...and another kind of animal at night.

Keo turned his head toward the window, but the curtains were pulled and he couldn't see out. That was fine with him, because it meant whatever was out there, whatever was *scratch-scratching* the glass, couldn't see in at him, either.

He slowly eased himself up from the bed, grimacing a bit at the slight stinging pain from his side. The throbbing from his temple that had been accompanying him since leaving Jonah's was noticeably missing.

Thank God. Any more of that, and I might have to crack open my skull to make it stop.

He attributed his reasonably good condition to the almost-full night's sleep he had gotten. A quick glance at his watch confirmed it was well past midnight: 2:14 a.m. He had lain down around six, before nightfall, so he'd gotten more than a decent eight hours—

Thoom.

It came from outside his room, from the living room.

Thoom.

The door. Someone (*something*) was striking the door.

Good luck with that, Keo thought even as he rose from the

bed and moved as fast as he could, which wasn't very fast at all. He might have been able to double time it, but the second or two he would gain as a result wasn't nearly worth aggravating the stitching at his side.

Besides, he wasn't concerned about the house's front door giving in. Henry had installed a giant slab of oak out there, and along with the three deadbolts, it was going to take a hell of a lot to bust through that thing. And the windows had burglar bars over them, securely fastened to the walls, so even without the glass panes—

The loud *crash!* of glass breaking.

Jinx, Keo thought as he opened his door and slipped out into the dark hallway.

There was nothing up the corridor to his right but the master bedroom where Henry slept with his wife; Keo had avoided the bigger room on purpose. The left side of the hallway led back into the great room and the front door—

Thoom.

Crash!

Thoom.

Crash!

He wasn't worried about the door. The impacts sounded almost puny by comparison to the breaking windows. It didn't take long for them to run out of glass to break, leaving just the insistent (but weak, so, so weak) pounding against the door.

Thoom. Thoom. Thoom.

It was almost pathetic, like little kids bumping their heads in frustration. Keo wasn't the least bit worried. It was going to take them all night just to make a dent in that door, even if every single creature out there pounded on it endlessly.

Good luck with that, boys.

It had been a while since Keo found himself trapped in one spot with ghouls on the other side trying to get at him. But there was no paralyzing fear or the overwhelming sense of dread that usually accompanied such moments. Instead, there was just a flush of annoyance as he stepped out of the back hallway and listened to them fruitlessly bang on the door.

Thoom. Thoom. Thoom.

They were insistent, he would give them that. But insistence wasn't going to knock down a door that probably took two grown men just to lift into place.

They had broken the glass panes on the two front windows and ripped the curtains loose, and hands now poked through the burglar gate. Dark faces, skins pulled tight against deformed skulls, peered in with lifeless black eyes. As soon as they saw him, they began frantically trying to squeeze through the tiny areas between bars, and the phrase "squares and round pegs" immediately came to mind.

Meanwhile, the *thoom* continued from the other side of the door.

Thoom. Thoom.

Again and again.

Thoom. Thoom.

Keep at it, boys. One of these days you might knock that door down, he thought, relaxing and letting the submachine gun hang at his side.

Even the obvious rise in intensity—*thoom-thoom-thoom*—didn't bother Keo too much. He didn't move from his spot, even when he heard shuffling from his right and Horse walked over—calmly, impossibly calmly—to where he was standing. Apparently the animal wasn't too concerned, either.

Ninja horse. It's survived this long for a reason.

Keo put a hand on the thoroughbred's reins. "They woke you up, too, huh?"

Thoom-thoom-thoom.

"Ghouls, man. No sense of courtesy whatsoever."

Thoom-thoom-thoom.

"Go into my room. It's quieter in there."

He directed Horse into the back hallway. The animal understood and walked past him, but Keo didn't look back to see if it knew enough to go into the kids' room that he had left open instead of the parents' bedroom farther back.

Instead, Keo focused on the creatures trying to squeeze in through the windows, slicing their skin on the jagged shards of glass that still clung to the frames. They were frenzied to gain entry, their eyes zeroing in on him from behind the bars—

THOOM!

His head snapped back to the front door. That latest blow had sounded a hell of a lot stronger than any of the previous ones.

THOOM!

The door actually moved that time, and Keo thought he heard both the hinges and deadbolts *clinking.*

What the hell were they using to ram the door? Something heavy, and tough. Maybe it was a car—

THOOM!

The ghouls had abandoned the windows, because Keo couldn't see them anymore. Where did they go? And why?

THOOM!

He faced the door again, reaching back and making sure he had the spare magazines for the MP5SD stuffed in his back pocket.

THOOM!

That time, the door did more than just slightly move—it actually *shook*—and Keo was certain one of the three hinges that held the heavy wood in place had also moved. The deadbolts, for their part, seemed to have held their ground.

A quick, panicked thought: Did Henry focus on the wrong side of the door? Was it the hinges that were the weak spots, and not the deadbolts?

That's not good. That's not good at all—

THOOM!

The door trembled, and one of the hinges snapped and the heavy brass *clacked* against the floor. The flat hinge rested where it fell, but the removable pin ricocheted into the air in Keo's direction, landing and rolling, before stopping two feet from the toe of his boots.

That's definitely not good.

Keo was looking down at the pin, trying to come up with a mental image of what was out there that could have possibly done that, when there was another massive—

THOOM! and the door flew open, and this time there was the echoing *clank-clank-clank!* of deadbolts as pieces of the locks clattered to the floor around Keo.

Aw, crap.

It stood in the open doorframe—tall and proud, and could have easily been mistaken for a human man even with its naked black flesh that seemed to glow against the darkness outside. Moonlight gleamed off its smooth domed head, its twin blue orbs pulsating as it looked in at him.

Blue Eyes.

Was it the same one? From the woods outside of Jonah's? Was it possible?

It looked so human and yet so inhuman. Keo thought he

could feel the simultaneous cold and heat radiating from the creature's pores reaching across the space of the living room to caress the exposed part of his own skin.

But that was probably all in his mind. Wasn't it?

There were just enough shadows around the monster that Keo couldn't tell if it was the same one that had attacked him outside of Jonah's. Not that you could really tell the Blue Eyes apart—or, at least, Keo never could. There had been one exception five years ago, but he was long gone.

Blue Eyes—whether it was the same one or not, it didn't really matter anymore—wasn't alone. Far from it. The black eyes scurried around its legs like little children unable to stay still in one place for more than a few seconds at a time. But Keo knew better: They weren't children, they were soldiers waiting for orders.

Someone had once tried to explain to Keo how it all worked, how the blue-eyed ones controlled the black eyes through some form of psychic connection. Six years ago, Keo wouldn't have believed such a thing was possible and might have even laughed in their faces. But then, six years ago the world still made sense.

He didn't know how long he stood there staring at Blue Eyes. It could have been seconds or whole minutes, but Keo didn't snap out of it until the blue-eyed creature smiled—or Keo thought it smiled. It really just looked as if its lips (were those even lips?) curved slightly. Before Keo could be sure either way, the black eyes had slid past its legs and into the bungalow.

One, two—a dozen.

Two dozen.

He stumbled backward into the hallway, even as he pulled

the trigger and the first wave of ghouls flopped to the floor and stopped moving. As soon as that happened, more jumped over the fresh corpses and into the living room.

There was a second or two as Keo debated the merits of trying to nail Blue Eyes—it remained standing at the door, fearless—in the head, because that was all it would have taken. Kill Blue Eyes, and the rest would retreat. He had seen it happen before; it was a proven tactic, time and time again. Without a commander, someone to control them, to point them at a target, the black eyes were almost like lost drones, unable to process the loss of their CPU.

But he never got the chance, because they were coming, flooding into the house, and Keo thought, *Jesus, where did they come from? Where have they been hiding all this time?*

He pulled the trigger again, swiveling the submachine gun from left to right, the whirring of gunfire and the *clink-clink-clink* of bullet casings hitting the floor, overwhelming every one of his senses, including the awful stench of undead things as they clogged up the big room.

He was in the hallway when he ran out of bullets. There was no time to reload, so Keo slung the MP5SD and drew the SIG Sauer, and still backing up, fired into the nearest ghoul. It was barely two feet away from him when his round pierced its chest, the creature's desiccated form no match for the powerful bullet that sliced through it and struck the two ghouls directly behind it.

Unlike with the suppressed H&K, there was nothing to hold back the loud *boom!* of each pistol gunshot. The narrow corridor he was squeezed inside only seemed to double (*Triple?*) the blasts, and just like that, the pounding headache

he thought he had gotten rid of was back but even more fero-
cious than before.

When it rains, it pounds!

But he had stopped caring about making a lot of noise,
especially with all the banging the blue-eyed ghoul had done
while it was breaking down the door, and Keo fired again and
again, all the while backing up.

*It broke down your door, Henry! Should have installed a
heavier one, pal!*

Even as three—then *five*—more ghouls dropped in front of
Keo, three and five and *ten more* filled the narrow hallway in
their place. It had been such a long time since he'd had to face
so many of the undead things at one time that the sight of
them, pushing forward without any semblance of self-preservation, took his breath away. They wanted him—they wanted
to get *to* him—and it didn't matter what he threw at them or
how many of their kind died doing it.

They kept coming, and coming, and *coming.*

And because there wasn't enough space for them to all
squeeze through at the same time, they began crawling over
one another, creating stacks, but at the same time *clogging up*
the hallway.

Keo squeezed the trigger again and again.

There were so many and in such close proximity he didn't
even have to aim. Everywhere he fired, one—two—sometimes
four of the creatures flopped dead...only to be almost instantly
stepped on by the stampeding herd of child-size monsters.

He could feel the weight of the 9mm dropping even as he
drained the magazine when he finally reached the bedroom
and stepped through, then grabbed the door and slammed it
shut. The deadbolt hadn't snapped into place before the crea-

tures crashed into the wooden slab on the other side, the *thoom-thoom-thoom-thoom!* like machinegun fire. The bedroom door wasn't nearly as heavy as the thick oak one in the living room, so the pounding sounded noticeably louder.

Keo stumbled back, reloading first the SIG Sauer, then the MP5SD.

Thoom-thoom-thoom!

He had two more mags for the submachine gun in his pack in the corner, and he hurried to it and grabbed them, shoving them into his pocket.

Thoom-thoom-thoom!

A loud whinnying sound from behind him, and Keo looked over to find Horse at the window, facing him while its hind legs kicked back repeatedly at bony hands trying to pull at the burglar bars. There was a dozen of them out there that he could see, but many, many more fighting each other to get to the window, to be the first one in.

Thoom-thoom-thoom! from the other side of the room.

Keo turned back to face the door. He hadn't felt it before, but now that he wasn't retreating for his life, he remembered the wound in his side and grimaced as pain lanced through him. He pushed through it as best he could.

Thoom-thoom-thoom!

Louder and more insistent, but the door was holding because the ghouls were weak creatures and it didn't matter how long they struck it; the bedroom door wasn't going to buckle.

God, I hope it doesn't buckle.

But the black-eyed ghouls outside in the hallway right now weren't what Keo was worried about. It was Blue Eyes. Sooner or later, it was going to appear and push the black eyes aside and knock down the bedroom door, and there wasn't going to be a damn thing Keo could do to stop it. If breaking the front door was nothing to it with *three deadbolts*, then what chance did this flimsier wood with its lone lock have?

Nothing. Not a snowball's chance in hell.

Keo willed his breathing to slow down, then tune out the whinnying of Horse behind him as the animal continued to assault the ghouls trying to reach inside the room. He lifted the submachine gun and took aim at the door, placing the red dot sight on the spot where a slightly tall human male's head would be if there wasn't a door in the way.

Thoom-thoom-thoom!

He tested the trigger, then blinked at a bead of sweat stinging his right eye.

Thoom-thoom-thoom!

The pounding seemed to be working in sync to the thrumming from his temple, which only added to the annoyance.

Thoom-thoom-thoom!

But at least the pain in his side had subsided. Thank God for that.

Thoom-thoom-thoom!

Keo waited.

He didn't move. He didn't dare move even a little bit for fear of lowering his aim because it was coming. He had no doubts about that whatsoever.

Thoom-thoom-thoom!

Once in the head. One bullet in the head, and it would be over.

Easier said than done.

Thoom-thoom-thoom!

Another bead of sweat, dripping into his left eye now. Christ, where was all the perspiration coming from?

Thoom-thoom-thoom!

He risked taking his hand off the trigger and wiping his forehead with his long shirt sleeve, then quickly slid the forefinger back into the trigger guard.

"Come on, you bastard. Come on. Don't keep me waiting."

Thoom-thoom—

It stopped. The pounding stopped.

What the hell?

Keo listened. He didn't move a muscle and barely breathed, and he just listened.

Nothing.

He couldn't hear anything happening on the other side of the door.

Not just in front of him, but there was nothing from behind him, either. Zilch. Nada.

Horse had stopped whinnying, but Keo couldn't risk the second or two it would have taken to glance back to find out why. He could hear the *clop-clop* of the horse moving around on the hard floor, which meant it was fine. Probably.

Then, out of nowhere, a loud *boom!*, like dynamite going off, coming from *outside the house.*

Keo spun around and looked toward the window. The ghouls had abandoned it.

A second *boom!* tore through the quiet.

Shotguns. Those were shotgun blasts!

Keo was still processing the new information when another one— *boom!*—shattered the night outside, except this time it was coming from the direction of the front door. Just when Keo thought whoever was shooting had moved over to the other side of the building, he was proven wrong, because there was another thunderous *boom!*, this time closer to his window.

More than one shooter!

He hurried toward the back of the room, glass crunching under his boots as he neared the window. He stayed far enough away that a ghoul reaching in couldn't get its fingers on him, but close enough to be able to see out just as orange and red flames stabbed out of a shotgun somewhere in the house's front yard with another resounding *boom!*, temporarily lighting a figure wearing a mask that covered only the lower half of his face.

The man wasn't alone; a second figure was with him, their backs pressing against one another as they both fired, racked their shotguns, then fired again. Keo recognized well-trained discipline and mutual trust in how the two men operated, as flames, like dragon's breath, spat out from the long barrels of their pump-action shotguns over and over again.

Keo thought it had to be the most beautiful sight he'd laid eyes on in a long time.

Horse looked over at him with a questioning look.

"Hey, don't ask me. I didn't invite them, either, but I'm damn glad they showed up."

Horse lifted his head in agreement. Or Keo thought he did, anyway.

Outside the house, one *booming* shotgun blast rang out after another, and another, and another, and it was all music to Keo's ears.

THIRTY

"Man, you're one lucky SOB," Lam said.

"*Really* lucky SOB," Willis said.

"I've been luckier," Keo said.

"Not this lucky."

"Definitely not this lucky," Lam said. "If we hadn't shown up, you would have been ghoul food, my man."

"Yeah, yeah," Keo said, but he grinned back at the two men because they were right. "What do you want, a kiss on the cheek?"

"That would be nice," Willis said.

"Maybe plant one on the bum," Lam said.

"You guys practice this?" Keo asked them.

"Nah, I'm just naturally charming," Willis said. "Lam's just naturally annoying."

"Ouch," Lam said.

They stood in the front yard of Henry's house, looking at the twisted and black pruned skin corpses surrounding them. Half of the creatures were shredded by buckshot and were missing limbs and large portions of their heads. A few had gaping holes that Keo could have shoved his fist through and still had leftover room for the rest of his arm.

Lam and Willis hadn't been Keo's only saviors—two others had shown up with them: a woman named Chloe and another man named Oliver. They were also both slayers, wearing bulletproof vests with half-masks hanging around their necks by straps.

Chloe walked over to them now, holding a bloody machete in one hand and a severed ghoul head with a big chunk of its skull missing in the other. The creature's eyes were wide open, and Keo could almost believe it knew what was about to happen just before it did, and the fear was frozen on its face when it died (*again?*). But he knew better, because the black eyes weren't capable of fear. They were primal beasts that survived on the basest of instincts.

The blue-eyed ones, on the other hand...

Was it hunting me? Was it the same one from outside Jonah's?

Keo might have shivered thinking about that possibility, but luckily Lam and Willis were too busy looking over at Chloe to notice.

"What're you gonna do with that?" Lam asked her.

The girl—she couldn't have been more than twenty or so, which would have made her a teenager during The Purge—grinned back at him. Blond and beautiful, if a bit on the short side. She reminded Keo of another blond teenager who would have grown into a twenty-something young woman by now. A gorgeous one at that.

"I dunno. I might use it as a decoration," Chloe said. She

placed the skull on her shoulder and did a pose. "What do you think?"

"I think you're gonna need another one to balance it out," Oliver said, walking up behind her.

"Everyone's a critic," Chloe said. She tossed the skull into the air, then kicked it like a soccer ball when it came back down. It flew into the darkness and disappeared somewhere into the woods beyond Henry's yard.

"Nice kick," Keo said.

"First Team All-District," Chloe said.

"I don't know what that means."

"It means she was a really good soccer player in high school," Oliver said. He was in his late twenties, and the way he stood protectively next to Chloe told Keo they were a couple. "So what's going on here?"

"What do you mean?" Keo said.

Oliver took out a rag and wiped the thick ghoul blood off his machete. The slayers had charged into the fight with shotguns, but once they'd emptied their weapons, instead of reloading, they had switched to their knives. It probably helped that they'd taken out the majority of the threats by then and were just finishing off the few that remained.

After it left. Blue Eyes. It left its minions behind to occupy the slayers while it fled.

Smart fucker.

"The only time I've seen this many ghouls in one place was about four years ago up in Nebraska," Oliver said. "The ones that didn't do The Walk Out. Since then, it's been nothing but small nests and a few ghouls here and there, nothing one slayer couldn't handle. But this..." He looked around at the bodies. "This is new. This is coordination." Then, back at Keo, "So what's going on?"

Keo walked over to the porch and sat down. All the activity had left him winded, and he'd had to grab two more pills from his stash just to stay upright. The meds were just starting to have an effect (*Think positive!*) as he leaned back against one of the foundation poles and looked around at the chaos.

It was a bloodbath, not that he could see any "blood" out here. What liquids he could make out over the shadows were all black, some gathering in thicker puddles than others. The creatures had swarmed the slayers to no avail. But there had been a lot of them, Oliver was right about that. Morning sunlight would give him a more exact count, but Keo thought there had to be at least thirty bodies out here.

The door was wide open behind him, and there was a long line of more undead things stretching from it to the back hallway. Horse had come outside along with Keo, and the thoroughbred was grazing in the open, far away from the nearest dead ghoul or their blood. Like Keo, it was taking advantage of the opportunity to stand around in the night. Even the birds in the trees and the animals in the surrounding woods had returned to making noises now that the threat was over.

Keo noticed the slayers were watching him, waiting for a response.

"I have no idea," he finally said. "I was trying to catch some Z's when they knocked on my door."

"And you've never seen them before?" Oliver asked. He didn't sound like he bought Keo's answer.

"These ones?" Keo shrugged. "One dead ghoul looks the same as another dead ghoul to me."

"That's such a living person thing to say," Oliver smirked.

"I've been accused of a lot of things, but that's a new one."

"You Japanese?" Chloe asked. Then, before he could answer, "I was always into manga when I was a kid. Then I graduated to anime."

"I don't know what any of that is."

"What kind of an Asian are you?"

"The kind that doesn't know what manga or anime is, apparently."

"I saw one of them staying away from the fight," Lam was saying. He had said it so somberly that they all looked over at him. "It had blue eyes."

"Yeah, I saw it, too," Chloe said, serious again. "I don't know when it took off, though." She might have shivered slightly while doing her best to cover it up. "That's the first time in a while."

"A lot of first times tonight," Willis said.

"I didn't see it," Oliver said.

"It was there," Chloe said.

"I believe you. I just didn't see it." He looked back at Keo. "What did *you* see?"

"They're right, it was here," Keo said. He jerked a thumb at the door behind him.

"It did that?" Oliver asked. When Keo nodded, he climbed up the porch, took out a flashlight, and inspected the damage.

"What're you guys doing back here?" Keo asked Lam and Willis. "I thought you were dead set on committing suicide by heading into Houston?"

"We were," Willis said. "Still might anyway. But that was before we ran into Chloe and Oliver." To Chloe: "Tell him."

"We were tracking them," Chloe said. "The ones that attacked your place."

Not my place, just some poor bastard who is probably dead, along with his family, Keo thought, but didn't think the information was relevant, so he didn't interrupt her.

"Like Oliver said, it's been a while since we've seen this many in one place," Chloe continued. "A literal swarm of ghouls. And they weren't staying put. They were moving. We stumbled across their tracks outside of Kerry's Mills, about ten miles from here. We were doing a job for the locals; three ghouls were snacking on livestock. Oliver thinks those three probably broke off from this group."

Lam glanced back at the bodies in the yard. "That's a goddamn lot of ghouls. You don't see something like this every day. At least, not anymore."

"It was definitely a blue eye," Oliver said. He hopped off the porch and put his flashlight away. "I've seen those things take out whole buildings. Strong bastards. Fast, too." He gave Keo what might have been a slightly impressed look. "And you survived it."

I survived it again, he thought. *Maybe.*

"Barely, thanks to you guys," he said instead.

"When did you get that?" Oliver asked, tracing one side of his face with a forefinger. "Before or after?"

"After."

"Wanna tell me about it?"

"What are you, writing a book?"

"He is writing a book, actually," Chloe said.

"The Ghoulish History of the World," Oliver said, before shrugging. "It's just a working title."

"You got a publisher for it yet?" Keo asked.

"Still looking. You know anyone in New York who might be interested? I'd hate to end up in the slush pile."

"Everyone in New York's dead, as far as I know."

"Dead schmead, as long as they know how to sell books," Oliver said. "Speaking of dead, you mind if we bunk here for the night?"

"You've earned it," Keo said. He stood up, before adding, "You'll have to, uh, help me clean up the mess first, though."

———

It didn't take them long to drag the bodies into the yard, and Keo got away with not doing the hard work by telling them he'd been shot earlier and showing them the bandages around his waist. Afterward, Oliver and Chloe took the master bedroom at the back, while Keo settled into the same kids' room. Horse remained in the great room with Lam and Willis, and the last thing Keo heard was Chloe moaning on the other side of the wall before he drifted off to sleep for the second time that night.

He dreamt of Blue Eyes, chasing him through the woods. He was alone, and unarmed, and it was just him and the monster.

"*Where are you going, funny man?*" the creature called after him. "*Tell me a joke. Tell me a funny story before I rip your guts out and eat your intestines.*"

But he didn't stop, and kept running, and running some more even when he didn't think he could anymore.

"*I'm going to play with you,*" Blue Eyes shouted after him. "*You'll beg me to kill you, to end it, but I won't... It'll be fun. For me, at least. But for you, it'll be an everlasting nightmare...*"

He woke up three times during the night and gave up sleeping after the third instance.

Lam and Willis were already up before Keo stumbled outside. The two slayers were dragging the leftover remains of dead ghouls—mostly bleach-white bones and deformed skulls now, in the light of day—into a large hole they had dug toward the edge of Henry's front yard. Both men had their half-masks on, covering their nostrils and mouth to keep out the smell, but even so they looked pale and were sweating profusely under the rising sun.

The stench of evaporated ghoul flesh clung to the air around the house and hit Keo like a semi truck as soon as he stepped onto the porch. He pulled his shirt up and over the lower half of his face and kept it there. No wonder the slayers always wore half-masks. It was ideal to stave off the stink whenever they had to "go to work."

Horse was already up and on the other side of the property chewing on leaves dangling off hanging branches. There were no signs of Chloe and Oliver, and Keo assumed they were still asleep inside the house.

It took Lam and Willis two more hours before they tossed the last bones into the hole and began to fill it back up. By the time they were done, there were just little bits of evidence—a bony finger here, a shattered limb there—that there were over thirty or more undead things here just last night.

He looked around him and wondered how many other hidden mass graves, similarly filled with deformed bones and skulls, were in just this part of the world. He could never forget that day when the creatures started pouring out of the buildings, stepping out into the sunlight and dying (*again*) before his eyes. One after another, after another. People called it The Walk Out, and only a handful of people really knew why it had happened. Some called it a miracle.

Keo went back into the house and came out with two warm bottles of water and tossed them to the slayers as they sat on the porch.

"Cheers, boys," Keo said.

"Appreciate it," Lam said, and drank his all in one gulp.

Willis went a little easier on his and pulled down his mask just long enough to down half of the bottle before pulling it back up. "So did you find them?" he asked, his voice slightly muffled. "The mother and daughter you were looking for?"

"I found one of them," Keo said.

He told them about Jonah's and his encounters with the Buckies. He left out the skirmish with Blue Eyes in the woods, mostly because he still couldn't decide if it, being the same one from last night, terrified him or—

Oh, who are you kidding. Terrified is definitely the right word for it.

"You think she's in Fenton now?" Lam asked. "How sure are you?"

"That's where they would have taken her," Keo nodded.

"Maybe they didn't," Willis said. "I've seen some bad things out there. A woman like that—the way you describe her..." He shook his head.

Keo knew exactly what he was trying to say. He remembered Wendy in her apartment with the line of Buckies waiting outside her door for their turn...

He sighed, said, "I gotta believe she's there. Even if she isn't, I have to make sure. I promised the kid."

"Don't make promises you can't keep," Willis said. "I never do."

"Yeah, well, now you tell me."

Willis chuckled.

"Fenton," Lam was saying, shaking his head. "That place... Something's going on in that place. Something I don't want any part of."

"Lam's right," Oliver said, coming out of the house behind them. "Chloe and I thought about going inside when we ran across it, but... I don't know. We both got this bad vibe, like we might not come out if we went in."

"Same with us," Willis said. "There's some seriously bad juju coming outta there, man. I'd steer clear, if I were you."

"These Buckies," Oliver said, "they're the ones with the *M* in the white circles?"

Keo nodded. "That's them."

"What's the *M* stand for?"

"I don't know," Keo lied. "But I'll be sure to ask them when I get to Fenton."

"I'm sure they won't mind telling you," Willis chuckled. "Just make sure they're not pointing their guns at you when you do."

"Sound advice if I ever heard some, thanks."

"Don't mention it."

"Still going to Houston after this?"

"We're actually thinking about going around it, try our luck someplace else before moving on to another state. Maybe eventually end up in Cali. See if there are more opportunities over there."

"Was it something I said?" Keo smiled.

"Don't look so proud of yourself," Lam snickered. "Mostly it's because we're running out of opportunities in Texas. Besides, ghouls aren't the only dangerous things out there these days."

"You scared, Lam?"

"I didn't get into this to kill people. I'd rather avoid that whenever I can."

"Too bad," Keo said. "I could definitely use your help in Fenton."

Oliver shook his head and gave Keo an almost sympathetic look. "It's your funeral, man. You should be careful, though; after last night, you might not have a whole lot of lives left."

Keo flashed back to the sight of Blue Eyes standing in the doorway, staring in at him.

Was it the same one from the woods outside Jonah's? And if it was, was it following him? Or was it *hunting* him?

"Yeah, careful's the name of the game," Keo said instead.

The slayers left an hour later to get a jumpstart on their journey. He heard Chloe telling the others that maybe they should "get a car, so we don't have to walk everywhere," as they disappeared into the woods.

Keo spent some extra time in the house checking on, then changing the dressing around his waist. The pounding along his skull had ceased when he woke up this morning and continued to be MIA, but he took a couple of more pills anyway just in case.

Horse remained outside the entire time, occasionally

disappearing into the woods but always returning. Keo didn't know where it kept going or why, but it was waiting for him in the yard when he came back outside, feeling as fresh as he had since, well, before he got shot.

After going through some of the supplies Jonah and Sherry had given him, Keo replenished what he needed from Henry's pantries that the slayers hadn't needed. He tossed the packs over Horse's saddle before giving the thoroughbred a tap on the head.

"You know where I'm going, right? It's going to be dangerous. So you should know what you're getting into."

The horse looked back at him before letting out a brief snort.

"Okay, but don't say I didn't warn you. Again."

When he climbed onto the saddle there was a slight irritating buzz from his side, but it was nothing like yesterday. Not even close. That was either a sign he was healing up nicely or the meds were working.

Either/or.

He left Henry's property, slipping into the woods before aiming northwest. He had memorized a map of the area, and his current route would take him around Winding Creek, then back near Princeville, before he would eventually end up at Fenton. Keo didn't really know what he would do once he reached his ultimate destination, but he guessed that would mostly depend on what he found.

"*Something bad's going on in that place,*" Oliver had said.

"*There's some bad juju coming outta there,*" Willis had added.

It wasn't like he had any choice, though. Emma was in there. Probably.

Probably? This is one hell of a trip just for "probably," pal.

Keo let out a loud sigh and thought to himself for the thir-
tieth time since leaving Jonah's behind about what he was
doing. All of this, because he had promised a little girl?

No, it wasn't just that. It wasn't that simple.

He liked Emma. He liked her a lot. She'd been good to
him, treated him well, and even allowed him into her bed. He
still regretted not staying the night at least once.

Couldn't you have done it just once, you idiot? Just once?

But he hadn't, and it was too late to change that.

Well, maybe not too late, but rectifying that mistake would
mean first finding Emma, then rescuing her from the Buckies,
and then...

And then what?

He had no idea.

He skirted around Princeville, listening for activity coming
from the state highway that ran through the city. There wasn't
any—no car engines, no human voices, and nothing that would
indicate human beings other than himself were present in the
area.

Fenton was farther north, and Keo continued on with a
mixture of dread and anticipation.

"There's some bad juju coming outta there," Willis had
said, and Keo thought he could feel some of that "bad juju"
right now even if he didn't necessarily believe in such things.
The only reason he kept going anyway was the thought of
Emma, in trouble, and Megan waiting for her mother.

He liked them. Both of them. God help him, but Keo had
come to enjoy their company. There was Emma's great food
and all those useless chats with Megan at his cabin after
school. But most of all, he just *liked* them.

And the Buckies had hurt them.

They had hurt Megan and Emma, and they still had Emma. They were probably hurting her right now, and the more he thought about that—the more he focused on that—the angrier Keo got.

By the time he was within a mile or so of Fenton, Keo was ready to kill someone.

THIRTY-ONE

There were three of them, and they were camped in a small clearing that looked as if it had been put to use previously in the very recent past. He identified them as Buckies right away by the white circled *M* in the middle on their assault vests.

They were armed with gun belts and had rifles leaning nearby, and all three had two-way radios clipped to their hips. They had built a fire and were spit roasting something that looked like a small fawn. Keo saw the smoke coming from their campfire a hundred meters away and climbed off Horse and walked the rest of the way over, listening for signs of more Buckies in the area the entire time. He was too close now that the last thing he wanted was to lose his element of surprise.

What element of surprise? You're walking right into a big ol' mess of bad guys.

He ignored the voice and pushed on.

He heard them talking—loudly—as he got closer; they clearly had no cares in the world. And maybe they didn't need them, this close to Fenton. He was the one who was almost behind enemy lines—if he wasn't already, depending on how wide those "lines" were. As far as he knew, there could have been a dozen camps like this one around Fenton, some kind of loose outer perimeter, perhaps. The slayers hadn't mentioned seeing them, but it would have been easy to walk right by given how thick and plentiful the woods were in this part of the state. Keo would have done exactly that if he hadn't spotted their smoke.

He made sure the MP5SD was on semiauto when he left Horse behind and walked the final ten meters or so. The thoroughbred seemed to understand his intentions and didn't follow. Either that, or it didn't care enough to follow him.

Either/or, Keo thought as he went into a slight crouch and looked out from behind a massive tree trunk into the clearing.

A man was working the metal contraption they were using to spit roast their meal, which further convinced Keo this was a regular spot because that rotisserie looked way too heavy to be moved back and forth. The Bucky—thirties, with sandy blond hair—was applying a generous coat of sauce from a plastic Tupperware box onto the skinned fawn with a brush, while another man peeled potatoes he was pulling out of a sack on the ground next to him. The third and last Bucky was digging into his tactical bag and finally found what he was looking for.

"My man," Sandy Blond laughed when he saw the third guy pull out a six-pack of beer, except there were only four left.

"Never leave home without it," Six-Pack said. He peeled one off and tossed it to Sandy Blond, then sailed the other one at Mr. Potato.

"Warm," Mr. Potato said as he caught the beer and made a face.

"Hey, beggars can't be choosers," Six-Pack said.

"You know we have ice in town, right?"

"Shut up and drink; or don't, and give it back."

"I'm just saying," Mr. Potato said.

"You say too much," Sandy Blond said. "That's your problem."

"I'm a thinker, that's all," Mr. Potato said. He was in his early twenties, with what Keo thought was the beginnings of a mullet.

Six-Pack was by far the oldest—maybe forties—and he popped his beer and took a long drink before lowering it. Warm or not, he seemed to enjoy the brew just fine. "Damn, that's good stuff."

"Does beer expire?" Mr. Potato asked as he turned his can over in his hand.

Six-Pack shrugged. "I don't taste any difference."

"I think they do," Sandy Blond said. "But that could just be Big Beer trying to trick you into buying more."

"Big Beer?" Mr. Potato said doubtfully.

"Yeah, you know, the guys who run the beer business. Telling you something expires is like encouraging you to drink it faster, then you'll have to buy more sooner. It's a vicious circle."

"It's a fucking delicious vicious circle," Six-Pack said, just before he let out a loud burp.

The other two chuckled, and Sandy Blond was still working on the fawn with the brush while Mr. Potato had gone back to peeling his potatoes, when Keo stepped outside and shot Six-Pack—who was closest to him by far—in the back.

As the man collapsed, Keo swung and shot Sandy Blond in the face.

Mr. Potato had his small tactical knife in one hand and a potato in the other when he froze in place. His eyes went first to Six-Pack, lying on his stomach on the ground, then to Sandy Blond next to the rotisserie. The MP5SD hadn't made very much noise at all when it fired both times, so it was taking the Bucky a little longer to fully grasp what had just happened.

Finally, the man's eyes found and stayed on Keo as he walked over. Keo was pretty sure the man would either scream or go for his holstered sidearm or even the rifle leaning against the tree behind him, but the only thing Mr. Potato managed to do was utter the single word, "What?"

Keo shot Six-Pack in the back two more times as he walked past the Bucky, both as insurance and to let the last survivor know he meant business. He didn't bother doing the same with Sandy Blond, who lay next to the campfire with one hand burning in the flames. Even if the man had somehow managed to survive a bullet to the face, he would have been jumping around by now.

Halfway to Mr. Potato, Keo motioned with the submachine gun. The Bucky didn't seem to understand, so Keo said, "The knife, idiot. Throw it away."

The man dropped it instead of throwing it away. Keo smirked and wondered if that was on purpose or if the Bucky was just too paralyzed with indecision to do more than just release the knife from his grip.

Keo kicked the knife away, then grabbed the gun out of the man's holster and tossed it. He did the same to the rifle before taking a few steps back and lowering the H&K.

The Bucky was still holding onto his half-peeled potato, which Keo found amusing and didn't tell him to drop. A part of him wanted to see how long the man would continue to hold onto it.

"What's your name?" Keo asked.

Mr. Potato stared at him but didn't answer.

"You got a name?" Keo said.

"Hatch," the man finally said.

"Like hatchback?"

"I guess?"

Keo glanced around the camp, listening for noises—voices, the *thump-thump* of horse hooves or even car engines. And like the last few times, he didn't find anything out there. That didn't really make sense this close to Fenton, which Keo expected to be bustling with activity with people coming and going at all hours. Unless, of course, he still had a long way to go in order to reach Fenton. Maybe he wasn't even close.

He looked back at Hatch. "Just the three of you?"

Hatch nodded. He was, Keo noticed, still holding onto the potato.

"What are you guys doing out here?" Keo asked.

"Patrol," Hatch said.

"How close are we to Fenton?"

"Two miles?"

"Are you sure?"

Hatch seemed to think about it. "I think so? Maybe more?"

Keo smiled. The man didn't sound sure at all, but Keo asked instead, "How many other patrols are out here?"

Hatch seemed to think about that one, too, and took longer this time. Either he was not sure about his answer, or he wasn't sure if he even *should* answer.

Keo decided to help him out and fired a shot into the

ground barely an inch from Hatch's right thigh. The man flinched with his entire body as dirt kicked at his face.

"How many other patrols?" Keo asked again.

"I don't know," Hatch said without hesitation. "Five, I think?"

"You think?"

"I don't know for sure. There might be more out here today."

"Why?"

"I'm not sure. Things were hectic all morning."

"Why?"

"Why?" Hatch repeated.

"Why were things hectic this morning?"

"I don't know. Something happened last night, I think."

"What?"

"Huh?"

"What happened last night?"

"Oh. I don't know."

"You don't know much, do you?"

"I guess not..."

Keo didn't think Hatch was lying. The man didn't seem capable of coming up with on-the-spot lies. Hell, the guy hadn't realized he was still holding onto the half-peeled potato. Besides, Keo had seen plenty of mooks like Hatch. They were grunts—and worse, they were happy to be grunts and to stay that way. Guys like Hatch lacked ambition and were content to be one of the guys holding the guns instead of having one pointed at them.

He crouched in front of Hatch, grimacing a bit (and hoping the Bucky didn't notice), and said, "Let's change subjects. Were you there? At Winding Creek?"

"Winding what?" Hatch said.

"Winding Creek."

"I don't know what that is."

"It's a town. South of here."

Hatch shook his head. "I told you, man, I'm just a patrol guy. I just patrol Fenton, that's all." His eyes snapped to his two dead buddies. "We don't go out with the others on the raids."

"So this is your regular gig?"

"Yeah, pretty much."

Keo stared at the man, trying to decide if he was scared and incapable of lying or just really good at acting.

Finally, he said, "The women and children from the raids. Why are they taking them?"

"I don't know," Hatch said. "I'm just—"

"On patrol, I know, you've said that before."

"I swear, man, I don't know anything that has to do with the raids. None of us do. You gotta be in Buck's unit to know about that stuff. He keeps things really close to the vest. Real need-to-know."

"You're not a part of Buck's unit?"

"Not really."

"Explain."

"Huh?"

Keo pointed at the circled *M* over one of Hatch's vest pouches. "Explain that, if you're not one of Buck's guys."

Again, that hesitation as Hatch tried to decide if he should talk or not.

And again, Keo decided to help him out by firing a bullet, this time just an inch above his right ear and splitting bark from the tree behind him.

"Jesus!" Hatch said as he flinched with his entire body again. "Stop doing that!"

"Don't be such a princess."

"Christ."

"You kiss your mom with that mouth?"

"My mom's dead."

"It was a figure of speech." Keo pointed at the circled *M* again. "You were in the middle of explaining that to me."

"Buck's guys trained us. Once we're done with training, we get to wear the *M*. It's like a privilege. But Buck doesn't really trust anyone who wasn't a part of his original unit. Not enough to watch his back when he's out on a raid."

"And he always goes out in person? Buckaroo?"

"Yeah. It's part of why his guys like him."

"Explain."

"You know, because he always puts his money where his mouth is? He won't ask his guys to go out there if he won't. That's why they like him."

"So you were in Fenton long before he showed up?"

Hatch nodded. "I was there even before the ghouls died off."

Not all of them, Keo thought, but kept that to himself.

He said instead, "What about the women and children that Buck's people brought back to Fenton?"

"Like I said, I don't know about that stuff."

"You've never seen them in town?"

"Maybe, I don't know. There's a lot of people in town. I mean, a *lot.*"

"How many is a lot?"

"A few thousand..."

"That's a lot."

"Yeah, it is."

"The guy who runs the place," Keo said. "Copenhagen. Is that his name? Like the capital of Denmark?"

"Yeah, that's him," Hatch nodded. "I don't know about no capital, though."

Keo chuckled. "You don't know much, do you?"

"Nah, I guess not."

"Tell me about him. Copenhagen."

"Like, his past or something?"

"Like, yeah," Keo smiled.

"I think he used to be a cop."

"You think?"

"Maybe he used to be a cop. I dunno. He was there when the ghouls were still running the place."

"One of the overseers."

"I guess you could call him that."

"Go on..."

"After The Walk Out, the people in town either left or stayed. He was one of the bosses that stayed. Then one day, it was just him."

"What does that mean?"

"Of all the bosses we had when the ghouls were still around, he was the only one left afterward."

"What happened to the others?"

"I don't know. I mean, no one knows for sure. Some think they decided to leave—you know, head back to where they came from. But others think he killed them." Hatch shrugged. "No one knows for sure, and it's not like anyone asked. Anyway, he's been running the place by himself since."

"When did Buck and his boys show up?"

"About two years ago, I think?"

"How many men did he have with him at the time?"

"Two hundred? Maybe more?"

"You think?"

"I think," Hatch nodded.

Keo smiled again. "How many men did Copenhagen have before Buck showed up?"

"You mean, guys that used to be soldiers, or everyone?"

"The former."

"Huh?"

"The first one."

"Oh. About a hundred, I think. But that ballooned pretty fast when people started showing up from other places."

Like Lewis and Vince from Winding Creek?

"How many guys are wearing that now?" Keo asked, pointing at the circled *M* again.

"Five hundred or so."

"What's the draw?"

"I don't understand..."

"Fenton. What's so special about it that so many guys are joining up?"

Hatch gave Keo a perplexed look, like he couldn't comprehend the question.

"What are they doing, giving away free virgins?" Keo asked. "Or maybe free new cars for everyone who signs up?"

Hatch shook his head. "It's nothing like that, man."

"So what's it like, then?"

"They're just...strong."

"Strong? How so?"

"Strong," Hatch said as if Keo should understand. "Have you been out there? If you're not strong, you get run over. People come and take things that you have, that they want.

That's just how it is out there. Fenton is strong. No one's going to take anything from us."

Because Fenton is the one doing all the taking. And who doesn't like a winner?

Hatch was staring at Keo when he asked, "Are you going to kill me?"

"Now why would I do that?"

The Bucky glanced at Six-Pack behind and to Keo's right, then Sandy Blond to Keo's left.

"Ah, them," Keo said. "I just wanted you to know that I was serious, that's all. Also, I was in a bit of a foul mood. But I'm all good now, so you don't have to worry."

"That's...good?"

"Absolutely. Now, I need you to do me two favors."

"Two?" Hatch said, more than a little nervously.

"First, drop the potato."

"Huh?" Hatch glanced at his hand, the one clutching the potato. He dropped it like it was on fire before looking tentatively back at Keo. "What's the second favor?"

"I need your radio, and then I need you to deliver a message for me," Keo said. "I guess that's three favors, now that I think about it..."

THIRTY-TWO

It didn't take Hatch long to deliver the message.

Keo was enjoying a big slice of the roasted fawn he'd taken from the Bucky campsite before moving back into the woods, retracing his steps away from Fenton, when the radio on the ground next to him squawked and a voice said, "EB. My old friend."

He recognized Buck's voice, but instead of answering, Keo took his time chasing the venison down with some water, then wiped his oily hands on his pants legs. He had been fully prepared to wait another hour before he acted just in case Hatch hadn't, for whatever reason, come through.

"You there?" Buck asked through the two-way.

Keo let him wait a few more seconds before he finally picked up the radio and pressed the transmit lever. "Buckaroo. How the hell are ya?"

Buck chuckled through the radio. "I could be better. You caught me at a bad time, EB. I'm a little busy right now."

"You know what they say: when it rains, it pours."

"More like a drizzle. But in any case, it's a good thing I'm adaptable. How've you been?"

"Can't complain. Busy killing a lot of your guys."

"Is that right?"

"You know the ones down at Jonah's yesterday?"

"That was you?"

"Yup. Saw more of your boys show up later, all gussied up and ready for a fight. Thought you might have tagged along."

"Unfortunately I had other matters to attend to. Ghosts from the past, if you will."

"Sounds like the beginning of an interesting story. Tell me more."

"Maybe next time, when we see each other again in person."

"Promises, promises."

"So, that was you making all that trouble for me down there?"

"Guilty as charged."

"Well, damn, EB. I don't know whether to put down this radio and immediately launch a one-hundred-man strong manhunt for you or offer you a job."

"Either way works for me."

"What would you do if I went with the former?"

"Nothing fancy. Just wait around and kill your guys one by one. It's not like I got anything else better to do. My calendar's wide open these days."

Another amused chuckle from Buck. Keo wondered if that was for his benefit, since Buck didn't have to keep his radio keyed while he did it.

"So, did you get my message?" Keo asked.

"Sure did," Buck said. "Quote: 'Let everyone you took

from Winding Creek go, or I'll kill everyone in Fenton, including you and Copenhagen.' Did I get it right? Hatch was a little nervous when he was repeating it to me, so he might have gotten some of it wrong. I just want to be sure."

"Hatch got it right."

"But just to be one-hundred percent certain: Let everyone I took from Winding Creek go, or you'll kill me?"

"That's about it."

"And Copenhagen?"

"Oh yeah, him too."

"He didn't like that. Copenhagen, I mean. He got kind of annoyed, actually. Here's this guy he's never met, threatening his life."

"You didn't tell him about me?"

"I did, actually."

"What did he say?"

"He was like me—he didn't know whether to hunt you down or offer you a position on his staff."

This time Keo chuckled—and he kept the transmit button keyed so Buck could hear it. "So what'll it be?"

"I'm afraid we can't give them up."

"Can't, or won't?"

"Does it matter?"

"No, I guess not."

"Besides, you have me curious, EB. I'm wondering which one of these Winding Creek residents you're so desperate to get back. It can't be all of them, I know that."

"Do you now?"

"Oh, I'm sure of it," Buck said. "Almost as sure as I know your name's not really EB. Am I right...Keo?"

Shit, Keo thought, but he didn't hesitate to answer back, "Good guess."

"Not really," Buck said. There wasn't quite the triumph in his voice Keo was expecting. "I asked the people from Winding Creek about you. It wasn't really hard to get an identification as it turned out: Male, Asian, six-feet-something, with a big ol' scar across one side of his face. I wasn't sure about the scar, but Hatch confirmed it."

"Good ol' Hatch."

"So who is it, Keo? Who do I have that you want back so badly?"

"I'm surprised you didn't ask them that, too."

"Maybe I don't want to."

"And why would that be?"

"Maybe what I really want is to see you make good on your threat."

"Oh, it's not a threat, Buckaroo. I don't threaten."

"You just promise, is that it?"

"You're smarter than you look."

Buck laughed. It wasn't nearly as convincing as he was probably hoping. "Smart enough to remember that name. Keo. It's a hard name to forget, after all."

Double shit.

"You know what the *M* stands for, don't you?" Buck asked.

"Yeah," Keo said.

"Of course you do. You killed him. Blew his brains out. I wasn't there when you did it, but I heard about it. I heard all the grisly details. Then you somehow escaped the hangman's noose." Buck paused. Then, "You're a hard man to kill, Keo."

"I've had a lot of practice."

"I don't doubt that whatsoever. A man of your skills. The

things you must have done even before the world went to shit. You are indeed impressive, Keo."

"I've been called worse."

"I'm sure you have."

"So now that we know each other better, where do we stand?"

"I think we both know the answer to that one," Buck said. "If you want the people from Winding Creek back, you'll have to come and get them. I'll even make you this promise, Keo, from one professional to another: I won't hurt them. I won't lay a single hand on them or try to find out which one you're so stuck on."

"That's mighty big of you."

"So thank me."

Keo clenched his teeth for a brief second. Then, "Thank you."

"You're welcome," Buck said. "Now, let's see you make good on your promise. You know where to find me."

"*Flectere si nequeo superos, Acheronta movebo,*" Keo said.

Buck laughed again. This time, it came through more convincing. "They did say you were an odd duck for a killer."

"So that's it, then." Keo added, in his best game show host voice, "Is *that* your final answer?"

"I'm afraid so."

"Don't say I didn't give a chance."

"Likewise."

"I'll see you again very soon, Buckaroo."

"Don't keep me waiting too long, Keo," Buck said, just before the radio went silent.

Keo put the two-way back down and finished the slice of venison.

What exactly had he expected?

Pretty much this.

He was wiping his hands on his pants legs when Horse, standing next to him, lifted his head and snorted loudly.

"Yeah, I know, I can hear them, too. Ol Buck was stalling me, that little scamp."

He stood up and unslung the MP5SD submachine gun, then took a second to think about what Hatch had said about Fenton:

"They're just...strong. Have you been out there? If you're not strong, you get run over. People come and take things that you have, that they want. That's just how it is out there. Fenton is strong. No one's going to take anything from them."

No, maybe not, but Keo had seen stronger forces buckle when you hit them at just the right spots. He had personal experience with that.

Right now, he swore he couldn't just hear them trampling around the woods, snapping branches like primitive apes, but he could also *smell* them.

And they reeked, all right, but it wasn't body odor in the air. They were emanating *excitement* because they were hunting *him*.

Keo grinned at Horse. "The more things change, blah blah blah."

The animal snorted back.

"Exactly," Keo said, before picking up Horse's reins and starting off, the two of them vanishing like ghosts.

Made in the USA
Coppell, TX
29 March 2021